Discord Jones

Something to Curse About

Gayla Drummond

Katarr Kanticles Press

Katarr Kanticles Press
Texas, USA
Edited by Tonya Cannariato
Copyright © 2014 Gayla Drummond

ISBN-13: 978-0615954172 (Katarr Kanticles Press)
ISBN-10: 0615954170

"Listen." He turned the volume up as I sat down. A woman's photo was in one corner of the screen.

"Hey, that's…" I sat down on the couch next to him, staring at the TV.

"Rose Middleton jumped from the top of the Ferris wheel at the county fair in an alleged suicide attempt, but someone was on hand to stop her deadly plunge." Video, probably from someone's cell phone, showed her stopping in mid-air and then slowly descending to the ground. I was congratulating myself on not being caught on camera when the anchorwoman spoke again.

"However, her guardian angel wasn't present at the hospital later, when Rose jumped through a fourth floor window."

My jaw dropped. "She's dead?"

The anchorwoman confirmed it just before Nick turned the sound back down to barely audible. "She really wanted to die."

"No, she didn't. I heard her thoughts. It sounded like something was making her do it. She actually thought 'I don't want to die'." We stared at each other until Nick put his arm around my shoulders.

"You can't win them all."

Acknowledgments

Many thanks to you. Yes, you the reader.

Also to my beta readers: Kate Smith, J.C. Montgomery, and Tonya Cannariato. Double thanks to Tonya for burning the midnight oil so we could release *Something to Curse About* a little earlier than scheduled.

Something to Curse About

One

Screams pierced the air, but I'd grown used to hearing them over the past year and change. The smell of cotton candy, popcorn, and other, standard carnival fare wafted by on a warm breeze. Music played from each ride, rising over the noise of the crowd as we paused to watch inept teens try to toss rings onto bottles. I licked a bit of spun sugar from the corner of my mouth, savoring the taste of having a normal day out.

Sean, my five-year-old brother, tugged on my hand while leaning toward a nearby concession stand. "I'm hungry."

"Again? Where are you putting everything?" We'd already purchased four different snacks between rides, and had only arrived about two hours before. "Your tummy isn't that big."

Nick laughed, both hands busy holding onto Jonah's legs. My younger brother sat on the shifter's shoulders, holding fistfuls of his hair and wearing a huge smile. He was enjoying being the "tallest" for a change.

"He's growing. We guys are always hungry during growth spurts."

"Maybe, but you're not the one who's going to get it if he gets sick from too much sugar." I ruffled Sean's dark blonde hair. "Let's go find the parents and see about dinner."

"Fwench Fwies," Jonah voted at the top of his voice, and everyone within twenty feet winced. Even me, though I had to smile. It's cute when little kids haven't gotten the hang of certain letters.

"Okay, let's go, men." The older adults were checking out the various expo halls after deciding not to waste the services of two perfectly good younger adults as babysitters. I led the way, glancing back a few times at Nick and Jonah.

My boyfriend had leaped at the chance to join a family outing, and really seemed to be enjoying himself. He wasn't even freaking out about all the sticky bits Jonah had managed to mash into his dark brown hair. Of course, Nick was a shifter, so maybe messy little kids weren't a problem for him.

One of the smaller buildings, rented by the New Age center where my mom worked, was my first choice to check. As I suspected, she was in front of the table that displayed the bars of soap and tiny bottles of perfume she'd made.

She also had Betty, my dad's second wife, cornered and was holding one of the little bottles right under her nose. Poor Betty. She'd been raised to respect her elders, and not only was Mom that at fifty-seven, but also one of Dad's best friends and the mother of his eldest child. She was stuck, standing there with a fixed smile on her face.

"Hey, where's Dad?" My question stopped Mom from trading out bottles. "Sean the Bottomless Belly is hungry, and I could use a meal break."

Seeing an opportunity, Betty was quick to snatch it with a loud *Oh, thank God* flying from her mind. "I'll go find him."

We watched her hurry off, and then Mom rummaged through her bottles, picking one up and turning to Nick. "Tell me if this one says 'Cordi' to you."

"Sure."

I shook my head at his agreeableness. She'd latched onto him the second we'd walked through the entrance gate, and kept him busy for twenty minutes, smelling perfume after perfume. Mom said she was trying to mix the perfect scent for me, but I thought she was just enjoying sharing the fruits of her newest passion. Nick was a willing guinea pig, eager to get along with my family even though he'd suffered a major sneezing fit after one smell test.

Sean began wiggling. "I gotta go."

"Me too," Jonah chimed in. Anything his big brother did, he had to do too.

"Okay, I'll take you."

Nick lifted him off his shoulders and set him on the floor. "There you go."

"You have cotton candy in your ear." Grinning at him, I caught Jonah's hand. "Let's go."

There was a restroom not too far away, and fortunately, it wasn't full. After undoing buttons and zippers, I sent both boys into one stall and stood by waiting for them to do their thing. Giggles followed as they relieved themselves, and there was a bit of discussion about who could pee the most.

Boys. Rolling my eyes, I traded a smile with a woman busy changing a diaper. "Don't forget to flush, guys."

"I wanna do it."

"No, I get to. I'm oldest." Sean won, flushed the toilet, and then both were ready for help refastening their jeans.

"Good job. Let's wash our hands." That went well, with a minimum of mess. Mixing small boys and water usually resulted in disaster. I led them back outside.

Sean saw something. Before I knew it, he'd shaken loose and taken off like a shot, disappearing into the crowd. "Sean! Oh, crap."

I picked up Jonah and ran after him. Panic was setting in by the time I spotted him watching people lined up and playing ski-ball. "Dude, don't do that. You know you're not supposed to wander off. You'll get lost."

"I can't get lost. You're here. Can I play this one?"

Confidence, thy name is little brother. Sean sort of understood my job was to find people and things, and that I had special abilities. Of course, he thought they were magic. I guess to a five-year-old, psychic talents were magic. "Maybe after we eat. Everyone's going to be wondering where we are. Come on."

He pouted, but gave me his hand. Looking around, I realized we were halfway down the midway and sighed. "You move fast and far when the mood strikes."

"I'm gonna be a ninja when I grow up."

Laughing, I started walking. "Perfect job for you."

"Discord?"

I stopped and turned around to find Logan a few feet away. "Hey."

There were some people with him, and he was holding a girl's hand. She looked about seventeen or so, very pretty with pale gold hair and light green eyes. Logan smiled. "Are these your brothers?"

"Yes. Sean and Jonah, meet my friend Logan. He can turn into a tiger." Their eyes went wide as they stared at him.

Jonah spoke first. "I can tiger too. Wanna hear?"

"Sure." Logan glanced at me, one eyebrow rising a bit.

"Waaaaaaaaaahhrrrrrrr!"

"Ow. My ear." I couldn't even rub it, with him on my hip and holding Sean's hand.

Logan chuckled. "That's a pretty good roar."

The girl shifted her weight, leaning against his arm, and he smiled at her. "This is my cousin, Terra. Terra, Discord Jones, the private investigator I told you about."

A smile lit up her face as her eyes zeroed in on mine. "Hello, I'm pleased to meet you."

"Hi. Same here."

Logan introduced the other two with them, both men. "Soames and Teague."

I nodded and smiled, receiving the same back. I'd seen Teague before, and remembered Logan saying he wasn't a tiger, but a lion. About to mention we were planning to eat and invite them to join us, I froze with my mouth half-open as *I don't want to die* resounded in my head, followed by a rush of cold, hard fear.

"Discord? What is it? A vision?" Logan took a step forward, Terra releasing his hand.

"No, it's...."

Why is this happening? Someone help me! Please!

I shoved Jonah into Logan's arms. "Hold him. Someone's in trouble. Sean, stay with Logan."

Turning, I closed my eyes and concentrated, trying to pinpoint the direction the fear was coming from. Catching hold of emotions in a crowd of people is hard. It's like playing a game of Hot and Cold. You move in a direction and see if it gets stronger.

Oh God, oh God. Please help me.

Eyes opening, I ran toward the Ferris wheel, vaguely aware of Logan and his group following. It was the right direction, and someone screamed just as I stopped at the edge of the loading platform. I looked up, as everyone else was, and gasped when a woman jumped from the top.

Thrusting up both arms, I called on my telekinetic ability and managed to stop her plunge to the ground. A few, slow breaths later, I was lowering her to the platform and feeling the stares of those closest to me.

She was unconscious. I rubbed my forehead and sighed as the ride operator called for help.

Two

At the first chance, I slipped through the crowd to find Logan and my brothers. A few people patted me on the back before moving out of my way, and I had to grit my teeth as their amazement transferred directly into my brain.

The group of shifters stood at the back of the crowd, Terra in the middle. She was holding Jonah, and Logan, standing on her left, had Sean. "Thanks."

"No problem. Are you all right?"

I realized I was rubbing my forehead again. "Yeah, just a little bit of a headache."

"Why don't we carry the boys for you?" he offered, glancing at his cousin. She was cuddling Jonah while he petted her hair.

"Sure. Everyone else is probably wondering where we are. We were going to grab some food. You're welcome to join us, if you want?" A few people were still staring and I really wanted to leave the area. It was one thing to use my abilities on cases. Wowing a bunch of carnival goers, even accidentally, wasn't my thing.

Terra answered. "We'd love to."

"Cool. They're in an expo hall." I led the way, wishing the shooting pains in my head would settle down.

I'd met Logan not long after my boss, Mr. Whitehaven, had hired Nick to babysit me. My job at Arcane Solutions has led to meeting interesting people. Some have become friends, like the witches and their familiars, while others have become enemies.

For example, vampires don't like me very much. The feeling's mutual.

At least one person has become more than a friend: Nick. He's a wolf, which causes friction when Logan's around. It's mostly a dog and cat thing, silly as that sounds. As much as I've come to care about him, the fact his job is to protect has caused some friction between us more than once.

Then there's Leglin. I kind of blackmailed a client into giving him to me after said client withheld information that resulted in my becoming favored demon prey. He's an elf-bred, part-demon hound who has a wolf shifter ancestor.

Needless to say, he's not an ordinary dog. For one, he's huge. He's also very intelligent, comes when called even if I'm stuck in a different realm because he has some magic of his own, and he can kill demons.

He's basically awesome.

Leglin and I are still figuring things out, because I'm not really comfortable treating him like a dog. It's only been a month since we became roomies, and things are going well. I'd taken him to spend the day with David and Jo, a couple of my witchy friends, at David's shop, The Blue Orb.

Nick turned around before we were halfway down the table-lined aisle, his brows drawing together and a faint frown appearing. Maybe he felt out-numbered, since there were four feline shifters with us. I'm still mostly in the dark about shifter relations. His "Hey" to Logan wasn't enthusiastic, even though I grabbed his hand and slipped my fingers through his.

Logan returned it, and then said, "Hello, Mrs. Jones."

Mom smiled. "I remember you. We met at Cordi's apartment. Call me Sunny."

Right after I'd been attacked by demons a second time. I'm surprised she remembered, since she hadn't really looked at him once Nick dropped that bomb on her.

I made all the introductions, mentioning I'd invited them to eat with us, and noticed Betty's smile growing more fixed. Poor woman would love to pretend everyone is human, because she's terrified by supernatural types. Including me, though she pretends she isn't for my dad's sake.

My dad shook hands with the newcomers. He's about as open-minded as my mom. Then again, he works in advertising and since his bosses know he has a psychic for a daughter, Dad's often pegged as the go-to-guy when supernatural clients hire the agency, so he's gotten used to meeting supes.

Logan noticed Betty's reaction, and put Sean down before nudging Terra. She followed suit, after a few seconds of cuddling Jonah with a light purr. "You're lucky, to have such handsome sons."

"Thank you." Betty's smile relaxed a bit, but she was quick to gesture both boys to her. I shot an apologetic look at Logan and company, but none of them seemed to be offended.

"I really need some food, people." Not the most gracious way to get things moving forward, but my head was still hurting. Being around large crowds is a strain for me, and using one of my abilities hadn't helped matters.

The strain is because I'm both telepathic and empathic. I hear people's thoughts and feel their emotions, even though I shield myself from both as much as possible. Several hundred people in a relatively small area was draining my reserves.

It's not like I can become a hermit though, and no way I'd miss out on my little brothers' first fair trip. I don't spend nearly as much time as I'd like to with them as it is; being psychic, I'm all too aware of Betty's discomfort around those who aren't "normal." She tries hard to be nice to me in spite of her fears for Dad's sake, so in return, I try to make things as easy as possible on her.

Mom looked at me, her forehead creasing. She's the original hippie chick, even legally changed her name to Sunshine Breeze back in the early '70s. "One of the local charities has a pizza parlor set up in a quiet corner."

I grinned at Jonah. "If they serve French fries too, that'll work."

With that, we were off. Nick put his arm around my waist after easing between Logan and me. "What took you so long to get back?"

Explaining, including Sean's excited contributions with sound effects, took the entire walk. My parents expressed their pride, which made me blush bright red, and even Betty looked impressed.

With eleven people, it took several minutes to go through the line to order, pay, and then push some tables together so we could all sit in a group. I ended up with Nick on one side and Terra on the other. My dad suddenly realized that Logan was the one rebuilding my car, which had been demolished by vampires during the same case that caused the shifter and me to meet, and resulted in my new roomie, Leglin. It gave dinner conversation a starting point.

Terra had the same calm vibe I'd noticed in Logan and my boss, Mr. Whitehaven. Calm people are like over-the-counter headache medication for me. While eating my two slices of sausage, mushroom, and green peppers, I paid attention to the other two shifters, Soames and Teague, and picked up the same vibe from them.

Soaking it in didn't hurt anything as far as they were concerned, and it certainly helped me. By the time everyone was finished and just chatting, my headache was gone. The rest of the afternoon and evening were fun, as we wandered around, playing games, looking at exhibits, and enjoying rides.

Three

The parents and boys peeled off from the group as we left the gates. I pulled out my cell phone to call David. "Hey, I'll be calling Leglin home pretty soon."

"I'm sure he's ready. Copernicus has decided your hound has prime nesting material on tap." Copernicus, a raven, was David's familiar. "Leglin's been good-natured about having hair pulled from his tail, but I think his patience is beginning to wear thin."

"Ouch, okay, I'll call him as soon as we get to Nick's truck. Thanks for letting him hang out." After saying bye, Logan cleared his throat.

"Terra was wondering if you might want to come over for lunch sometime. She just moved here, so doesn't really know anyone yet." He silently added *I would really appreciate it. She's lonely.*

I nodded, smiling at her. "Sure, it'd be fun. How about Wednesday?"

She smiled back. "Wednesday's good. I'm living with Logan right now, over the garage."

"Cool. I'll try to be there about one, if that's okay?" It was, and the four of them left after additional good-byes.

Nick frowned after them. "I'm not sure that's a good idea."

"Why? She seems nice, and being new kind of sucks for anyone."

"Cordi." He sighed my name, wearing his "you're being thick" look. "She's going to be their Queen. You don't want to get involved in shifter politics."

I thought that over as we walked to his truck. "Aren't I already involved in shifter politics? I'm dating you. Wait a minute before answering. Leglin?"

My hound, all two hundred or so black and tan pounds of him, appeared next to me. He grinned, tongue lolling out the side of his mouth, and wagged his tail. It hit the side of Nick's truck with a loud thump. "Hey, bub. How was your play date?"

Scoping out his tail while the hound grumbled, I spotted a bare spot. "We're not buying that bird a Christmas present this year."

Nick laughed, and opened the rear passenger door. Hot air billowed out. I really needed to introduce him to windshield shades. "Here you go, Linny."

Once we were all in the truck, I tugged my tee away from suddenly sticky skin. "Turn on the A/C before answering, or I'll melt before I can hear it."

He started the truck and switched the air conditioner on high. Another blast of hot air struck me in the face. "I won't ever be a pack leader, so dating me doesn't stick you in the middle of shifter politics."

I adjusted the vents and fastened my seat belt. "Why won't you ever be a pack leader?"

"Because it takes over your life, and I like mine the way it is." He eased the truck out of its parking spot, changed gears, and we began rolling forward. "Besides, I'm not patient or dominant enough to lead a pack."

"Okay, but it's not like I'm never around shifters. I've had cases involving them."

He grinned. "But you don't discriminate, and neither does the boss. Any shifter's case is welcome, so that makes you a neutral party."

The idea of being friends with a future Queen of something was cool. "Yet I'm dating a wolf and hello! My roomie is also part wolf shifter. If those two things don't remove my neutrality, why would being nice to Terra suddenly involve me in shifter politics?"

"It's complicated."

It was my turn to sigh, and I looked out the passenger window. "Stuff with you guys always is."

I didn't mean just shifters, but all supernatural people. It's not like humans couldn't be complicated, but some supes had made "complicated" into a fine art. Returning my attention to Nick, I admired the flex of muscles in his forearms as he guided the truck into a turn. "How do you know Terra's going to be their Queen?"

His response was a shrug. "Everyone knows."

"I didn't."

"Right now, the only organized feline group in Santo Trueno is the Pride. Now more tigers are coming here."

"Because of Terra?"

"Only a white tiger can be a clan Queen, and she's a white tiger."

I knew Logan was a black tiger, and he'd told me that was rare, rarer than white. "Why only white?"

"I don't know. I'm not a tiger. Are you hungry again yet? We can pick something up."

Leglin shoved his head over the seat and between us, his ears perked. I scratched under his chin. "I'm not, but he is."

Nick didn't treat the hound like a dog either. "Mexican or Chinese?" The hound grunted. "Mexican it is."

I leaned forward to look at him. "Do you really understand what he's saying, or do you guess?"

"For us to know, and you to find out." With a grin, Nick signaled a right turn.

Arriving at my apartment, Mexican seemed to have been the correct choice, since Leglin parked his big rear beside the table and poked the food containers with his nose. "Give me a minute, and I'll feed you."

He had a bowl for water, but I always put his food on a plate. It seemed more fitting for someone with an ancestor who could take human shape, even if Leglin couldn't. Probably a good thing elf hounds couldn't shift, or they might have beaten up the elves. Elves don't like shifters, and the feeling's mutual, since the pointy-eared snobs sometimes hunted them.

With elf hounds, at that. Leglin had never hunted shifters, and that was part of the reason I'd wanted him.

Arranging his double order of beef fajitas onto a plate, I grabbed a placemat off the table, and put both down on the floor for him. "There you go. Enjoy."

Nick collected a plate and utensils for himself before sitting down. "Are you sure you don't want any?"

"I'm good." Pulling out a couple of beers, I joined him. "Here."

"Thanks." After popping the top, he took a drink and asked, "So are you going to eat lunch with her?"

Her? Oh, Terra. Was it some weird interspecies prejudice he didn't use her name?

"Yes. It would be rude not to show after I accepted. Besides, Logan's still working on my car, and I want to see how much he's done on it." I missed my little sports car. Nick never let me drive his truck, so my transportation choices were limited to being chauffeured or teleporting.

He sighed around a mouthful of fajita, shook his head and

swallowed. "It's a bad idea."

"See, you're telling me that, but you're not giving any solid reasoning."

"It's…"

"Complicated. Yeah, you said that." Rolling my eyes, I had a drink of my beer. "I'm going. Deal with it."

Nick scowled. "You never take my advice."

"I do too."

"No, you don't. You listen, but then you just do whatever the hell you want to anyway." He glared while taking a huge bite.

"Maybe that's because most of your advice is to run and let you get whomped on." It was true. He always wanted me clear of sticky situations. "I mean, it's nice that you care enough that you'd rather get your butt kicked than see me get hurt, but you know, I'm…"

"Not helpless. Yeah, I know, and I do not always get my butt kicked. It was one of the interview questions: How many times have you gotten your butt kicked? Mr. Whitehaven wouldn't have hired me if I got beat down every time I came up against someone."

I couldn't prevent a grin from surfacing. "Aw, did I hurt your widdle male ego?"

His glare returned. Laughing, I rose enough to lean over and kiss him. "I'm sorry. No, you don't always get your butt kicked. And Mr. Whitehaven did not ask you that question."

Our boss was far too formal to use the word "butt". He's the only person I know who calls everyone by their full names; the only one who doesn't call me Discord or Cordi, but Discordia.

The only exception to the rule is Kate, our co-worker and another witch friend. She's not fond of her full name, Katherine, and they must've struck some sort of deal about his not using it before I began working there. Or maybe she just refused to answer to the full version. I could totally see her doing that.

Nick gave up glaring at me in favor of finishing his late dinner and then moving to the living room to watch the 11 o'clock news. I took care of clean up, and had just hung the dish towel over the sink's edge to dry when he called for me.

"What?" I grabbed my beer before leaving the kitchen.

"Listen." He turned the volume up as I sat down. A woman's photo was in one corner of the screen.

"Hey, that's…" I sat down on the couch next to him, staring at the TV.

"Rose Middleton jumped from the top of the Ferris wheel at the county fair in an alleged suicide attempt, but someone was on hand to stop her deadly plunge." Video, probably from someone's cell phone, showed her stopping in mid-air and then slowly descending to the ground. I was congratulating myself on not being caught on camera when the anchorwoman spoke again.

"However, her guardian angel wasn't present at the hospital later, when Rose jumped through a fourth floor window."

My jaw dropped. "She's dead?"

The anchorwoman confirmed it just before Nick turned the sound back down to barely audible. "She really wanted to die."

"No, she didn't. I heard her thoughts. It sounded like something was making her do it. She actually thought 'I don't want to die'." We stared at each other until Nick put his arm around my shoulders.

"You can't win them all."

Totally true statement, though it didn't make me feel better. He noticed, pulling me into his lap for some cuddle time. One of the things I really liked about Nick was the fact he enjoyed cuddling, in or out of bed. Cuddling made him happy, and with my empathic ability, his happiness felt like a warm, fuzzy blanket covering me.

One of the other things I liked about him came along once we called it a night and went to bed. It hadn't taken Nick long to tune into the fact I needed a little extra attention during sex in order to have an orgasm. Once he'd realized, I had absolutely no complaints in that department of our relationship.

None popped up that night either.

Four

There were six more suicides over the weekend. When I arrived at the office Monday morning, I discovered Santo Trueno's mayor, Richard Wells, and the chief of police, Tom Stannett, meeting with Mr. Whitehaven.

"This is Miss Discordia Jones," my boss introduced me.

"Hi." Not liking the grim atmosphere, I nodded and smiled my way across the room to stand next to Nick, who leaned against the wall at Whitehaven's left shoulder. "What's going on?"

"Miss Jones," the mayor began, but Stannett cut him off. The police chief was a burly built man with thinning, sandy hair and faded blue eyes. He looked out of place, sitting next to Wells. The mayor's hair was golden-blonde, his eyes dark gray, and his expensive suit hung well on his trim body.

"It's about the suicides. There are some who think you may be responsible."

My jaw dropped. "What?"

Wells scowled at Stannett. "This isn't how we were going to handle it."

The police chief shrugged. "No, you were going to talk circles before getting to the point. Jones has helped solve several cases, and deserves some respect for that."

"She's also been responsible for several deaths."

Anger lubricated my voice. "They were all vampires or demons, except one. I don't run around killing people for the hell of it. Each one was trying to either kill or kidnap me."

"Was Ginger Moore trying to kill you?"

My breath caught, hot tears pricking my eyelids as I closed my eyes at the unexpected mention of my friend's name. "No."

"Yet you staked and killed her."

I opened my eyes to glare at him, wondering how he knew while curling my hands into fists. "She hated being a vampire."

Mr. Whitehaven held up his hand. "Mayor Wells, I have a notarized document on file, signed by Miss Moore, in which she requested to be euthanized and stated her reasons for the request. Discordia simply fulfilled that request."

He had what? I hadn't known about that.

"That doesn't make it le…"

My boss leaned forward. I wondered if his eyes were glowing red when both men paled. "We aren't human, and have certain long-honored traditions. One of which is that a vampire who wishes to cease his or her existence may do so, by any means necessary. Miss Moore was a young vampire, a thrall of a far more powerful master. She couldn't end her second life without aid." Whitehaven leaned back. "It wasn't murder, gentlemen, but mercy."

The present faded away, and I stood in a small room lit by a single overhead bulb, facing a metal door. I slowly turned around. Ginger lay on a worn blanket spread over a metal framed cot. Above ground, the sun was shining. Down here, everything seemed grimy in the weak light. The room, located below a mansion in the Barrows, wasn't anything more than a dusty, concrete box with a metal door.

She appeared to be sleeping, but her chest didn't move. Vampires don't need to breathe, except to speak or pass themselves off as human. They don't breathe while taking their daily rest.

I had a stake in one hand, a small sledgehammer in the other, and the echo of Ginger's pleas from the night before ringing in my ears. "Please, Cordi. Do it today. I can't live like this anymore!"

Nearly three weeks had passed since I had made the promise to her. I'd spent those weeks practicing on, of all things, cantaloupes. The object was to do it as fast and painlessly for her as possible: stake right over the heart, then one blow of the hammer to drive it through.

If I did it right, she wouldn't feel a thing. If I didn't, she would wake. So would her master, and one of them would likely kill me. In her right mind, Ginger wouldn't hurt me, but no vampire startled out of sleep by a stake would be in its right mind.

Encased in yellow rubber cleaning gloves, my palms were sweating as I crossed the small space. Looking down at her, I almost lost my nerve. Vampire or not, Ginger was my best friend. We'd been friends since we were three years old. Ginger was the only friend who visited me while I was comatose. Who stuck by me while I figured out all of the psychic stuff.

All of which was the reason she'd asked me, and I'd promised. Real friends would do anything for each other, and the only way out of her nightmare life was to die a second time.

If I didn't help her, no one would. Taking a deep breath, I put the sharp tip of the stake over her heart. My arm trembled as I lifted the hammer, and I lowered it again, closing my eyes to take and release a couple of deep breaths.

When I opened my eyes, I lifted the hammer at the same time, and slammed it down onto the end of the stake. My grunt of effort ended with a whimper as Ginger jerked, her eyes opening. A second before blood began soaking the nightgown she wore, her eyes focused on mine.

She smiled.

She smiled, her eyes closed, and as she went limp, her skin turned gray.

I yanked my gloved hand away from the stake with a loud sob, and teleported home to my bathroom, where I stripped and scrubbed myself raw in the shower, crying for Ginger, and for myself.

"Cordi?" Nick's voice shattered the memory. I looked up then around the room, realizing I was on the floor, huddled against the wall, and he'd crouched next to me. "What happened? Are you okay? You're crying."

I wiped my cheeks, and shook my head. "It was a flashback. I'm okay."

Okay except for the embarrassment of having an episode in front of not only non-friends, but prominent citizens. Also the first super flashback in front of Nick, which would probably cement his opinions about my inability to take care of myself and lead to yet another "you run, I fight" argument. Hopefully not during a situation when we didn't have time for one.

At least Nick had enough sense not to make a big deal out of it. He helped me up, and kept an arm around my waist. The boss handed me a couple of tissues. "Thanks."

"A flashback?" Mayor Wells stared at me, his lips turned ever-so-slightly upward. I wanted to rip the smug expression off his face. "You have PTSD?"

"It's common among psychics with certain abilities," Mr. Whitehaven said. "Retro-cognition is one of them. Discordia has unfortunately experienced several traumatic events while assisting law enforcement."

"More traumatic than killing an innocent girl?"

Anger blazed. I found my voice again. "He tortured her. Made her do things she couldn't live with. She wanted out, and that was the only way out." I paused, staring at Wells until he blinked. "I didn't want to do it, but it was the only way she'd find peace, and she had no one else to turn to."

The mayor opened his mouth, but Stannett spoke first. "Jones, have you ever controlled anyone's mind?"

"No."

"Are you capable of doing it?"

"I don't know, but even if I could, I wouldn't. It's wrong."

"Tell me where you were over the weekend."

Nick shifted his weight, lifting his chin while pulling me closer to his side. "I stayed the weekend with her. We were at her apartment, except for a trip to the park and grocery store."

"He left late last night, after we had dinner and watched a movie." I shook my head. "We were at the fair when that woman jumped. I'm the one who stopped her. Why would I—if I could make someone commit suicide—turn around and stop them from doing it?"

The two men traded a glance, before Stannett asked, "You were there? Were there any witnesses?"

"Yeah, some of my friends and people standing in line at the Ferris wheel."

Wells leaned forward. "How did you know?"

"I felt her fear first then heard her thoughts. She didn't want to jump. I don't know why she did."

He frowned. "You make a habit of listening to people's thoughts?"

If Nick hadn't been holding onto me, I might've crossed the room to punch the mayor right in the mouth. "No, I make a habit of *not* listening so that I don't lose my damn mind. But sometimes, people's emotions are so strong, their thoughts are like screams, and they break right through my mental shields. She was scared. She screamed."

Stannett cleared his throat, and I turned my glare toward him. "What?"

"Were her thoughts coherent?"

"Yeah. Give me a minute." I scowled, trying to recall the exact thoughts that had passed from her mind to mine. "She thought 'I don't want to die', 'Why is this happening? Someone help me' and 'Oh God. Please help me'. I'm not God, but I could hear her, so I helped her."

The police chief frowned while sitting back. "Yet later, she did it anyway." He stared at the thick carpeting for a few seconds, his brow furrowed. When he looked up, he was still frowning. "You're certain she didn't want to commit suicide?"

"As certain as I can be, between the thoughts I caught, and feeling how afraid she was."

Stannett nodded. "Nothing we've uncovered so far indicates any of them were suicidal. That means someone made them do it."

"Which means my name popped to the head of the potential suspect list?" I pushed away from Nick, but didn't walk past the front edge of the boss's desk. Any closer, and the urge to smack both men around would become too strong. "Why? Because I'm a psychic?"

"You're on several lists, because you're the only known psychic in North America with so many abilities." Wells crossed his arms, calmly meeting my gaze. "You're unusual, Miss Jones. Unusual and powerful. By all accounts, you're dangerous."

I smirked, hooking a thumb over my shoulder to indicate Whitehaven and Nick. "Yeah? Try telling them that."

"Discordia does have more abilities than other psychics, and thus is more powerful; however, her abilities do not always work. Using them is a physical drain." Mr. Whitehaven's chair creaked. "I can assure you that controlling another's mind requires constant surveillance and a certain finesse. Not only is Discordia young, but she's had very few years of practice with her abilities. No human psychic in the world could currently control another person to the required degree. None of them have enough experience or practice to be able to overcome another's primitive survival instincts."

Both men turned their full attention on him. I leaned a hip against the side of his desk, crossing my arms as he continued. "Gentlemen, you aren't looking for a psychic. There are only two potential suspects: Either a master vampire, or an exceptionally strong magic practitioner who specializes in curses."

Five

Before they left, Stannett asked if I'd be available to help. I agreed, on the condition that I was paid my regular rate by the city, not the police department. Mr. Whitehaven approved, mentioning my current "heavy workload" and our commitments to clients to handle their cases in a timely manner. The only current cases I actually had were a lost dog and a wealthy grandmother who suspected her grandson of stealing things from her home to sell for drugs. I can't take more than two or three cases at a time, because my relevant abilities don't play the logic game. Concentrating on one case doesn't mean any psychic "hits" I have are related to that case.

Wells didn't like it, but after he and Stannett stepped outside for a private conference, he agreed.

"Certainly stuck it to them," Nick said while we watched the two men cross the parking lot to their vehicles.

I shrugged. "I was going to help anyway, but the mayor and his buddies obviously thought I was guilty just because I'm a psychic. That's insulting, and against the law anyway. We're supposed to be innocent until proven guilty, damn it."

He stroked a hand down my back, ending it with a pat between my shoulder blades. "Welcome to the real world."

"The real world sucks."

"You get used to it."

I stepped away, turning to face him. "But I don't have to like it."

"No," Nick agreed. "You don't, but being angry over it is a waste of energy."

"Maybe not. Wells thinks I'm dangerous, and he pissed me off, but I didn't do anything to him."

Nick raised his eyebrows. "And…?"

"He thought I was making people kill themselves all over town, so it should occur to him that I could've done something to him, and was angry enough to, but didn't."

"Considering both you and the boss made it clear you can't

control people the way he thought, I doubt the possibility will cross his mind."

"Gah." I threw my hands up and stalked to my office. Nick was probably right, which sucked. So much for my attempt at making lemonade from lemons. I started a pot of coffee, not having much else to do until after lunch, which is when I agreed to go to the station and begin helping by handling the clothing worn by the victims.

There were a million things I'd rather do, up to driving to the sea park in San Antonio and subjecting myself to the misery and anger of its aquatic residents. Or maybe the city pound. You haven't really visited that sort of place until you've walked through and felt dogs afraid of being beaten or begging like hell for you to take them home before it's their turn to visit the "Bad Room" no one ever returns from.

Becoming a psychic makes life a thousand times more difficult.

The only upside is using your abilities to make a difference, and that's limited for two reasons. First, you can't stay unshielded all the time, looking for opportunities to help people, because you'd go bonkers. Second, there are a lot of things you can't change without crossing lines that shouldn't be crossed.

Only people with major issues crossed those lines. Maybe I have some major issues, but megalomania isn't one of them.

I pulled out the file on the lost dog, and poured and doctored a cup of coffee before sitting down to stare at the dog's photo again. Princess was a registered Chihuahua with an "excellent pedigree" who'd gone missing, or had been stolen, five days prior.

Her owner, Vera Headley, was a nice lady whose reddened eyes made it clear she missed her little Princess. The Chihuahua looked like a tiny white doe, with her long legs, slender body, round skull and large, dark eyes. Precious, in a slightly freakish way.

So far, I'd had two flashes I knew were related to the case, unless my other client's thief was less than a foot tall and had a hobby of hiding under bushes. I wouldn't rule out the possibility, what with the variety of small folk living in Santo Trueno.

Closing my eyes, I checked my mental folder to make certain the golden shimmer that represented Princess hadn't disappeared. It was still present, which meant the tiny dog was alive.

Miss Headley had a dog walker who picked up Princess around noon every day for walkies, along with a half-dozen other small dogs. I'd already cleared the dog walker—not that my client thought the other woman guilty of anything except a momentary lapse of attention.

The dog walker, Eileen Smith, had stopped at a coffee shop's walk-up window, and looked down while leaving the window to discover Princess missing. The dog either slipped her collar, or someone helped her do it, because it remained on the end of the leash.

Why they didn't use a harness, I couldn't guess. Those were safer for dogs with itty bitty necks.

Miss Headley had brought Princess's royal purple doggy bed with her, and both Nick and Leglin took the Chihuahua's scent from it. Neither had any luck trying to track her though. Too much traffic in the area where she'd disappeared. At least I'd gotten my first look at Nick as a wolf. I'd missed out on the only other time he'd changed due to being a little emotional after seeing myself sacrificed and realizing precognition had joined my other abilities.

He was a large wolf, covered in fur the same dark brown as his hair.

We'd basically gotten nowhere, and I really wanted to find the little dog. The city had been having some trouble with organized dog fighting. There'd been a big story on it a couple of months back, when someone found chewed up canine bodies, mostly small ones, dumped a few miles outside city limits.

The larger dogs had lost their fights, and the reporter said the others were "bait dogs". I'd gotten sick reading the explanation.

I didn't understand how anyone could look at a cute, tiny dog like Princess, and then deliberately throw her in the jaws of an abused, aggressive, much larger dog to be torn to pieces.

Of course, I can't understand why anyone would want to abuse animals anyway, regardless of size or type.

With a deep sigh, I closed the folder and set it aside, wishing my tracking ability would kick in. Most of my abilities didn't work just because I wanted them to. I'd put in enough practice with teleporting that it almost always worked.

Practicing didn't mean success with my other abilities. My pyrokinesis and cryokinesis—fire and ice—worked about seventy-five percent of the time. Telekinesis—moving things around, including people—was one I had to block constantly, if I didn't want stuff near me to start floating or zipping around. Fortunately, my telekinesis has a limited range of influence, not more than about two dozen feet, and I can't lift a car or truck more than a few inches off the ground.

My empathy and telepathy were on all the time too, as far as receiving went. My other abilities—the ones I needed to help solve cases—tended to appear when they felt like it. Fortunately, they felt like it often enough to be useful, or I wouldn't have my job.

At a tap on my office door, I looked up to find Mr. Whitehaven. "May I come in?"

"Sure."

He did, closing the door before gingerly settling into one of the two chairs in front of my desk. My boss is eight feet tall, and the chair complained in response to his weight.

"Are you alright?"

"Yeah, I'm okay." Whitehaven's never judged me for my PSTD-related episodes. He's always checked with me after any he's aware of, but he doesn't tend to push. The boss and Damian are two people I can talk to when I feel a need to talk. They've both seen some awful things. Not much shocks them.

It's not like I can talk to my parents about my flashbacks or nightmares. Mom's name isn't Sunshine for nothing, and while my dad dealt calmly with my first case, he's in advertising and doesn't even watch scary movies.

I've never felt right burdening them with the horrors retro-cognition tends to leave me with. They'd both listen and try to help. I have no doubts on that score. But they don't really live in the same world I do, and haven't experienced the crap that comes with it.

Which is good, in my book. I don't want them to have to deal with the blood and craziness. Some of that's selfishness, because I need the break spending time with them offers. Most of it's that I just don't want them to have to deal with the crap I do.

Mr. Whitehaven smiled briefly. "Do you have any questions about the document?"

I did. "Why did Ginger come to you for that? Is it really a standard thing?"

"Yes, it is." The chair creaked when he shifted slightly. "There are people among us who are trusted to keep various records. I'm one of them, and someone sympathetic to her wishes referred her to me."

"Oh."

"It's a tradition from before the Melding, to avoid vendettas," he said. "We simply added notarizing since humans place trust in it."

Made sense. I nodded. "Okay."

"While I don't wish to pry, it appears that recently, you're having fewer episodes."

"Being busy helps." Between work, the still-new relationship with Nick, and having Leglin as a roommate, I had less time to sit around and just think about stuff. Or rather, try not to think about stuff and have it fight back by flooding my brain.

He nodded and rose from the chair. "Remember I'm available when you feel the need to talk, Discordia."

"I will. Thanks, boss." We smiled at each other as warm fuzzies attacked my insides. I really do have a great support system, and count myself lucky because of it.

Whitehaven left, and I pulled out the file for my other case. I never know what might trigger my tracking ability, though questions seem to be in the Top Twenty list of things that wake it up.

At least, when they're the right questions.

Six

The right questions didn't show themselves. Nick and I left the office early for lunch, in order to make our daily stop by the pound. He parked across the street and went inside with a photo of the Chihuahua while I waited.

Once had been enough of a visit for me, but Miss Headley's work hours made it difficult for her to check daily before closing time. She worked as a dental hygienist and her boss wasn't exactly an animal lover. Nick didn't enjoy the task because the dogs reacted badly to his presence, barking, snarling, and howling.

After seeing what a concentrated doggy dose of frantic hope, fear, and despair did to me, he'd said he would do the daily check. I let him handle it, willing to compromise between his need to protect and my need to prove I could take care of myself. It's not like he'd be physically hurt doing it, as he could be in other situations.

Mr. Whitehaven hired him specifically to protect me, and that was the one real problem in my relationship with Nick. When your job involves bad guys in any way, there's always a risk of injury.

I can't cut and run every time things get a little hairy, and really, what kind of person would I be to run out on someone I care about every time things get ugly when I have the abilities I do?

Answer: Not the kind of person I wanted to be.

Nick returned, shaking his head. "No sign of her."

He handed me the photo, and I tucked it into the glove box. "I guess lunch and then the station."

"Are you sure you want to eat before?"

"Yeah." Food is fuel, and using my abilities takes energy. Ergo, a well-fed and -rested psychic is a well-armed psychic.

We decided on Indian food for lunch. Nick hadn't tried many different types of cuisines before we met, and when I'd learned that, I made it a mission to introduce him to every sort of food I could think of.

"Spicy." He gasped the word out, his eyes watering. I pushed his ice water closer, and grinned as he lifted it for a huge swallow.

"Too spicy?"

Nick shook his head. "No, I like it."

I tried not to laugh as he took another large bite, more tears appearing in his eyes. He ate every bit of his curry, and drank five glasses of ice water to accomplish it. You had to admire a guy who finished the job at hand, no matter how painful it was.

***

"I'm not catching anything to tie them together." I put down the woven rose shrug. "They all seem like normal people."

Stannett frowned. "Not helpful."

"Sorry. My tracking sense might decide to wake up later, or a vision might hit. I'll let you know if that happens." That was all I could offer through the headache determinedly smashing my brain. Heavy emotion left tracks, and I'd had to deal with the impressions left by seven terrified people as they died painful deaths.

Nick put his hand on my back. "She's finished."

"Go home and rest," Damian said. "Let us know if you gain any insights."

"I will."

The four of us trooped out of the morgue into bright sunlight. I repressed a groan, digging in my purse for my shades. My phone went off, the first few bars of "Dancing in the Moonlight" playing. "It's Logan. See you later, Damian."

"Bye."

I answered while we walked toward Nick's truck. "Hey."

"Hi. I don't suppose there's any chance you could come by today? I have a couple more things I need your signature on."

"Sure. In fact, we can head over now," I said, ignoring Nick's frown as he opened the passenger door for me.

"Good. See you shortly."

"Yeah, bye." Call ended, I looked at Nick. "What?"

"You're in pain, yet Logan calls, and you're jumping to respond."

"I want my car back. He can't order parts and stuff without my okay."

Nick shut the door once I was inside, and started right back up as soon as he slid behind the wheel. "It could wait."

"I want my car back." I buckled the seat belt. My friends understood what my car meant to me, but Nick didn't really get it.

Plus, he had a jealousy problem where the older shifter was concerned. "You'd miss your truck if you didn't have it."

"I'd drive one of the pack vehicles."

Releasing a groan, I laid my head back. "Until you have a car or truck you fall in love with, you're not going to understand why my car is so important to me."

He started the engine. "You sure it's the car?"

"Oh, you didn't just...argh." Lifting my head, I snatched off my shades to glare at him. "What is your problem with Logan? You aren't jealous of Damian or David."

"They're human."

"Debatable, since they're witches—I mean warlocks. But what the hell does that have to do with anything?"

Lips compressed, Nick didn't answer. I pushed. "Seriously, is this one of those canine versus feline things? Because you guys are part human too, and really shouldn't let..."

"I don't like him, okay?" The words burst out of him. "He's conveniently around whenever you're alone and in trouble. He's conveniently a mechanic who could fix your car. Everything about him is too damn convenient."

"I...you...he was a mechanic before my car got trashed. He lives in the Palisades, Nick. It's not like he can make my tracking sense flip on or anything." I nearly poked an eye out, putting my shades back on. "And he is not around every time I run into trouble. Besides that, he covered your ass when you were down when we were fighting demons. You should be nicer to him for that, if nothing else."

His jaw set before Nick ground out, "He likes you."

"I hope so, since we're friends and he's putting my car back together." I released a sharp sigh. "Look, you don't need to be jealous of him. You're the guy I'm seeing and sleeping with. I picked you, remember?"

"Before you met him."

"Oh for God's sake." I threw both hands into the air. "Dude, seriously, drop it right now. I'm getting mad."

"Why?"

"Because you obviously don't trust me, that's why. Thanks a lot." I folded my arms across my chest and turned my head to stare out the window. A few minutes of silence and a mile of honey mesquite passed.

"I trust you, Cordi."

I snorted. "Sure."

"I don't trust him."

"If you trust me, it shouldn't matter whether you trust him or not." The drum in my head pounded double time. I hated relationship drama.

"He's bigger and stronger than you."

Squeezing my eyes shut, I twisted around in the seat to face him, and opened them. "So?"

"The stronger males always get the girls." Nick's grip on the steering wheel turned his knuckles white, and a muscle twitched in his clenched jaw.

"Oh, wait a minute. Is this a shifter thing? Because human women don't necessarily pick the big, strong guys. A lot pick the smart guys, and not every smart guy is big and strong. Besides, I'm not a shifter."

He chewed that over for a minute. "They really don't?"

"Maybe they do in your pack, and yeah, I guess the club scene's full of girls going after the good-looking types, but that's not necessarily reality the world over, okay?" God, I hoped this would put an end to his jealousy toward Logan. It was completely irrational.

Sure, Logan was good-looking and I'd noticed. More than once. But we were just friends, and I was dating Nick. I'd told an elf interested in me that Nick was my boyfriend. An elf!

Okay, that particular elf, gorgeous as he was, had a problem being truthful and had nearly gotten me killed, making me Number One on the demon hit list, but still. I probably could've had him for a boyfriend if I wanted to, and hello? Gorgeous elf.

Aware Nick hadn't said anything, I frowned. "That doesn't mean I don't think you're good-looking. You're a heaping helping of hot and sexy."

He half-smiled. "Thanks."

"Besides, do you honestly think Logan would try to, I don't even know how to word it. Um…force me into a relationship with him? Exactly how would he go about doing that, what with my being psychic and all?"

His shoulders hunched a bit. "I don't know. I guess I didn't think about that."

I unbuckled my seat belt and scooted over. "I'm with you, okay? You're my guy. Quit being jealous. It pisses me off."

"I'm sorry."

"Apology accepted." I kissed his cheek while buckling the lap belt. "Just look at him the same way you do Damian and David. He's a friend, that's all."

"I'll try." He put his arm around my shoulders. "I'm sorry."

"You already said that."

"I'm saying it again."

I laughed and put my head on his shoulder. It looked like our drama bout was over. "Then I guess I'll accept it again."

When we arrived at the garage, Nick pulled into the drive of the first bay door, which was open. I got out on his side instead of scooting back over, and looked around for my car. The four vehicles I could see were larger than my "little tin can," as Nick called my beloved 280ZX.

Logan came around the front of the truck, a clipboard in hand. "I need you to sign these, and if you want, come take a look at my progress."

"Sure." I took the clipboard and pen he offered, following as he set off for the far end of the garage. Nick touched my back, steering me past a pair of legs sticking out from under a car, while I signed the first purchase order.

"Well, what do you think?"

I looked up from the clipboard at Logan's question, and my mouth fell open. Closing it, I squealed and shoved the clipboard into Nick's hands. "My baby!"

My car sat gleaming in the afternoon sun coming in through a high-set window. Even the tires shone. I hurried around it, touching the smooth, root beer brown metallic paint and peering into the windows. The only sounds I could make were *oohs* and *ahhs* between excited squeaks.

He'd brought my car back to life. Not a scratch or dent marred its metal hide. The interior smelled like new car when I flung the driver's door open and sank behind the wheel.

The only thing different was the stereo. It wasn't stock, but having considered upgrading it before, that wasn't a problem. Noticing the key in the ignition, I pushed in the clutch and started it.

My baby roared to life and settled into a deep purr. Putting my forehead against the steering wheel, I nearly cried as a rush of pure happiness filled me.

"I'm sorry about the stereo," Logan said. I sat back, discovering that he and Nick had come around to the driver's side. My boyfriend's eyebrows were raised, but he wore a smile. "Finding a stock st…"

"Doesn't matter. The new one is awesome. My car is awesome.

You're awesome. I can't believe it looks so damn good. It looks better than before! I owe you forever."

Both of them laughed, but I didn't care. I had my independence back.

Seven

My eagerness to spend time driving my car won out over any other together time. Nick and I went our separate ways for the day after the three of us figured out how to connect my phone to the stereo's hands-free feature. My way was the highway, the windows rolled down and the stereo blasting "Girls Just Want to Have Fun".

The flash and appearance of an abnormally thick golden thread caused me to swerve onto the shoulder, bringing the car to a halt.

Gold wasn't a color I'd seen in my tracking threads before. Silver, red, green, and brown I'd seen before, but gold was a new one.

Then again, I'd never dealt with forced suicides before. Maybe that's the case it was for?

Pulling back out into traffic, I followed the thread off the highway and through the city, the surroundings growing more familiar as I went.

My stomach clenched painfully when I reached the elementary school only a few blocks from my apartment. There were a lot of cars clustered around a line of police vehicles, which blocked off the front of the school. I spotted SWAT members up on the roof.

I drove by, scanning the crowd and nodding at the cop who impatiently waved me on. Kept driving until I reached my apartment's parking lot, where I left my car before teleporting back to a spot across the street from the school.

The thread, still active, led me into the crowd of frightened, angry parents and through it, straight to a terrified Betty. I touched her shoulder, noticing Damian and Stannett just beyond her, and she jumped nearly a foot into the air. "Cordi."

She reached, and I took her hands, my anxiety shooting through the roof at her initiating physical contact. Betty had never touched me before. "What's happening?"

Damian heard me, and turned around. "There's a gunman inside. No one's been hurt."

His unspoken "yet" earned a shudder from Betty. I squeezed her hands. "Can I help?"

The warlock looked at Stannett. "She may be useful."

Stannett nodded. "Stay close, we'll see…"

"He's coming out" crackled out from the radios nearby. Everyone's attention went to the school entrance. Betty's head whipped around so quickly, I heard her neck pop.

Then her breath sobbed out, and I saw why.

Oh, God. Out of all the kids in school, he had Sean.

My voice cracked as my grip on Betty's hands tightened. "That's my little brother. Damian, he has Sean."

"You're out, Jones." Stannett waved a hand. "Get back."

"What do you mean, she's out?" Betty freed her hands, her eyes narrowing. "She can do things you can't. She can…"

"Screw this situation six ways to Sunday with her emotions running wild," he said. "So, she's out."

I took a deep breath, tearing my gaze away from Sean's tear-streaked face and the gun muzzle pressed to his blonde hair. "I won't do anything to risk my brother."

Schumacher, Damian's burly, balding partner, cleared his throat. "With respect, sir, we're the ones who work most closely with Jones. I trust her to have my back in any situation."

"If my son dies because you won't let her help, I'll make it my life's mission to ruin you." Betty's low, vicious tone drew Stannett's gaze to her face.

"I understand this is a terrifying situation, ma'am, but what exactly can she do? He has a gun to your son's head, not to mention a dozen other children as shields."

"She may be able to read his mind," Damian said. "Get a line on whether this is a suicide by cop situation, or something else, since he's not talking."

I nodded. "I can try."

"If she's successful, we'll be making more informed decisions."

The police chief blew out a breath, glancing at the gunman and kids. "Will he feel it?"

"No, I'll focus on him and try scanning his thoughts. He won't notice at all." I forced my hands to relax out of the fists they'd curled into. "I need to be a little closer than this though."

Stannett frowned. "How close?"

"There's a lot of interference with this many scared people around." I bit my lip, looking at the front of the school. "Maybe twenty feet."

He shook his head. "Anyone going that close could set him off."

"Not if he doesn't see her." Damian lifted his chin slightly. "She can teleport to the entrance's roof. He won't see her up there, but she'll be close enough to focus on him."

Close enough to have trouble blocking out the terror the kids were probably feeling too, but I didn't mention that.

"There's enough room for two," Schumacher pointed out.

"Let her do it." Betty's quiet request had us all looking at her pale face and red-rimmed eyes. "Please."

Damian edged forward. "I'll go with Cordi."

"All right." The police chief glared at me. "Do it and get back here. Do *nothing* else."

I nodded, reaching for Damian's hand as he held it toward me. We stepped behind the SWAT van, and teleported. Reappearing on the entrance's overhanging roof, we both immediately crouched down. A slight lean forward and I could see the group below us. *Damian?*

I hear you. He squeezed my hand. *Go ahead and try.*

Focusing on the top of the gunman's head, I took a deep breath and let it out quietly before beginning to scan. My breathing hitched as I hit the wall of fear emanating from the kids. It took me a minute or so to block them out.

I won't do it. I won't do it. The thought, repeated over and over again, had other thoughts attached to it, but I couldn't quite catch them. I stared down, studying the man with the gun. We were close enough to see the faint tremors racking his arm.

Crap, he was another victim of whoever had caused the suicides. Had to be. I scanned his mind again, as carefully as possible, trying to pick up those other thoughts hanging behind his mantra of "I won't do it."

A sense of urgency that wasn't mine crept into my head. I didn't fight it, taking what I could pick up before teleporting us back behind the SWAT van.

"Well?" Stannett asked the second we stepped into view.

I offered everything I'd been able to glean. "His name is Mike Chapman. He's being forced to do this, I think by the same person who caused the others to commit suicide."

Schumacher grunted. "Then this is a suicide by cop thing."

"He doesn't want to hurt anyone, and is fighting the compulsion." I swallowed hard. "But I think he's losing."

"He's shaking," Damian confirmed. "We need to act fast."

"Sniper." The police chief scowled. "We'll take him out."

My eyes widened. "You're going to shoot him?"

"To save those kids? Yes. Do you have another suggestion?"

I thought fast. What could I do? There had to be som... "Yeah, I do."

"I'm listening."

"I'll teleport right beside him, and teleport away with his gun. He'll be disarmed, no need to shoot him, and we'll have a living lead to figure out who's behind this."

"Are you faster than a bullet, Jones?" Stannett stared into my eyes.

"Time me." I teleported without waiting for his go-ahead, before his question created any doubt. A blink and my fingers closed around the gun's muzzle. Another and I bent, laying it on the ground before Stannett.

Before he could speak, I teleported again. Mike Chapman's mouth dropped open, his dark blue eyes wide as I punched him square in the nose. He released Sean and staggered back a half-step. "Sit down!"

All of the kids dropped like rocks at my shout, and I moved backward while raising my hands, my knees shaking enough that I almost fell down. "I know you didn't want to hurt them, Mike. This isn't your fault. Everything's going to be okay."

I hoped I wasn't lying to him as two SWAT members rushed up and took him down.

A pair of black dress shoes appeared at the foot of the stairs, where I'd sat until the rest of my adrenalin shakes faded. Dropping my hands, I lifted my head and met Stannett's faded blue eyes. The lines at the corners of his eyes relaxed after a few seconds of surveying me. "I came over here to read you the riot act for acting without permission. But it doesn't look like it's necessary."

"Are all the kids okay? Their teachers?"

"Yes, and so is Mr. Chapman. He's strapped down to a gurney to keep him from doing anything else."

I sighed, briefly closing my eyes. "I'm sorry I didn't wait for you to say go, but I'm not sorry it worked."

"I'm not sorry it worked either." He squatted, resting his wrists on his knees. "But I'm going to make it damn clear, here and now, that any time in the future you're on a scene with my people, you wait for the word from me or whoever's in charge, Jones. Acting without thinking everything through, and not everyone knowing the plan, can lead to people being hurt or dying."

A simple nod was all I offered. He was being a lot nicer about it than I'd been to myself, after they'd hauled off Chapman and I had a few minutes to think about things. I couldn't even find it in me to point out he'd been willing to kill the guy, when Chapman wasn't at fault for anything except being a victim himself.

Maybe if he'd threatened to arrest me, or to stop using me as a special consultant, I could've dredged up a little righteous indignation. But he hadn't, and I wasn't feeling very righteous. More like a little sick to my stomach, and a whole lot of relieved.

The police chief studied my expression for a solid minute, before standing and offering me a hand up. "I think your mother wants to talk to you."

"Betty's my step-mother." I made it to my feet with his help, and blinked away a bout of dizziness as we let go of each other's hand.

"Are you all right?" Stannett frowned. "You look pale."

I didn't want to admit how shaky I still felt over my actions. "Yeah, I'm just a little tired. Teleporting kind of takes it out of me."

We began walking toward the vehicles. Once we reached them, I braced against Sean's charge and leap. "Whoa!"

His hug nearly choked me. "I knew when I saw you everything was gonna be okay."

Dear God, please never, ever let me fail him. I looked at Betty over his shoulder. She wore a smile, but her lips were trembling. "Are you okay?"

"I'm fine now," she said, coming closer before reaching out to touch Sean's back. "He's safe."

I squeezed my brother while what she wasn't saying thumped into my brain with all the power of a speeding train. *I've been so scared of her, and she saved him, the other kids, and even that man. I don't know what to say to her. How can I repay her for saving Sean's life?*

Betty's hand slipped down, her fingertips touching my arm, and she whispered, "Thank you."

I smiled. We stood there for a few minutes, until Sean wiggled to be let down. Betty's phone jingled and she pulled it out of her purse to check. "It's your father. He's here."

"Let's go find him." I held my hand out for Sean to grab, which he did at the same time he took hold of her free hand. We found Dad within a few minutes. He scooped Sean up for a hug, giving Betty and me each a smile that melted the worry from his expression.

"What happened? Last I heard, it was still a standoff."

"Cordi happened," Betty said, stepping closer to my side and putting her hand on my back.

"I wasn't scared." Sean followed that declaration with, "Well, a little at first, but then I wasn't."

Dad chuckled. "You're a tough kid."

"She's a hero."

I looked at Betty in shock. "No, I'm not."

"Of course you are. You saved at least fourteen lives."

"I'm just someone who happens to have a few talents most people don't. That's all. And I was scared, even if Tough Kid here wasn't."

"Scared or not, you acted, and your actions saved lives. That sounds like a hero to me," she said, a genuine smile blooming on her face. Then she surprised me with a hug. I closed my eyes against another wave of dizziness while returning it.

"Cordi, what are you doing?"

I blinked, and found Damian, Dad, Stannett, two uniformed cops, Betty, and Sean staring at me. My dad was the one who'd spoken. "What?"

"You need to put the gun down, Cordi," Damian said.

"Gun? Wha…" Becoming aware of a weight in my hand, I glanced down and found a gun in it, pointing at the ground. "Where did that come from?"

"It's mine." Damian pulled his jacket away enough for me to see his empty shoulder holster.

"Okay, but how did I get it?" I hated guns, kept the one Mr. Whitehaven insisted I learn to shoot locked up in my desk at the office.

"You teleported it." He moved forward once I changed my hold to the gun's barrel and held the grip toward him. "Are you okay?"

"Confused, but otherwise, yeah."

He took hold of the gun. "You have to let go."

"I can't," I said from between gritted teeth. "I'm telling my fingers to, but they're not listening to me."

Damian frowned. "You touched him."

"Huh?"

"You touched Chapman."

"Oh." Still trying to make my hand obey, I scowled. If he yanked it free, I'd lose some skin. "You think the curse is passed by touch?"

"Well, it could be, or at least this particular one may have been." Damian removed the clip from the gun and shoved it into his jacket pocket. "Let's not have any accidents."

"If the others were passed by touch, we'd have a lot more dead people."

Damian nodded. "Yes, we would. All right, I'm going to let go of the gun now. Nobody get excited."

It suddenly occurred to me that holding a gun in the middle of a number of armed cops wasn't the best place to be. That realization didn't work to loosen my fingers. "Can I sit down?"

"Good idea."

After I sat down on the pavement, I nearly freaked out. "He touched Sean too. Betty and Dad have touched Sean and me."

Stannett spoke. "Chapman had Sean's arm, and Sean's wearing a long-sleeved shirt." He turned to Betty, who held Sean. "Did the man touch your skin?"

Sean thought for a minute then shook his head. "I don't think so, except with the gun. Is Cordi going to be okay?"

"She'll be fine," Damian assured him. "I don't think it's working on her the way it's meant to."

While willing my hand to let go of the gun, I said, "Betty, you touched me and Sean both. Are you feeling okay?"

She nodded. "I think so."

Stannett sighed, looking at Damian. "Well, now what?"

"I think I'd better call David and take them to the shop. We'll do a cleansing spell."

"On them." I nodded toward my family members. "If the curse did jump from Chapman to me, I'm the biggest piece of evidence you have right now. You can try something else out, see if you can learn anything, and then do a cleansing spell on me."

Damian grimaced. "Are you certain? That could take a while."

"Yeah, I'm sure."

Boy, was I. The odds of Chapman picking out Sean had to be hundreds to one. I hoped that thought wouldn't occur to Betty.

Eight

Nearly two hours later my hand hurt from holding the stupid gun, but Dad, Betty, and Sean were clean of any magic. Dad sent Betty and Sean home after deciding he'd stay with me until the situation ended. Sean protested, but Betty agreed because Jonah's babysitter needed to get home.

"Okay." David sat down on a chair across from the one I'd dropped into as soon as we arrived at the Blue Orb. He ran a hand through his fine blonde hair while blinking owlishly at me. "Tell me exactly what happened."

I related the events up to the hug from Betty, trying not to squirm. Having a handful of gun made a restroom trip a little on the problematic side. "And then I opened my eyes, and boom! Everyone was staring at me and I had Damian's gun in my hand."

"You didn't hear any voices?"

"No."

"You don't remember anything that happened between hugging Betty and realizing you had the gun?"

"Nope."

He ran a hand through his hair and turned to Damian. "Your turn. What happened?"

"We walked up to them just as Cordi let go of Betty and stepped back. Next thing I knew, my gun was missing."

"I can't teleport stuff I'm not touching, so…"

Jo interrupted. "You've never tried to, have you?"

I thought about it. "Actually, no, I don't think I have. When I need to move stuff, I use telekinesis."

"It looks like you can teleport things you aren't in contact with, it's just that you never thought of trying before." She half-smiled. "Hell of a way to find it out, huh?"

"You could say that." I'd have to practice since I had no clue how I'd done it.

"Anyway," Damian said. "Cordi turned around to face us, and had my gun. She began to raise it…"

"And I asked her what she was doing," Dad broke in. "She lowered it, and seemed normal, except for not being able to let go of it."

David leaned back, tugging at the cuff of his gray cardigan. "Hm. That's interesting. You're certain you didn't hear any voices?"

"No voices."

"Are you hearing any now?"

"Just yours." My reply earned a chuckle from Jo.

"Do you feel any urges to shoot yourself or anyone else?"

"No."

He half-closed his eyes, brow wrinkling while his fingers plucked away at his cardigan. "I think we can rule out any sort of possession if she's not hearing voices or feeling extreme urges."

I was so beginning to feel a certain extreme urge, and crossed my legs to suppress it.

"Which leaves what? Compulsion spell?" Jo ran her hand through her auburn hair when David nodded. "Those are tricky, especially if designed to jump from person to person by touch instead of being created with a certain person as the target. I wouldn't know where to begin with creating a spell like that."

I didn't like the sound of that. My friends were pretty accomplished witches. Each of them had a specialization or two, which combined, made them one of the most powerful covens in Santo Trueno. "Is this going to be one of those spells that requires a sacrifice? Because I had enough of that with the whole demon thing."

Damian cleared his throat. "The most well-known compulsion spells are love spells, but those tend to be created as potions or objects."

"Yes, but a person could be used in place of an object." Pursing his lips, David sank lower in his chair. "Yet the more people who touch an object that's been spelled, the more it tends to dilute the compulsion."

"So this isn't a sacrifice thing?"

"Well..." he hedged. The three witches traded looks, and I sighed.

"It could be. That's what you're not saying, right?"

"Any spell can be made more powerful by a sacrifice of some sort. It doesn't have to be a sacrifice that ends in death though." Jo shrugged. "I can't wrap my mind around one thing in particular. If this particular compulsion spell is strong enough to pass from one person to another, why isn't it affecting Cordi the same way it did the guy she apparently got it from?"

"Good question," Damian said. "There wasn't any expression on her face, any more than there was on Chapman's. When she began to lift the gun, her arm trembled like his did."

David sat up and turned to my dad. "And she snapped right out of it when you asked her what she was doing?"

"Yes. Is that important?" Dad looked from him to me. I shrugged, wincing when the movement caused a pang in my hand.

"The sound of your voice apparently swung the odds in her favor to fight off the compulsion. This could be," David nodded at me, "where blood comes into play, with the familial bond between you."

"Thanks, Dad."

"Any time, kid." We grinned at each other.

"We can figure out how the spell was done later. Right now, we need to try and isolate it, in case Cordi's resistance to the compulsion wears down. It's still present, or she'd have let go of my gun by now." There was a faint worry line between Damian's brows. "I'd rather not be surprised again."

"It's unloaded," I pointed out.

"You teleported it. You could teleport the clip. We're not going to take chances."

"Okay."

My dad rubbed his chin. "I'm clean of magic, right?"

"Yes," Jo said.

"Would I make a good place to isolate it?"

"No." My response came at the same time as David's "Yes". He didn't flinch when I glared at him. "You are not using my dad as a jar."

"I volunteered," Dad said. "I can't teleport guns and the four of you should be more than enough to keep me from hurting anyone."

Everyone ignored my protests. David dug out a leather glove for Dad to wear so his wrist would be protected before Damian cuffed him to the banister of the stairs. I balked when waved over. "I don't like this."

My dad smiled. "I'll be fine."

Huffing out a swear word, I rose from the chair and crossed to the stairs. He held out his free hand, and I gave him mine. "I don't feel anything happening."

No sooner than I'd finished speaking, than the gun thumped to the floor. "Okay, I guess it worked. Ow, my hand. Dad?"

"I'm fine," he said after shaking his head. "Better let go, in case it moves back or something."

I did, stepping away to massage my aching hand while Damian

retrieved his gun. The warlock's tense posture relaxed and he smiled at me while tucking it into his shoulder holster.

Jo's familiar, a gray tabby cat named Beatrix who answered to "Trixie", wove her way through legs and jumped onto the banister. Copernicus, David's raven familiar, fluttered over and landed beside her. Both intently watched my dad while Damian called his familiar, Illusion.

The goofy-looking husky popped into existence, a piece of toilet paper sticking out from the side of his mouth. Damian dropped his head, covering his face with one hand. "Did you leave any alive?"

With a wag of his tail, Illusion grinned. He noticed the other two familiars, and tilted his head. His soft "Rroowrroo" earned an equally soft caw from Copernicus. At that, the husky sat down at the foot of the stairs and joined the other two in staring at Dad.

Though I couldn't feel anything, I moved back a few steps. All three of my friends watched their familiars as intently as the animals watched my dad, who winked at me.

"Feels like I'm giving a presentation to hard-to-impress clients."

"I'll bet." I dug my thumb into the palm of my hand, trying to rub out some of the ache. "It's good pra…"

Illy barked, and I glanced at him before looking at the other two. Trixie's fur puffed out and Copernicus half-spread his wings while opening his beak. When I looked back at my dad, his amusement had become blankness. "Okay. It worked. Do whatever you need to and get it off him."

"Mr. Jones, do you hear voices?" David's hushed question gave me the creeps. I rubbed my arms, smoothing down the sudden rise of gooseflesh.

Dad's reply was a slip of sound from between barely parted lips. "Voice."

"Male or female?"

"Man."

The three witches traded glances. David asked another question. "What is he telling you to do?"

Dad's response wasn't immediate, which made it more shocking when he lunged to his feet, roaring out the word, "Kill!"

Trixie and Copernicus shot out of the way, but Illy rose on his hind legs, butting Dad in the stomach and knocking him back onto his butt. The husky locked gazes with him and barked once. It sounded like a command. Dad froze.

"Okay, enough. Get it off him." I followed the demand with a smack to David's arm. "Now."

He rubbed his arm and pouted. "There's no call for violence."

"Calm down," Jo said. "Illy has him. We have to move him to the circle."

They did while I hovered behind Dad as he shambled along, following Illy. The husky walked backward, never lowering his gaze from my dad's eyes—or running into anything. Illy herded Dad right into the middle of the circle engraved in the polished concrete floor of David's workroom.

"What's he doing to him?"

"Nothing that will hurt him." Damian's assurance didn't help much. I chewed on a fingernail and watched Dad's expressionless face while they moved around, preparing to work the cleansing spell for the fourth time.

Halfway through, my dad blinked. His brow furrowed and he looked around at the three chanting witches, pausing on me when I said, "Don't break the circle. They're not done yet."

Dad nodded, scrubbing both hands through his brown hair. It stuck out in all directions when he finished, as though he'd just woken up from sleeping.

"Are you all right?"

"I think so."

Jo shushed us in between words. I paced back and forth, glaring at the back of her head. Inside the circle, Dad chuckled and ran a hand over his face.

After they'd worked the fifth cleansing spell, I stepped out of the circle, tired, grumpy, and in desperate need. "Be back in a minute."

After I returned from my speedy trip to one of the upstairs bathrooms, I asked, "So what did you find out?"

"They're still conferring." David gestured at the three familiars, clustered together in the reading area. Jo and Damian began clearing away the candles and other things they'd used in the spells. "Why don't you two go home? One of us will call when we have something to report."

"That sounds like a great idea." Dad stretched. "Come on, kiddo. I'll take you home."

We told the others good-bye and walked out. "That was freaky."

"I'll say." He shivered while unlocking his car. "Remind me not to do that again."

"I didn't want you to do it in the first place." My reminder received a shrug.

"Parents help their kids."

I winced. "Sorry. Thank you, Dad."

He laughed. "You're welcome, Cordi."

Halfway to my apartment, I remembered something good had come of the day. "Hey, my car's finished. Wait until you see it."

"Where is it?"

"At home. I teleported to the school from there. It was weird. My tracking sense blipped on while I was cruising the highway, led me straight to the school." I checked my pinky nail. I'd chewed it ragged. "But the thread wasn't a color I've seen before."

"What color was it?"

"Gold." I remembered something, from the case involving demons and the liar of an elf's book. "He told me to pay better attention to the colors."

Dad glanced at me. "Who did?"

"Um," I hadn't gotten around to telling him about the event that let me know precognition had joined my stable of psychic abilities. Probably because I'd actually died for a whole four minutes. "He's either a stress delusion or a spirit guide. Says his name's Sal."

Lips pressing tight, Dad lifted a hand from the steering wheel to rub the end of his nose. "Sal?"

"Sal," I confirmed. "Looks like a little old Indian man."

"Let's go with spirit guide."

"Okay. Anyway, he told me to pay better attention to the colors. I hadn't really thought about it since, but I guess he means the colors of my tracking threads."

Turning into the parking lot, Dad nodded. "Makes sense." He saw my car and his mouth fell open. "Wow. That Logan does some amazing work. It looks new."

"He does. Come look at the inside." I hopped out as he parked and led the way over to my returned baby. Dad oohed and ahhed as much as I had, but he skipped the squeaking.

After several minutes, he sighed. "I'd better get home. Betty's probably worried half to death."

"Okay." We hugged and I waved him off before locking my car and heading inside.

Leglin sat in the middle of the living room, his long, black and tan face somehow expressing stern disapproval.

"I'm sorry. There was a problem. Do you need to go outside?" He lowered his muzzle, brown eyes rolling up while his ears swept back. "I wish I could figure out what you're saying as easy as Nick does. Hungry?"

Leglin barked, his ears perking. "I'm too tired to cook. We're ordering pizza, okay?"

From the way he leaped to his feet, tail wagging, I guessed it was okay. "I'll tell you the toppings, and you bark for the things you want on yours."

My four-legged roommate's tail wagged faster.

Nine

I sat on the living room floor next to the coffee table, holding a piece of pizza for Leglin while writing down the colors of tracking threads and the cases I felt pretty certain they were related to. Since I usually had more than one case at a time, "pretty certain" was as close as it got.

"Silver has to mean vampires. Red is for demons—and let's hope we don't see any more threads that color."

Thump, thump. Leglin nibbled another bite off his super meat and cheese pizza.

"It's my turn to eat a slice next. Okay, brown...um, I think that's animals and like, natural stuff. Because I had to find a carving once, and a brown tracking thread finally led me to it. But a brown thread helped me find clues to find that missing racehorse too."

I stopped to wipe the hound's lips, which had some strings of cheese dangling from them, with a paper towel. "Okay, green must be magical stuff. Or maybe 'not evil' magical stuff, because if it was for all magical stuff, then there would've been some green threads going on while we were looking for Thorandryll's book, right?"

Leglin sneezed.

"Eww. Eat the rest of it. I have to wash my hand." I shoved the last third of the slice in his mouth when he opened it. The hound's shoulders quivered as he chewed. "Are you laughing?"

He gave me wide, innocent eyes. "You are. Gah."

I went to wash my hands. Returning, I grabbed a slice of my pizza—mine had veggies—and went back to work. "I don't remember any other colors, except for today, when the gold one popped up. So is gold for curses, or something else?"

No response from the hound, who eyed the slice of pizza I held. "It's mine."

I took a bite, thinking while chewing. "I guess it must be for cursed stuff, considering what happened." Leglin bumped my elbow with his nose. "What?"

He jerked his chin at my pizza. "I told you, it's mi...oh, you want me to hurry up and eat it?"

Thump, thump.

"This is a working dinner, dude. I talk during those." I took another bite anyway, and remade a shorter list with just the colors and what they must be related to next to each. "There. I wonder how many other colors might show up?"

Leglin grunted, poking me in the arm again. "Okay, okay."

We finished our dinner, and I let him out the front door before I cleared away the pizza boxes. Once he returned, I took a shower and put on one of my new PJ sets. Sleeping nude had become a thing of the past, because the hound slept in my room when Nick didn't stay over. He slept on the couch when Nick did.

Since discovering Leglin was part wolf shifter and therefore more of a person than most people who loved dogs considered them to be, I'd decided to treat him like I would any guy I wasn't dating. That meant no running around naked in front of him.

He probably didn't care one way or the other, but I did. It felt respectful.

After I'd turned off the light and climbed into bed, Leglin jumped up on the other side and plopped onto his side, back to me.

"Ronnie's been after me about moving into a house again," I said, watching the shadow of the tree outside my bedroom window dance across the mini blinds. He grunted, turning his ear back. "You know, because it's easier to set wards on a house since it doesn't share walls with other people's homes."

He grunted again.

"Derrick's paying my credit card bill for my car repairs, and I saved my bonus from Thorandryll's case." I rolled over onto my side and scratched the hound's neck. "I saved last year's Christmas bonus too, and I've put money in savings every check. Dad taught me to do that."

Thump.

"Anyway, I think I have enough to make a good down payment. You could have your own room and a yard. That'd be cool, right?"

Grunt.

"Is that a yes?"

Thump.

"I'm thinking a three bedroom, so we'd have a guest room. It's just," I hesitated, scratching under his chin. "There's a lot more things to worry about when you buy a house. Stuff you don't have to deal with when you rent an apartment."

"Hrr?"

"If something breaks, I tell the apartment manager, and she

sends a maintenance guy or whatever. I don't have to pay for it or worry about getting someone to fix it."

Leglin grunted again.

"So it's a big deal. A big responsibility. It's scary."

The hound snorted, and I laughed, rolling back onto my back. "Okay, not as scary as fighting demons or vampires, but it's still scary. Night, roomie."

Thump, thump.

Barely three hours later, my tracking sense flared, yanking me from a nightmare of having a house falling apart around my ears. I groaned, seeing the thin black thread it presented me with. "Great, a new color."

Leglin sat up and yawned.

"Go back to sleep, dude. I'll call Nick, and if I need you, I'll call you." He plopped back down as I threw the covers off and hurried to dress.

Five minutes later, I locked the door behind me and shrugged into my leather jacket. While walking to my car, I called Nick, only to be shunted directly to voice mail. In a fit of sleep-deprived pique, I didn't leave a message.

It didn't matter. If I needed back-up, all I had to do was say Leglin's name, and the hound would come to me, wherever I was.

It was a nifty bonus of the magical blood bond between us— though I still didn't like that it made the hound a servant of sorts. I yawned my way out of the parking lot, enjoying the purring of my car's engine.

I realized the thread led into the Palisades and muttered a few choice words. The last time I'd left my car unattended in that area resulted in the need for its nearly complete rebuilding by Logan.

Making a U-turn, I parked it under a working light in the lot of the strip mall across the highway from the Palisades. After locking it, I focused on a familiar memory and teleported into the warzone, as the *Santo Trueno Daily* loved to label the Palisades.

The thread held, its darkness leading me down several streets and into an alley. I poked around the spot it ended, but didn't find anything. "Not useful. Thanks for nothing."

As I straightened, the soft sound of a footstep came to my ears. Before I could turn around, an arm slid across my throat and began applying pressure. I grabbed for a hold, intending to try and throw him over me.

"You're an irritating, interfering little bitch," my attacker muttered. "I made this one just for you."

With that, he bent us backward and poured something nasty-tasting into my gasping mouth. I tried to spit it out, but he proved faster, dropping the bottle and slapping his hand over my mouth and nose.

The liquid, thick and sour, slid down my throat and my vision went dark.

Looked like I'd found the guy responsible for cursing people.

Ten

Upon regaining consciousness, I clambered to all fours while opening my eyes, and froze. My hands were gone. In their place were two bony white paws tipped with short nails. I fell over with a thump when my gaze focused on the black nose at the end of a black and white muzzle.

Climbing to my feet—paws—again, I bent and tucked my head to look under me. Yep, I was a dog, with white hair, pink belly, and hind legs ending in two more bony-looking paws. A long, black and white tail tucked between my hind legs as I watched.

Holy crap. Crazy Curseman had turned me into a dog.

I looked up, and then around, realizing I was still in the same alley. My clothes were gone, along with my keys, wallet, and cell phone. *Okay, don't panic.*

Kate and the coven could break this spell. I just had to get to them. Closing my eyes, I pulled up an image of my office and tried to teleport.

Nothing happened.

I tried to call fire, to lift a rotting piece of newspaper, and finally, since I was in the Palisades, to contact Logan telepathically.

Not a damn thing resulted from those attempts, and a whimper escaped as realization crashed down onto me: For the first time in my entire life, I was truly alone. Worse, my abilities were gone, leaving me utterly helpless.

Numbness filled me, but I tried walking and made my way to the end of the alley. Everything seemed quiet, and I crept around the corner to look up at the street sign, wanting to know exactly where I was. My ears kept flicking, which felt extremely weird, and it took me a couple of minutes to make the letters be letters.

Wasn't a street name I knew.

Turning, I saw my reflection in the large window of the corner store, and walked over for a better look. Ears flattening, I saw a largish, black and white mutt staring back. Definitely not as large as Leglin, and probably part Border Collie from the coloration, but not as long-haired. I turned my head from side to side. *At least I'm not an ugly dog.*

I opened my mouth, lips quivering upwards. Long, wicked looking canines appeared. I closed my mouth, lips falling back into place. *Okay, maybe I'm not entirely helpless. I'm not little, and I have big, sharp teeth.* My stomach gurgled. *And I'm hungry.*

Not dog enough to Lassie my way home, I decided the closest safe place was Logan's garage. At least, it would be if lion and tiger shifters didn't consider dogs chew toys. I hoped they didn't. My immediate issue would be finding it.

I turned away from the shop window to look around the street. Nothing looked familiar on this block, so I trotted down to the next, pausing to look both ways before crossing. In the middle of the street, a better idea struck, and I halted to act on it, mentally calling Leglin.

Being magically bound to me, the hound could come when I called him, whether out loud or mentally, no matter how far apart we were.

At least, that's what was supposed to happen.

It didn't. Maybe Crazy Curseman's magic was stronger or something.

I heaved a big sigh and began trotting again. Three blocks down, I spotted the little fast food joint where Nick had bought burritos for us during a previous trip to the Palisades. It offered some orientation, and after standing still for a few minutes, I had a mental map of how to reach the garage.

Progress! I set off at a run, my paws thumping across cement and asphalt, and quickly learned to slow down when making turns. The weight of my tail threw me off on the first one, my hind end going sideways while my front paws scrabbled for purchase.

I hoped I wouldn't stay a dog long enough to figure out all the fine tuning of four-legged locomotion. Proceeding at a lope instead of dead run, I put the brakes on two streets away from the garage as a light breeze brought a new smell to my nose.

It seemed familiar, and I sniffed, attempting to figure out why. Another deep sniff caused an explosive sneeze, briefly clearing my nose. I took a more cautious sniff, catching the smell again, and realized why it seemed familiar. The scent was the same as the taste of Logan's kiss, the night we'd shared Thorandryll's bed and I'd accidentally dragged the shifter into a retro-cognition dream.

Rich, nutty, and slightly sweet. I lifted my head, looking down the block on my left. There were cars parked along the curb, blocking my view of the other side of the street. I moved past them, still couldn't see because of more cars parked on the other side, and hurried across to slip between two.

Excitement seized me when I saw a dark figure walking down the block, away from me. The smell had grown stronger. Logan had told me, back when we first met, that he liked to take late-night walks. It had to be him.

I ran after him, catching up faster than expected, and he halted as I collapsed at his feet. My legs had tangled when I tried to stop and turn, dumping me on my side. He looked down as I looked up, rolling to my back and waving all four legs in the air to untangle them. "Well, hello."

Man, am I glad to see you! The guy throwing curses around turned me into a dog. Can you believe that? I need a ride to David's, like pronto.

Logan pulled his hands from his pockets and squatted while I managed to sit up. He held the back of one hand toward my nose. Some automatic reflex made me sniff it. He smiled. "Are you lost, little girl?"

*Crap, he can't hear me. If it looks like a dog...*I sighed, staring at his face. He slowly reached to begin scratching behind my left ear. "I guess you're okay with shifters, huh? Good girl."

He scratched a little harder, and to my embarrassment, my spine curved, one hind paw bouncing on the sidewalk. Ear scratches felt *good.* I vowed to scratch behind Leglin's ears more often.

You know, if I ever had hands again.

The shifter stopped scratching, both his hands sliding down my neck and halfway down my sides. "No collar, but well-fed and not very dirty. You haven't been lost too long."

I whined, trying to catch his eyes again. Logan's narrowed as he stared into mine. "Now, that's odd."

What? I wondered, feeling my tail begin to wag. He ruffled the fur on the back of my neck before standing.

"Why don't you come home with me, girl? I'll take you to a vet tomorrow, and see if you have one of those microchips so we can get you home to your family."

Jumping to my paws, I said "*Yes!*" but it came out as a bark. The shifter smiled again, bending slightly to pat my head. "Good girl. Come on."

Note to self: Logan really is a good guy. I fell in on his left, walking with him. Apparently, finding a stray dog ended his walk for the night, because he led the way to the garage.

For the moment, I had safety with someone I knew. Definitely a step in the right direction. I couldn't help but feel a little proud of myself. As far as I knew, no one had even realized I was missing yet, and I'd already managed to make contact with a friend.

Soames stood guard, and raised both eyebrows as he saw me standing next to Logan. "A dog?"

"She's lost, and seems to like shifters okay." Logan shrugged. "I'm going to try and find her owner."

"Okay." The other shifter stepped aside, and locked the door once we'd walked through. Logan's fingertips brushed the top of my head.

"This way, girl. Sorry, we have to climb stairs."

Crap. I hoped I could make it up them.

I did, but only because Logan picked me up after I took a tumble down a few on the third set when a back paw missed the edge of one. He put me down right outside his apartment's door, opened it, and waved me inside while calling, "Hey, Terra, look what I found."

The teen came out of her bedroom. Her eyes widened, and she took a half step backward. "That's a dog."

"Yes, a real dog, not an elf hound, and she's friendly. It's okay." His assurance didn't soothe her, because she stayed exactly where she was. A faint, acrid smell wafted from her. I didn't like it, and sat down just inside the door. It clicked when Logan closed it. He dropped down to one knee beside me, putting his hand on my shoulders. "I wouldn't bring home a threat. She's lost, and hasn't even growled once. It's okay."

Terra edged forward a few inches, her pale green gaze never leaving my face. "It's staring at me."

He ruffled my neck fur. "Yeah, she does that." He'd emphasized the "she" and moved to stroking the top of my head. "But it's really okay."

"I can't believe you brought a dog home." She moved sideways to sit on the couch, and pulled her knees to her chest. "A big dog."

The acrid scent had grown stronger, and I sneezed before dropping to my belly and scraping a paw over my muzzle. The teen froze, her eyes so wide I thought her eyeballs might pop out. Call me slow, but it was only then that I realized she was afraid of me.

Well, of Doggy Me.

A soft whine worked its way out of my throat, and I sat up,

turning to look at Logan. Why was she scared of dogs? Okay, I could understand shifters being afraid of elf hounds, since those were used to hunt them, but scared of normal dogs?

Terra could shift and eat a dog my size for lunch. A Chihuahua wouldn't even be a snack for most shifters.

He put his arm around my shoulders, his other hand rising to scratch my chest. I leaned into him, suddenly worried her fear might end with her jumping on me and biting my head off or something. "Do we have any leftovers from dinner? She's probably hungry and thirsty."

"Yeah." She unwound her arms from around her legs and slowly unfolded them. Her feet touched the worn carpeting, and after watching me for several seconds, Terra stood. "You're sure she's not going to bite me?"

"Some normal dogs like cats. Maybe she's one of them." Logan didn't rise, and kept his arm around me. "All I know is she came right up to me while I was out. Flopped at my feet and showed her belly. She didn't growl at Soames when we came in either. Pretty sure she's okay."

I did not show my belly. I tripped.

Of course, he couldn't hear me. I sighed and lay down, my muzzle propped on my legs. This was going to take some getting used to.

Eleven

I woke up the next morning to a confusing welter of scents. The disorientation made me briefly forget what had happened and where I was. Long enough to flail around and fall off the bed with a loud yelp bursting out when I hit the floor. The comforter dropped on top of me.

"Easy, little girl." Logan scooted off the bed to kneel beside me, and began untangling me from the comforter. "Just a minute."

Untangled, I stood and shook. After a second, I shook again because it felt good and weird, my skin sliding back and forth over my shoulders and back. With a chuckle, he patted my head and rose. "You meant to do that, right?"

Oh, absolutely, because I love to embarrass the hell out of myself at every opportunity.

"We'll have breakfast, and then I'll take you to the closest vet."

While that sounded good, there was something else I really needed about then. Logan disappeared into his bathroom. It'd been a relief to discover he slept in sweat pants. I went to the bedroom door, which he hadn't shut completely, and nosed it open. Terra stood at the kitchen counter, reading the back of a box of pancake mix. She glanced my way, her lips compressing into a thin line.

I whined, padding to the front door. She ignored me. *Come on, Terra. I don't want Logan taking me for walkies.*

That would be far too embarrassing once I was human again. At my next, louder whine, she put the box down and frowned at me. "What?"

I pawed the bottom of the door, wagging my tail.

The teen sighed. "You need to go outside?"

I bounced up and down before pawing at the door again.

"All right. I guess I can take you out to the yard."

Oh, thank you.

Unfortunately, I'd forgotten about the stairs. Terra started down, noticed I wasn't beside her any longer, and stopped. She looked over her shoulder. "Well, come on."

Crap. I half-crawled down a few, placing each paw carefully. She bounced down to the landing, turning to watch my descent. By the time I reached it, I was shaking. Stairs were difficult with four legs and no arms.

The future tiger Queen of Santo Trueno stared down, her brows drawn together while she nibbled her bottom lip. I looked away, toward the next set of stairs, and felt my tail curl until it was between my legs and against my belly.

"You're scared of stairs." Her fingertips brushed my ear. "Okay. Don't bite me."

Before I could look at her, she'd bent and hefted me, one arm under my rear, the other across my chest. I almost peed when she took the first couple of steps, certain she'd trip and we'd both go tail over tea kettle.

We didn't. Her faint wobble disappeared, and we thumped down to the next landing, then the following two without any trouble. Once on the first floor, she put me down and grinned. "There, that wasn't so bad. Right?"

You asking me, or yourself? I wagged my tail, noticing the acrid smell of her fear was nearly gone. Still grinning, Terra patted my head before leading me down the hallway to a door at the back. It opened onto a small, fenced area full of old and new overgrowth.

I found a hidden spot as quickly as possible, and concentrated on the day ahead. Fortunately, my doggy body didn't need instructions on how to take care of business. Finished, I stepped forward and kicked dirt like I'd seen real dogs do.

When I rejoined Terra at the door, she patted my head again. "Good girl."

The smell of fear had completely disappeared. I guess helping her get over her dog phobia could be counted as a plus to the situation. We went back inside, and she coaxed me up the stairs, appearing ready to catch hold if I tripped or fell.

By the time we walked into the apartment, Logan was ready to leave.

"I was going to cook pancakes," Terra protested.

"That's okay, I'll pick something up on the way," he said before lowering his head to rub his cheek against hers. He followed that with a kiss on her forehead. "We'll go to the grocery store when I get back, okay?"

"Okay. Um, what if the vet doesn't know who she belongs to?"

He looked down at me. "I don't know."

"You can't take her to the pound."

My blood ran cold. *No, don't take me to the pound!*

"If they can't help me, I'll run by to see Discord. I guess if she can't help, I'll bring her home and we can put an ad in the paper or something."

Whew.

Terra seemed satisfied with that, and patted my head. "Okay, see you later."

Roughly two hours later, we knew that I wasn't microchipped. We also knew that I was a seven-month-old Border Collie mix—the last thing I'd already figured out—weighing sixty-five pounds, and that in spite of the fact I'd refused, with a loud growl, bared teeth, and rear firmly planted, the indignity of having my temperature taken, I seemed to be a healthy pup.

I made a note to repay Logan for the cost of the checkup, as well as the purple collar and leash he bought before we left the vet clinic. Back in his truck, I sat quietly while he put the collar on me. He grimaced, checking to make certain it wasn't too tight. "Sorry, girl. There's a leash law and we have to follow the rules."

Not a problem. Come on, let's go. I need Kate.

Logan fastened his seat belt, turned the key, and a few seconds later, we were on the move again. Curious, I edged down the bench seat and stuck my nose out the passenger window. A minute later, my whole head was hanging out and my eyes were half-closed as information flooded my nose. I couldn't make heads or tails of most of it, aside from exhaust fumes, fast food smells, and the overall odor of a lot of people mixing with sunshine, man-made materials, dirt, and growing things.

It was pretty damn cool.

I pulled my head back inside to look at Logan, wondering if he got the same information all the time, or just when he shifted to tiger. He held out the leftover hash brown from our fast food breakfast. "Here, girl."

I ate it, hesitated then licked the crumbs off the vinyl seat. Dogs can't blush, and I was still hungry. I eyed his coffee with longing. Logan noticed and lifted a large cup of ice water from the second cup holder. "Thirsty?"

Promising myself a whole pot of coffee two seconds after I became human again, I lapped up some water.

"You made friends with Terra pretty fast. Maybe if we can't

find who you belong to, you can live with us," he said, replacing the cup. "Though a human family would probably be better."

You could give me to my dad. Permanently being a dog would be one way to spend a lot more time with my little brothers without causing Betty freak fits. *Woohoo, a glimmer of light in the worst-case scenario.*

I tucked the idea away, along with sudden worries about a much shorter lifespan and Betty's conscientiousness as a pet owner. Amadeus, the Cocker Spaniel she'd selected for the boys, was neutered. I loved my little brothers, but being spayed wasn't on my bucket list.

Logan braked, throwing his arm out to keep me from falling into the floorboard. He frowned at the car in front of us. "Idiot. You okay, girl?"

Pressed against the back of the seat, I nodded. The shifter's lips quirked as he dropped his arm. From the talk the night before, I knew he hadn't had much to do with normal animals people kept as pets before or after the Melding. He'd been around my friends' familiars a few times, and Leglin a little more, but they weren't normal pets by any stretch of the imagination.

Aside from that, he was a feline shifter, which had to add another layer of difficulty in communicating with him. Unless I figured out a way to talk or did something extremely abnormal, he would keep on thinking that I was simply a lost dog.

I brightened. Nick was a wolf shifter, and he communicated with Leglin. Maybe he'd understand me. Holding that hope close, I looked through the windshield, eager to reach the office.

When we arrived, Kate wasn't sitting at the receptionist's desk. I followed Logan to my empty office, which he glanced inside of before turning to walk down to Kate's office. She wasn't there either. Our next stop was Mr. Whitehaven's office. He was there, but on the phone and speaking in a foreign language. It sounded harsh like German, but wasn't.

He smiled, gesturing for us to come in and have a seat, his reddish brown eyes focusing on me. For a second, I thought he recognized me and my rear wagged back and forth with my tail. But no, he continued his conversation without pausing.

Recognition would've made him drop the phone, or look

surprised, or something. Maybe the boss just liked dogs.

I sat on the floor once Logan sank down onto the couch. He unsnapped the leash, trusting Doggy Me to behave. His trust wasn't misplaced; no way I'd attempt jumping onto the couch after failing to manage to jump up on the bed. I'd had to climb instead, which proved pretty awkward with four legs and no hands.

A whole new respect for dogs had taken root in my heart.

Mr. Whitehaven finished his call, and gave Logan a cordial greeting, which the shifter returned before explaining why we were there. He ended with, "I hoped Discord might be able to shed some light on who this little girl belongs to."

Discord can shed all the light. Too bad you can't understand me. I watched my boss's expression, and knew that he had no clue I'd gone missing yet.

"She should be in soon. How is your Queen-to-be settling in?"

I'd been turned into a dog by a crazy man, and they were making chitchat. Maybe Mr. Whitehaven would sense something if I got closer? I stood and crossed the room to walk around his desk and sit beside him. He pushed his chair out, turning it enough to look at me.

When he bent to pet me, I caught a nose full of oddness that included a hint of strange-smelling smoke and metal. I'd never noticed it before. It had to be his personal smell, but I didn't recognize anything else in it. It wasn't unpleasant, just…odd.

Odd and sort of wild smelling.

Busy concentrating on it, I heard the faint squeak of the front door opening and closing. Someone had arrived, probably Nick since I didn't hear Percy, Kate's parrot familiar, complaining. The boss gently ruffled the back of my neck. "She's quite friendly."

"And smart," Logan said as Nick appeared in the doorway. My first reaction was joy. Surely he'd figure out I was me.

My second, as his scent wafted across the room, wasn't intentional but something instinctive. I backed away from Mr. Whitehaven, so that I could see Nick clearly, the hairs down my spine bristling, and growled.

Nick stank of something Doggy Me didn't like at all. My growl climbed and fell when he focused on me. In spite of my deep warning sound, he dismissed me in favor of asking Logan, "Is it yours?"

"Not exactly. She's lost." The tiger shifter patted his leg. I ignored him, fighting to stop the growl.

"She's going to be dead if she jumps me," Nick said in a flat voice. His eyes flashed gold when he looked at me again, but his next words were for the boss. "Cordi's missing."

Everyone forgot me, and their lack of attention allowed me to stifle my growl.

Whitehaven turned his chair to face him. "Are you certain?"

"I stopped by her place. Her car's gone and Leglin's there alone. He said she went out last night and didn't come back. He can't find her."

A thrill of warmth swept through me, hearing that my hound buddy had been trying to find me. Nick raked a hand through his hair. "She didn't call me. Again. And now something's happened to her."

Though I felt bad he was worried, my lips drew back in a silent snarl. Since no one was paying attention, I decided to return to Logan by way of the room's perimeter. Going too close to Nick didn't seem like a good idea, what with something internal loudly insisting the wolf shifter was "bad" and "wrong" and pushing me to attack him.

Whitehaven's full wall display case was on that side of the room, and as I neared it, my ears perked at the faint sound of voices. At least, I thought they were voices, but I couldn't make out any actual words. I stopped and tilted my head, listening to the continuous murmur of sound.

The next thing I knew, Logan had snapped the leash onto my collar. Startled, I looked up, but he'd already straightened. "I'll take her home and come back to help search. I can bring a couple of others to help."

Nick blew off his offer of help with a rude snort. "I can have a dozen from the pack here in twenty minutes."

I felt like biting him until Mr. Whitehaven spoke. "There's no sense gathering a search party until we know if Damian is able to lock onto her cell phone. If he is, we'll be grateful for any assistance you can provide."

Logan nodded, but I felt the tension in him and saw the way his eyes narrowed at Nick. "We'll be ready."

I moved when he gave the leash a gentle tug. Nick left the doorway, crossing the room to begin arguing with the boss. Once outside in the parking lot, Logan heaved a quick, hard breath. "Sometimes, I really want to kick the ever-loving shit out of that arrogant puppy." He stroked my head. "He rubs you the wrong way too, huh?"

Doggy Me. Human Me likes him. I wondered if being turned into a dog made me a better judge of character. People were always talking about how animals knew it when someone was bad. Nick could be damn bossy, and he was downright rude to Logan most of the time, but I didn't think he was a bad person.

Then again, Doggy Me was part Border Collie, a dog bred to watch and tend herds, while Nick was a wolf, one of the hereditary predators such dogs guarded against. It could be that simple.

"I hope Discord's all right," the shifter muttered, twitching the leash. We walked to his truck in silence.

Twelve

Logan didn't drive straight back to his apartment. Instead, he stopped at a pet store outlet. "Finding your family is going to have to wait, girl, so we need to pick up a few things for you."

By then, I'd begun to wonder why he talked to Doggy Me so much. A lot of people talk to their pets, but it wasn't something I expected shifters to do. Whatever the reason, it was nice to find out he didn't drop something the second it became inconvenient.

I did feel bad they were worried, but it was kind of funny too. *Here I am, right under your noses. I'm not nearly as lost as you guys think.*

We went inside, and Logan proved to be a fast, decisive shopper. His idea of a "few things" resulted in a mixed case of canned dog food, a large bag of kibble—the good stuff, not an off-brand—food and water bowls, a box of organic doggy biscuits, a big square dog bed, a brush, and four toys. Internally cringing at the total, I followed him back out to the truck while adding it to what I already owed him for the vet checkup.

I needed to return to human before taking care of Doggy Me emptied out his bank account.

Twenty minutes later, we pulled into the garage. A couple of other shifters helped unload and carry things upstairs, and he told them to clean up in order to go with him to help look for me.

"Discord's missing?" Terra asked, looking up from the bags he'd placed on the table.

"Looks like it." Logan unsnapped the leash then touched her back. "Don't worry. We'll find her, if she doesn't handle whatever's going on herself."

I nosed his other hand, pleased to learn that he really thought I could take care of myself. He looked down with a smile. "I decided our new friend here is staying until Discord turns up. Would you mind taking care of her for a while?"

"I don't mind, but what about going to the grocery store?"

"Alanna and Teague will take you."

The teen nodded, emptying the bags. She surprised me by asking, "Did you try contacting her?"

"The second Nick said she was missing. She didn't answer. I think there's a limit on her telepathic range." Logan began pulling tags off of the toys. "But I'll keep trying."

"What about her elf hound? Can't he…"

"Nick said he can't find her."

I sat down as Terra's face paled. "That's not possible. He's bound to her by blood magic. He should always be able to find her."

"Yeah, I know." They gazed at each other for several seconds. Logan shook his head. "There could be another reason for why he can't find her."

Than what reason? I looked from her to him.

"So you think she's still alive?"

Oh, that reason.

He smiled. "I won't count her out until I see her decomposed body. Discord's smart, tough, and powerful. It's more likely someone or something is hiding her from Leglin. She'll either escape, or figure out a way around it and call for help if she needs it."

My tail started wagging. *You are my new bestest friend, Mr. Sayer.*

Logan glanced down and patted me on the head. "I need to get downstairs, let Alanna and Teague know, and head back to Arcane Solutions." He pulled out his wallet, handing over a card. "Don't go crazy over the junk food at the grocery store."

Terra sighed, accepting the card. "I won't."

With a chuckle, he lowered his head to rub his cheek against hers, kissed her forehead, and headed for the door. I followed, but he gently shooed me back and shut the door in my face.

Curses, foiled again.

The teen fed and brushed me after putting away my new belongings, and then took me downstairs to the yard. A woman came out before I went in search of a private spot. Since she asked if Terra was ready to leave, I decided she must be Alanna.

"Yeah. Do you think she'll be all right out here while we're gone?"

"Should be. I'll tell Jake to check on her a few times."

Terra knelt to hug me. "You be good and stay here. I'll be back soon."

I wagged my tail, seeing an opportunity. As soon as they went inside, I hurried to take care of business and began searching for a way out of the yard. Sooner or later, Kate would do a locator spell.

Since I knew where the garage was, I could find my way back to where I'd left my car. Finding Doggy Me with my car should give them a hint.

The yard's walls were cinder block, but the gate was wood, and there wasn't anything but dirt under it. I couldn't open it, but fifteen minutes later, I wiggled under it thanks to the hole I'd dug. After a good shake to rid my coat of the worst of the dirt, I took off at a run.

Daytime traffic proved daunting. Vehicles were a lot bigger when you were a dog. I had a few narrow misses before reaching the highway, and paused to catch my breath before braving the underpass. The strip mall waited on the other side. I couldn't see my car yet, and hoped it hadn't been towed, or worse, stolen.

"Hey!"

I looked over my shoulder and found Terra hanging out a car window three vehicles back. *Crap.*

Turning, I hurriedly looked both ways and took off across the access road as the light turned green. She yelled again, but I couldn't make out the words over the sounds of engines revving. Thanks to the green light, I didn't have to stop on the other side of the underpass, but kept going across the other access road and to the sidewalk around the strip mall's parking lot.

It was full of cars, so I halted to look around. Of all the things to forget, I couldn't remember exactly where I'd left my car. Under one of the lights, but there were a couple dozen or so of them. *I need to pay a lot more attention before I teleport.*

"There she is."

Aw, hell. Terra and company had followed, and were pulling into the closest entrance. I flattened my ears, aimed for the closest light pole, and plunged into the parking lot chaos. The sound of doors slamming followed me, as did Terra's cries for me to stop.

Guilt was quick to rise at her frightened tone, but if I could find my car before they caught me, she would recognize it, and call Logan. It wouldn't necessarily let them figure out Doggy Me was actually Cordi, but beggars can't be choosers.

I do not recommend playing chase with determined shifters. The steady car and foot traffic was one of the reasons they didn't quickly catch me. However, having three people chasing after me did provide enough incentive that I learned to jump. Mostly over Teague, who tended to dive for me each time he caught sight of me.

The other reason they were having trouble? Terra wasn't the only one phobic about dogs. Teague did finally manage to grab hold of my tail, but when I instinctively turned with my teeth bared, he let go and backed away with wide eyes.

Alanna, a petite brunette with big blue eyes, called him a wuss as she shot past him, hot on my trail. I poured on the speed, only to slam on the brakes as Terra stepped out from between two parked cars. They had me sort of surrounded.

I turned, intending to dart between cars before one of them was close enough to grab my collar, and froze, the tip of my nose not eight inches from the front bumper of my beloved chariot.

"Bad dog!" Terra's hand closed on my collar. "You scared me. Someone could've hit you. I'm going to buy a chain and…"

I looked up when she fell silent and felt a doggy grin spread. She'd noticed my car, and her mouth stayed open as her eyebrows slowly rose. She recovered quickly, closing her mouth and swallowing. "Teague, call Logan. Tell him we found Discord's car."

Yes! I wanted to do a victory dance, but settled for wagging my tail when she knelt and hugged me, still staring at my car.

An hour later, I wasn't nearly as pleased. I stood in the center of a knot of shifters, five tigers, a lion, and nearly a dozen wolves. Damian was present, with his partner, Detective Schumacher, and two uniformed cops.

Discord Jones had officially become a missing person, because they'd found my cell phone on the edge of the highway, four miles away. No sign of my clothes, wallet, or keys.

"We need to clear the area and block it off," Damian said, watching the wolves pass around a plastic bag with something in it. "What's that?"

Nick answered. "It's a shirt she wore a couple of days ago. We're going to spread out and see if we can pick up her scent."

"Discord doesn't like to park her car inside the Palisades. If it's here, she probably teleported," Logan said. He had a tight grip on my collar, because I'd been growling continuously for twenty minutes. Doggy Me didn't like the smell of any of the wolf shifters.

"He's likely right. I'm going to do a spell that will show us whether she did or not." Damian knelt to open the dark blue duffle bag at his feet. I knew it held his department-approved spell paraphernalia. I even knew the spell he planned to do didn't always work. Even though the odds were one in a hundred, if this spell got results, they were accepted in court, so it was worth his while.

My witch buddies often said having a personal connection to

someone helped, which meant the spell should work this time, especially with a focus object as large as my car. A good thing, since Damian didn't have me and my abilities as backup this time—not that they always came through.

While watching him set his things up, I tried to reach for my telepathic ability again. *Damian?*

Nothing. I tried Nick, Logan, and even Schumacher, but none of them heard me.

Disgusted, I leaned against Logan's leg. He crouched down, his dark green eyes meeting mine, and proceeded to quietly lecture me for running off and scaring Terra.

Schumacher approached. "Is the dog a shifter too?"

"No, she's a normal dog."

The beefy detective grinned. "Then she probably didn't understand half of what you said. Maybe not even that much."

Logan sighed, his fingers closing around my muzzle to give it a light shake, and then he straightened. "Yeah. Guess I'm not used to normal animals."

"What's her name?"

"I don't know. Found her last night. I'm Logan Sayer." They shook hands, and the shifter filled him in on his attempts to find my imaginary owners. Schumacher held his hand out for me to sniff and patted my head after I'd done so. There were traces of burger on his skin. I hoped I'd eat one again, preferably as a human.

"If you don't have any luck, and decide not to keep her, let me know. My sister's been looking for a dog. She'd take good care of her."

"I'll keep that in mind, thanks."

Meanwhile, Terra had edged closer to Damian, watching his preparations with interest. She cleared her throat. "What does this spell do?"

"It'll show time passing in this specific location, from about ten last night until dawn, like watching a video on fast forward."

The teen frowned, glancing up at the light post. I followed her gaze to a security camera mounted on it. "Why don't you just look at the security camera footage?"

The warlock snorted. "Because there isn't any. That camera's a fake."

"Oh."

We waited for the customers who owned the cars parked around mine to move them, until the area cleared enough for Damian to spray paint a gray circle around my car. Terra asked if the color was important, and Damian smiled.

He loved answering questions about magic, and explained that gray was one of the colors conducive to vision and neutrality. "Which means I won't accidentally influence a vision with what I want to see, but we'll see the truth of what happened during the time we're viewing."

"If you can see the past, can you see the future too?"

Damian shook his head. "The future isn't written. Or at least, not written in stone, though David—he's a member of my coven—thinks there are some events that are. Only psychics with precognition ever catch glimpses of the future."

He finished spraying the circle and straightened. "You should come by the Blue Orb sometime. David owns it, and another of our coven members, Jo, works there with him."

The girl glanced at Logan, who smiled and nodded. "I'll take you after we find Discord."

"This will take a few more minutes." Damian traded his paint for chalk. I wished he'd call for Illy, but couldn't remember him needing his familiar for this spell before. Maybe that's what it'd take: Getting to one of my witch buddies' familiars. I didn't really understand what they were, other than not really the animals they appeared to be.

After the episode with my dad, I was glad they all seemed to like me.

Since I'd watched Damian do the spell before, I watched Nick instead. He'd taken my shirt back and sealed the bag. He spoke to another shifter, and I realized they looked quite a bit alike. Were they brothers? Nick hadn't ever mentioned his family. He only talked about his pack in general terms, aside from his Alpha. Then again, he'd never really offered much information about him either.

He'd made the suggestion that I visit, but I'd turned him down after learning a lot of them preferred skin to clothes most of the time.

The other noticed my staring, and nudged Nick. "Dog's watching you."

My boyfriend turned around, his eyes flashing to dark gold. "Would you take that damn dog home or whatever?"

Logan patted my head. "She's not going to do anything."

"Better hope it doesn't," the other shifter said. "We'll rip it apart."

Terra whirled around, her light eyes narrowed. "And maybe I'll rip you apart. How'd you like that, wolf boy?"

"Come at me, kitty. I'll tear your head off and use your skull to piss in."

Wow, what a freakin' douchebag. If he was Nick's brother, I

already didn't like him. Logan released his hold my collar, taking a step toward the other shifter. "Don't threaten our Queen."

"She made the first threat," Nick said, but he put a hand on the other wolf shifter's arm.

"I did not. He threatened Angel."

The other tigers, and Teague the lion, closed ranks behind the three of us. Nick's brow creased, and brown flooded his irises, pushing the gold out. "The dog is a threat. It's waiting for its chance to attack one of us."

Schumacher wandered over, stopping so that he stood between the two groups. "Okay, folks, let's everyone calm down. We're here to find a missing person, not argue over the pretty puppy who can't help her instincts." He looked at Logan. "Just keep hold of her, okay?"

"Sure." Logan patted his thigh, and I moved to stand beside him. He didn't grab my collar, but his fingers rested on it.

The beefy detective winked at us before turning his head. "Now, you…what's your name?"

Nick had to elbow his companion before the guy would answer. "Patrick Maxwell."

They were related. I studied him, and decided they were definitely brothers. They looked too much alike to be anything else. Patrick stood an inch or so taller than Nick, and he was a little heavier built. I thought he could be a couple of years older, and could almost smell the arrogance oozing from him.

Definitely a douchebag.

"Nice name, kid. Why don't you apologize to the little lady here for being ugly to her and the puppy and we'll call it even instead of starting some kind of shifter war?" When Patrick scowled, Schumacher drew himself up to his full height and spoke in a less friendly tone. "That wasn't a suggestion."

"Discord likes dogs," Logan murmured, so quietly Schumacher didn't hear. But Nick must have, because he elbowed Patrick again.

That did the trick, though Patrick's sarcastic tone didn't suit the flowery bow he executed. It looked silly with his cutoff jeans and muscle shirt anyway. "My apologies."

Terra hissed, but said, "Accepted."

"There now, see? No need for anyone to get their undies in a bundle." Schumacher grinned, smacking his hands together. "Much better, kiddies. Let's focus on business now, okay?"

"I'm ready." Damian's announcement drew everyone's attention. A few minutes of rearranging occurred, as everyone moved to find a spot to watch. I ended up standing between Logan and

Terra, off to the warlock's right side. The other cat shifters lined the edge of the circle from Terra around, ending with Teague standing between the tigers and Nick.

Damian began chanting. The candles he'd placed at the four cardinal points popped, their wicks lighting. The breeze tried to put them out, but my witch buddies had long ago learned to combat the wind. They used the same wicks in their candles, which Jo and Ronnie made, that joke birthday candles did. You had to pinch them to put them out.

Zing! The circle flashed and formed a half-bowl of swirling grayness, obscuring my car from view. With a little more chanting, the gray changed, becoming dark and then clearing enough for us to see an empty parking spot within a circle of yellow light.

"So cool," Terra breathed.

Damian spoke a final word before telling them, "Now, we watch."

Several minutes passed with not much happening inside the impromptu theater, other than the light flickering and an occasional bit of dust skating over the asphalt.

Finally, my car pulled into the spot and my former human self stepped out of it. The warlock said something, freezing the scene. "Well, she was fine that far."

I heaved a sigh, staring at myself, and heard an echoing, quieter sigh from Logan before he said, "She looks cranky."

From the other side of the magic theater, Nick spoke. "She must've been asleep. Her hair's messy. I bet her tracking sense woke her with something."

Human Me's long, brown hair did look kind of tangled with spots of fuzziness. Her narrowed eyes and faint scowl definitely indicated crankiness. I wanted to hide when I realized her tee was inside out.

At another word from Damian, the scene began moving again. Human Me locked my car, dropped the keys into the inside pocket of my jacket, and disappeared. I'd never gotten to see myself teleport before. It wasn't something you could watch yourself do in a mirror or anything.

For about five minutes, my car sat there by itself, the sun eventually rising and overpowering the parking lot light, and then the magic dissipated, leaving my real car in the center of those watching.

"Right," Damian said. "She went into the Palisades. I'll call Kate, see if she can pinpoint a location."

"We'll go in, start looking for her trail." Nick glanced at his brother. "In pairs."

"We'll help." By "we", Logan didn't mean Terra, her two guardians, or me. Our "we" was sent home.

Thirteen

Once home, Alanna and Terra filled in the hole I'd dug before leaving me in the backyard. I took care of a suddenly pressing need and then wandered around, looking for another way out.

A whimper on the other side of the fence drew my attention. I trotted over to the gate and barked as quietly as possible, hoping my question was understandable. *"Who's there?"*

"Princess."

I hit my nose on the gate, trying to look through the wooden slats. After a few seconds of adjusting, I could make out white fur. *"I'm Cordi. I've been looking for you."*

The Chihuahua seemed to understand my whining without any trouble. *"Why?"*

"I know your mom, Vera."

"You do?" Princess pressed her face to the other side of the gate. *"I want to go home. Can you take me home?"*

Marveling at the difference being a dog made in communicating with one, I said, *"Not right now, but as soon as I can. You need to find a way in here. I'm staying with friends, and they'll take care of you too until we can take you home."*

She yipped and began scrabbling at the ground. *"There's a rock."*

"Yeah, I kind of dug out earlier. Let me see if I can move it." Hooking a paw over the rock, I scraped at it. It moved a little. *"I can. Wait a second."*

"Hurry. I saw the bad man looking for me."

Still working the rock away from the gate, I asked, *"What bad man?"*

"He took me away from Mom's friend, Eileen. He had others in a place that smelled bad. I couldn't open their cages, but I opened mine."

With a final hard pull, I managed to move the rock several inches back from the gate. It would've been a lot easier with hands instead of paws. *"Can you get in now?"*

More scrabbling and Princess wiggled under the gate. She shook dirt from her fur before looking up at me with bright, brown eyes. *"You're big!"*

I debated telling her that I was actually a human, but decided against it. *"Yeah. Do you know what shifters are?"*

"The animal people?" She shrank back against the gate, looking around while her ears flicked back. *"They're scary. The bad man's an animal people."*

What? Shifters were stealing dogs? *"What kind of animal is he?"*

Princess sneezed. *"Wolf."*

Okay, I needed some time to think about that. However, I didn't get it right then, as footsteps sounded in the alley. *"Someone's coming. Go hide."*

The Chihuahua didn't waste time, scooting away from the gate with her little whip of a tail tucking between her hind legs. I didn't move, watching the gate and listening.

"Last damn thing we need to be doing is looking for that yappy scrap of fur again." A heavy thumping sound followed the words, and someone yelped. Pressing my nose to the gate, I sniffed.

The person who'd yelped spoke. "I didn't let it out of the cage."

"Dogs are stupid, they can't open their own cages." Another thump and yelp. "I swear, if he finds out, you'll be the one getting your tail cut off."

They were coming closer, and the breeze carried their scents to me. A growl rose in my throat. They were wolf shifters. "Did you hear that?"

"Yeah." A few seconds later, the two were outside the gate. The larger one grabbed and shook it.

I went nuts, snarling, barking, and throwing myself at the gate, saliva flying everywhere. My doggy instincts shrieked *Kill, kill, kill!*

"Hey, looks like we got ourselves a candidate for the ring." The gate rattled. "It's locked. Step back."

"Wait, don't you smell..."

Behind me the door opened. I redoubled my efforts, aware that backup was on the way. I hoped it wasn't just Terra. Splinters of wood peeled away from the wooden planks as I raked my nails down them.

"Hey! Calm down." It wasn't Terra, but Teague. I spun away from the gate, dashing toward him, only to turn and run back, throwing myself against it again. The wolf shifters beat a hasty retreat down the alley.

Alanna appeared in the doorway. "What's going on?"

"The dog's lost its mind."

I stopped, cocking my head with my ears perked, and then gave a satisfied bark. *"That's right, run! Cowards."*

"She hasn't lost her mind. Can't you smell them? There were wolves here a minute ago." Alanna shook her head. "And they weren't any of those doing the searching. Better call Logan and tell him we had visitors."

Teague sniffed the air as I turned around, scanning the small yard for Princess. The Chihuahua had shoved herself under a tangle of weeds, and neither of the shifters had noticed her yet. *"You can come out. These animal people are my friends. They won't let the wolves get you."*

"Are you sure?"

"Yes. Come on." I walked toward her as Teague dashed back into the building. Alanna stayed, watching me, and sighed when she spotted Princess. "Great, another dog."

Terra seemed delighted I'd brought a friend home, swooping down on Princess to pick her up for a cuddle. "You're precious. Are you hungry? I bet you're hungry. You need a bath too. You're a little stinky."

I settled on the floor to think about the wolf shifters. Why would they be stealing dogs? Who was the "he" mentioned? Their pack leader? Were they members of Nick's pack?

None of them seemed to like dogs, but why would they steal them if they didn't like them? To eat?

A shudder worked its way down my spine. Surely not. I couldn't see Nick eating someone's pet, or being able to play dumb about our missing dog case if one of his pack had stolen Princess.

I laid my head on my forelegs, watching Terra fuss over Princess. The smaller dog had stopped shivering, reveling in the attention. At least she was safe. I'd have to figure a way to get her home. If Logan would take her to the office, Mr. Whitehaven, Kate, or Nick would recognize her and that would take care of that.

One case mostly solved. Not bad for someone who'd been turned into a dog.

I still needed to figure out why those wolf shifters had taken her, for whom and to what purpose. Lying there, watching Princess chow down on the doggy kibble Terra poured for her, I sighed. She was registered, and there was that "excellent pedigree" to consider. Maybe they were stealing dogs to sell them?

Wait. The larger shifter had said "candidate for the ring" when I went nuts at the gate.

Dog fighting. They'd stolen Princess to use as a bait dog. I shuddered again, in spite of feeling glad the little dog wouldn't be facing such an awful fate after all.

Okay, then I had the "why" in addition to recovering Princess, but who were those shifters working for?

I should probably be worrying about returning to human form instead of that, yet couldn't stop wondering who the mentioned "he" was.

When Logan rushed into the apartment a half hour later, I was still wondering.

"Are you all right?"

Terra frowned, busy drying off Princess, who hadn't thrown a fit about being bathed. "Yes, why are you here? You're supposed to be helping look for Discord."

"I was, but..."

"There were only two of them, and they were wolves. Do you really think wolves are working with tigers?"

Head up, I looked from her to Logan with my ears perked. Something was going on.

"Less than half the tigers moving to Santo Trueno have approached us. Establishing a clan here with a Queen as young as..."

She interrupted him. "I know, I know. But I'm safe here. You've made sure of that."

Logan dropped into a chair at the table and sighed. He ran a hand through his hair. "You're as safe as possible. That doesn't mean we can't be attacked here." His head tilted as his gaze zeroed in on Princess. "Where did that one come from?"

"She's a friend of Angel's."

"Angel?"

Terra nodded at me. "She needed a name, so I gave her one."

Logan glanced my way, his brow furrowing. "Huh. Why 'Angel'?"

The girl shrugged, picking up the dog brush to begin on Princess's coat. "I don't know. Kind of fit."

I wagged my tail. He knew my middle name was Angel. Maybe he'd keep thinking about it and something would click. I could hope, anyway.

"Okay." He patted his thigh, and I went to him, receiving a neck scratch for my trouble. "I should stay here. My first duty is to you."

"Don't be silly. We have twenty-four people here. One more isn't going to make me any safer."

Logan scowled. "Thanks."

She reached over to pat his shoulder. "I didn't mean it like that, and you know it. If I'm going to be Queen, I have to trust my people, not just my protector. You're not going to be that forever. I'll have a mate one day."

"It's my job to make sure that day is when you decide, not when someone else decides for you." He scratched harder at my neck. I poked him in the leg with my nose. Logan's fingers eased up. "Sorry, girl."

"I'm not a kid anymore."

"You're not an adult yet either. Diana should've waited until you were before sending you here."

Terra laughed. "She wanted to, but Dad was tired of breaking up fights."

"I bet he was," Logan muttered. I laid my head on his thigh, my eyes closing. Their conversation gave me an interesting look into their lives. "Keeping you safe was easier when you were little."

"That's what Dad said, before complaining about how old he's getting." The girl shrugged, setting the brush down. "There, Precious. You smell a lot better."

"Alanna's good at keeping people under control, but I really should stay here."

"No, you should go help find Discord." Terra latched onto his forearm, her pale green eyes swirling to a green-gold. "She's the one who needs help right now."

Logan's lips pursed as he stared at her. "You really like her."

Releasing his arm, she sat back. "Yeah, but that's not the only reason I think you should be helping find her." The teen bit her lip, her gaze dropping to Princess. "I'm hoping she'll help me pick the right mate."

Whoa. I lifted my head to look at her. That was a tall order. Why the hell would she want me to help her with that?

He leaned, catching hold of one of her hands. "As long as you make your choice freely, he'll be the right one."

"Everyone says that, but you know that's not always true."

Logan spoke, a purr underlining his words. "I have faith that you'll choose someone who will be a good Consort. Someone who will love you and be strong enough to protect you."

"I have to be strong enough to protect myself."

He chuckled. "That's a given with our bloodline. You will be."

Terra sighed, her back and shoulders straightening. She seemed to shake off her doubts in a second. "Right. Now, go. I have Alanna and Teague to help me. You concentrate on finding Discord."

There were a few more minutes of back and forth, but Logan finally gave in and left. It appeared that Terra and I had some stuff in common, sort of. She might have been born into a world of magic, but she had the same kind of self-doubts I did. Not that I'd tell anyone, but I worried a lot about coming up against someone and not being strong enough to protect myself. That was one of the reasons I hadn't thrown a bigger fit about the boss hiring Nick.

Yet I'd never be Queen of a shifter group, like her. Having people look to her for leadership for the rest of her life...boy, that sounded like a few thousand pounds of pressure. And they had to watch out for other tigers trying to kidnap her and force her into marriage? Wow.

I'd never have to worry about that kind of stuff, and it made my life look like a breeze compared to hers. Poor kid.

* * *

"*Don't pee on the floor. She'll take us outside in a minute*," I promised Princess, who danced around my front legs, her already bulging eyes bugging out even further.

"*I can hold it.*"

I whined again, looking over my shoulder at Terra. The teen looked up from her book. "Oh." She put the book down and rose from the couch. "Sorry. Let's go outside, girls."

Teague sat on a folding chair in the hallway outside, reading a magazine. "Do you need something?"

He smelled different than Terra, and I remembered he wasn't a tiger, but a lion. Even so, he smelled better to Doggy Me than the wolf shifters did. Border Collies probably didn't run across lions and tigers on a regular basis. Yeah, I still held out hope that was why Doggy Me didn't like wolf shifters.

"To take the dogs outside."

"I'll go with." He stood, dropping the magazine onto the chair's seat. "Logan said you'd named them?"

The teen grinned. "Yeah, Angel's the big girl, and the little one's Precious."

"Cute names."

Also pretty darn close to our real ones. Well, Angel *was* my real name. I wondered how Terra had managed to pick one of my names and one close to Princess's real name.

I made it down the stairs without any help, watching the two of them. Teague didn't seem interested in Terra. He called her "kid" a couple of times. Maybe lion and tiger shifters didn't mix the way natural lions and tigers sometimes did. I'd seen a liger once, during a family vacation to Las Vegas, back before the Melding. It had been bigger than Logan was in his tiger shape, and he was larger than natural tigers.

It would've been silly to leave a tiger standing guard over her, after what I'd heard, unless that tiger was Alanna. Teague must be the safest choice Logan had available.

Out in the yard, Teague walked to the gate and poked around while Princess quickly found a spot not far from the back steps and squatted. I chose a hidden spot again, and was aware of Terra's gaze when I left cover to rejoin Princess. The Chihuahua bounced around. *"Let's play!"*

I tried, but had no clue how to go about it. Princess yapped and ran, dodging under me and out while nipping at my legs. I pushed her a few times with my nose, careful not to be too rough. She gave up on me, sitting down with her tongue hanging out. *"How come you don't know how to play right?"*

"Um...ooh, a bird!"

The Chihuahua leaped to her paws and spun around, barking as she raced off to charge the pigeon that had landed in the yard. I sat down to watch her.

Terra was still watching me. Done scaring the pigeon away, Princess pranced back and sniffed my mouth. *"Why, you're a pup. You should know how to play."*

"Sorry. I haven't been around other dogs much." Leglin didn't play. Maybe I should try taking him to a dog park. Hell, I'd probably be joining him. Returning to human was beginning to feel like it wouldn't happen.

"You're sad." The Chihuahua cocked her head, her bat ears so perked, they trembled. *"Why are you sad?"*

"I'm sad about all those other dogs in the bad-smelling place." Talking to Princess reminded me of talking to Jonah. *"Do you know what will happen to them?"*

"No, what?"

I hesitated, worried I'd give her nightmares, but continued anyway. *"The bad men will make the big dogs fight. They'll teach them how on the little ones."*

Princess's eyes bugged out again, and she whimpered. *"That's bad. Bad, bad, bad!"*

"Yeah. I wish we could help them." I did, whether doing so would lead to discovering the identity of the mysterious "he" or not. No dog deserved either fate.

The Chihuahua sniffed, her ears drooping and perking. *"I remember where the bad-smelling place is."*

"I can't get out." I heaved a sigh, glancing at Terra, who watched us intently. *"And you don't need to go back there."*

"We could lead your animal people friends to it. She's," Princess pointed her nose at the teen. *"Nice. She would help."*

"I'm sure she would, if we could explain. But it would be dangerous for her too."

"Why?"

Yeah, just like talking to Jonah. Question after question. *"Some animal people that smell like her aren't nice. They'll be mean to her if they catch her."*

"Oh." The little dog's ears folded back. She stood and shook so hard, her twiggy hind legs flew from side to side. Too cute. *"Want to run?"*

"You go ahead."

Princess did, taking off and running in gradually widening circles. Teague left the gate, pausing to avoid stepping on her as she crossed his path, and shook his head. "Dogs are crazy."

"She's playing," Terra replied, transferring her gaze to the Chihuahua. A smile appeared on her face. "And having a lot of fun."

"Heh, hah, heh," Princess panted, zooming between the teen and me. She made a lot of noise for something so small. Probably didn't weigh five pounds. She came back around. "Hah, heh, hah."

I felt tired just watching her. Where did she get all that energy? Dropping to the ground, I stretched out on my side. The sun felt warm on my fur. I closed my eyes, keeping one ear up to listen to the Chihuahua's frantic progress around the yard.

"Heh, hah, heh."

Wow, that grew annoying really fast. I opened an eye the fourth time she began to zip past. *"Aren't you tired yet?"*

Princess skidded to a stop, almost going tail over nose when her hind end flipped upward. *"You act like an old dog."*

"Hey, I ran the wolves off, remember?"

"Oh, and you're still a pup. You're tired."

"All right, let's go in, girls. Come on, Angel. Here, Precious." Terra picked up the Chihuahua. I climbed back to my paws and stretched.

Upward dog. Downward dog. Heh. I stretched each hind leg out until they quivered. Stretching felt way better as a dog. Finished, I followed the teen back into the building. A couple of shifters came in from the garage as we neared the stairs. The door took a few seconds to close. Long enough for me to bolt through it. I eyed it. Maybe I could still do something about those other dogs.

"Can you tell me how to find the bad-smelling place?"

"Sure," Princess yipped.

Fourteen

Silly me, thinking it'd be easy. Princess couldn't read, though she understood letters were shapes that meant something to humans. Her directions consisted of smells and landmarks in the form of notable-to-a-dog places.

I had her go over it five times before Terra fed us dinner and began to cook, to make certain I wouldn't forget anything. The Chihuahua couldn't quite describe the "bad-smelling place" but she was quite firm there was a "meat-cheese-lettuce place" directly across the street from it. I thought she meant a taco or burger place.

"How do you know what lettuce is?"

"My mom taught me all sorts of foods. Chocolate is bad." Princess listed several other foods Vera had given her as treats. It was a pretty impressive list for three-year-old, much less a tiny dog whose whole body would fit in Doggy Me's mouth.

I repeated her directions back, and felt proud when she said I had everything correct.

"Can you open cages?"

Oops. Potential stumbling block. *"I don't know."*

"They're easy if they're not big or stuck. You pull out and push them if you're outside them. You push and push if you're inside." Princess sat up, waving her front legs in an effort to illustrate her directions.

The sound of stirring stopped, and I looked up to find Terra watching us again, a faint line between her brows. "What are you two doing?"

I nudged Princess's shoulder, pushing her over. She jumped up and ran around me, then dove under me to tug on one of my front legs. I fell over, pretending she'd pulled me down, and she pounced on my neck, worrying a mouthful of fur.

The display seemed to take care of the teen's curiosity. She returned to stirring. I winced as the faint aroma of scorched tuna rose. If I returned to human, I was going to give the girl some cooking lessons. Though she read the directions, Terra didn't quite have a handle on cooking temperatures.

Hearing footsteps outside in the hallway, I jumped up and barked at the door. It opened and Logan came inside. Princess danced around on her hind legs, waving her front ones to get his attention, but he patted my head first.

"Any luck?"

He shook his head, bending to pick up the Chihuahua. She settled in the crook of his arm. "We found her car keys and her wallet, but no sign of her."

"Where were they found?"

"The keys in a trashcan, outside a taco place." He shrugged off his jean jacket, transferring Princess from arm to arm. "Down on Augustine, across from that old brewery that's been condemned. Her wallet was in the middle of an empty lot over on Thompson."

I wasn't sure where Thompson was, but thought I remembered driving down Augustine when we were following my tracking sense and found Carole Bronson's body a month or so prior. It didn't seem close to where I'd regained consciousness and discovered my new body.

Logan sat at the table, absently stroking Princess's side with his fingertips. He frowned, staring at the tabletop. "I'm worried this could mean a demon got her."

"That hound could find her in the demon realm." Terra shook her head, lifting the pan from the stove. She carried it to the table and set it on a hot pad. "Why would a demon scatter her things? It'd be easier to take everything, where it wouldn't be found."

"To throw off any searchers?" He shrugged, leaning forward to peer into the pot, and sat back. "We won against them because of her, and demons bear grudges."

Argh. Totally wrong direction. I turned to cross the room and climbed onto the couch, feeling pretty disgusted. Shifters, witches, and whatever Mr. Whitehaven was, yet not a one of them seem to have considered the possibility I'd been cursed—again!—by the asshole who'd been making people commit suicide all over town. I wondered if he was still busy killing people, and growled quietly in frustration.

I spent the night on Logan's bed again, staring at him between naps and trying to make telepathic contact. As much as my abilities scared me at times, they'd become a part of me. Not having them proved scarier.

Sometime close to morning, I had a nightmare about a dog trapped in my body, running around without being able to control my abilities. The dog's fear choked me as I chased after myself, positive if we touched, we'd return to our rightful bodies.

I yelped and snapped when something touched my head, eyes opening as Logan snatched his hand back. "Easy, girl. Bad dream?"

You have no idea.

He slowly extended his hand again, and I licked it, thumping my tail a couple of times in apology. I didn't like the possibility the nightmare offered. What if that was what happened? I'd need to find my body to return to human.

Terra and Princess weren't awake when we left his bedroom. Logan called me to the door. "Come on, I'll take you outside before I leave."

Ugh. I followed anyway.

Halfway down the last flight of stairs, I heard the sound of one of the garage bay doors opening. Logan reached the foot of the stairs ahead of me, and turned to walk toward the back door.

As I hit the last step, someone came through the door leading to the garage. I bolted, slipping through before it closed and ignoring the shouts that filled the air. A shifter I hadn't met jumped in front of me. I leaped, hitting him in the chest with my front paws, and eeled through his arms as he went over backward, trying to close them around me. Upon reaching the open bay door, I turned right and ran as fast as I could, nearly knocking a few more people over before reaching the end of the block.

From somewhere behind me, I heard Logan calling. "Angel!"

I made another right at the end of the block, paused briefly at the alley entrance to orient myself, and took off again, directly across the street. Princess had stuck close to hiding places, traveling down the alleys as much as possible.

Anxiety, more than exertion, made me pant. I hoped no one would catch up before I found the right place. With no clear way to help myself, attempting to help those dogs was the least I could do.

Before long, I had to slow down and backtrack. The Chihuahua's legs were a lot shorter, and I'd overshot one of the markers.

"Hey, chica! What you doing?"

I lifted my head to find a dog nearly as tall as I was padding toward me. He looked like a pit bull of some sort, mostly white with a few brown spots, all broad head and big chest. There were scars on his muzzle and neck, and he limped. *"You a fighter?"*

He stopped, lifting his head. *"A fighter? Naw, chica. I'm a champion. I lived."*

I noticed his tail drooping. *"How did you get out?"*

"Kept my head. The others," he paused, cocking his head to one side. Most of his left ear was missing, leaving a nub. *"They go crazy, you know? Insane."* He dragged out the last word. *"Go crazy, you lose."*

I sat down. *"My name's Cordi. I helped a little one hide from the bad men. She escaped from a place where they're keeping a lot of dogs."*

"I'm Bone." Three other dogs slunk out from concealment behind him, one red, one black, and one mostly white. *"This is my pack."*

Uh oh. I rose and backed a few steps. *"I'm not looking for trouble. I want to help those dogs."*

"Why?" Bone cocked his head the other way, after glancing back at the other three. They stopped, one of them sitting down. Each of them looked like pit bulls too. From the scars showing, they'd fought as well. I noticed two toes missing from the right front paw of the red one.

"It's wrong the bad men make dogs fight each other. That they make big dogs hurt little ones."

Bone shook his head, his lips flapping. *"Chica, you can't help them."*

"Do you know where they are?"

His good ear swept back. *"Maybe."*

I offered them the only reward I could think of. *"If you help me, I'll help you find homes."*

The red dog snorted. *"Bitch is crazy, Bone."*

"Hey! I'm not a…" I stopped. Dog, female…yeah, I was a bitch to them. *"I'm not really a dog. I'm human. A bad man cursed me, turned me into a dog. And my name is Cordi, not Chica."*

The black dog, missing part of one lip so that his teeth showed, growled. *"I'm outta here. Don't want no part of people again."*

"You stay put, Diablo," Bone growled back, gazing steadily at me. I tried not to wince at the other dog's name. "Diablo" meant devil, and devils were usually demons.

"You fall for every line a bitch throws your way. Always ends in trouble."

My adventure offered a fascinating education of dogs, one I'd definitely keep in mind. If—when—I returned to human, I hoped I could retain enough from it to communicate with them better than before. *"Look, dude, I'm not asking for anything but help to find the place. I can handle things from there myself."*

"She's telling the truth. She's not natural." The last dog, white with merle markings and a graying muzzle, moved up to Bone's shoulder. *"Look at her."*

All four stared. I lifted my head, ears perking forward. *"What's wrong with me? I think I'm doing a pretty good job of being a dog."*

"I see it," Bone said. *"Okay, we'll show you the place."*

"But we're not getting involved. We did our time," the red dog grunted. *"Right, Bone?"*

Their pack leader didn't answer.

I felt out of place, trotting between Bone and the older dog, with the other two bringing up the rear. Doggy Me was taller, and stuck out like a sore thumb with my somewhat longer coat and lack of scars.

"You really human?"

"Yes. I have a car, an apartment, and a job. I work as a private investigator."

Bone cocked his good ear back. *"A what?"*

"Like a cop dog," the older one said.

"Oh, yeah. So why do you smell like those animal people that live over on Haymill?"

I nearly tripped. *"How do you know what street they're on?"*

Bone snorted. *"Might be missing an ear, but I can hear people talking."*

"Right. Sorry. A couple of them are my friends. Well, they are when I'm human. Guess right now, they're kind of my owners." Whom I'd run away from, again. I hoped that wouldn't be the last straw for Logan or Terra. It'd suck to end up in the pound.

No, it'd more than suck, whether someone came along to adopt Doggy Me or I visited the Bad Room. I'd either be dead or spayed and consigned to a shorter lifespan. I shook my head to dispel those thoughts. They didn't help jack. *"How come they don't understand dogs?"*

"Too much human in them. They don't understand cats either." Bone jerked his muzzle upward. *"It's up ahead. They keep 'em down in the cellar, so no one hears all the barking."*

We were nearing a street sign, and I glanced at it: Augustine.

Interesting. "*My cases are related.*"

"*Huh?*"

"*Princess, the little dog I helped, I was looking for her before I became a dog. She said there's a taco or burger place across from the bad-smelling place where the dogs are. And my animal person friend said my car keys were found in a trash can at a taco place, across from,*" I halted, looking at the three-story building taking up two full blocks further on, surrounded by tall, chain link fencing. I remembered it. "*The old brewery. We're close to the outskirts here.*"

"*Yeah.*" Bone sat down and scratched behind his nub. "*There's a taco place across from it, a block down. Why does that make them related?*"

"*The man who changed me into a dog dumped my phone out by the highway, my wallet on Thompson, and my keys here on Augustine. Right across from where the other dogs are being kept. I don't think it's a coincidence.*" I sat down too. "*Where's Thompson?*"

Diablo moved closer. "*Four streets over, between the highway and here.*"

I sneezed. "*I bet money he was coming here, that he's the one those two wolves were talking about. They were scared of him.*"

"*Wolves?*" The red dog pushed forward. "*Weren't no wolves running things when I was in.*"

"*Not when Diablo and me were in either. How about you, Sal?*" Bone asked the older dog, and I turned my head, staring at the white dog. Naw, couldn't be. Could it?

"*No.*"

Bone stood up, something in the set of his shoulders and neck indicating readiness. "*I don't like that at all. How about you guys?*"

They chorused, "*No.*"

He snorted, dropping his head and lifting a front paw to swipe at his muzzle. "*I say we do something about it. I say we help her get those other dogs out.*"

"*It's okay,*" I said, noticing Red's hesitation. "*Just tell me how to get in.*"

Bone laid his ear back and showed me his teeth. "*We're going. Come on.*"

"*Okay.*" I followed him across the street, secretly relieved I wouldn't be alone as the other three trotted after us.

Fifteen

"Ow, ow, ugh, ow." I panted, struggling to pull myself under the fence while leaving a lot of hair behind. Once through, I shook. *"I think I'm bleeding."*

"You're definitely not a dog." The observation came from Bone, who'd already eeled under the fence. *"You whine too much."*

The fence rattled as first Diablo then Red came under it. Sal had gone first, disappearing from sight through a low window with all the glass broken out.

"Do you like little kids?"

He cocked his head to one side. *"Why?"*

"So I'll know whether finding you a home with little kids who'll pull your tail and poke their fingers in your eyes is good revenge."

Bone chuffed. *"I like kids. They share food."*

Giving an exasperated growl, I made a note to find him a home with little kids. That might prove impossible, the way he looked. Who in their right mind would want a scarred up pit bull around their children? I'd have to find someone who really enjoyed doing charity work. I mentally smiled as a possibility crossed my mind, and tucked it away for future reference.

Sal barked from the window. *"It's clear."*

"Let's go," Bone said before turning around and dashing off. He leaped and flew through the window. Diablo took off, and jumped inside the building just as easily. I looked at Red.

"I may need some help."

He sighed. *"Come on."*

It took three tries before I managed to drag myself through the window. My back paws kept slipping off Red's back. After I made it, he jumped through and landed with a grunt, dust puffing up from his front paws.

The inside of the brewery was a wreck of dirt, broken glass, trash, and rusting metal. Our paw prints weren't the only prints. There were prints from other animals and humans too. It stunk to high heaven. *"What is that smell?"*

Diablo answered. "*People potty.*"

I looked at him. "*What?*"

"*People that ain't got nowhere else sleep here. They potty.*" He flicked an ear. "*You going to find them homes too?*"

The feel of my tail tucking had me looking away. "*I would if I could.*"

"*You know what the first rule is, when you're born in a home?*"

"*No.*"

Diablo grumbled. "*It's 'love humans'. When you're born on the streets, it's 'fear humans'. When you're on the streets, you see how bad people act to each other, and to us.*"

"*You were born on the streets.*" My guess turned out wrong.

The black dog chuffed. "*I was born in a home, sold away from my mom not long after my eyes were open. The kid I ended up with didn't want me. He traded me to a man for a pair of shoes, and I ended up in the pit.*"

I wanted to pick him up and cuddle the hell out of him, promise him nothing bad would ever happen to him again. Instead, I crept forward and tried to lick his cheek. "*I'm sorry.*"

Diablo jerked away. "*Let's get this done.*"

I watched him stalk off, my ears drooping. Red nudged my shoulder. "*It's harder for the home-born. They got lied to, you know what I mean?*"

"*Yeah.*"

Our path led through the deepest recesses of the brewery. Here and there, I saw places where the homeless had created nests for themselves, using whatever was handy. Boxes, broken wooden pallets, and even some pieces of furniture. I wondered how they'd gotten the larger stuff through the windows.

"*They live here, so they have to know what's going on. Why haven't they told anyone?*" I asked Sal, whom I'd ended up walking beside.

"*If they told, who'd listen to them? They're outcasts, like us. No one listens to outcasts,*" he said.

Diablo overheard. "*You're too dumb to be a dog. Pretty dumb for a human too.*"

I swallowed a growl. "*I can't learn if I don't ask questions.*" Having another one to ask, I did. "*Have we met before, Sal?*"

"When's the first time you saw me?"

Well, as a dog… *"About an hour ago."*

"Then I guess we haven't met before." He left my side, catching up to Bone, his tail wagging twice.

Maybe being a dog had begun doing something weird to my brain. Why would my so-called fairy godfather turn himself into a dog? Of course, that would also mean he wasn't a figment of my imagination.

Conversation with Dad aside, I did sort of think the little, weathered Indian was a delusion. A helpful delusion—sometimes— but a delusion all the same. There weren't any long-term studies on what having psychic abilities did to a person. Maybe we'd all end up crazy, locked away in some magical mental hospital constantly gabbing to our imaginary friends.

Ooh, cheerful thoughts, Cordi. Let's move on. My stomach rumbled. I'd taken off before being fed breakfast. *"I'm hungry."*

"There's mice," Red said.

Ugh. *"No, thank you."*

"Okay, gather around." Bone wagged his tail once after we'd obeyed. *"We have a problem. The door's closed."*

Our heads turned in concert, all of us looking at the large, metal sliding door. I sniffed, smelling the tang of spray oil. *"They've oiled it. We can push it open."*

"Yeah, but they'll hear us." He glanced at Sal, who left the group to sniff around the door.

"Two wolves, and something else. Don't know what it is. Haven't smelled it before."

Not liking the sound of that, I looked at the dirty concrete between my paws. The old dog kept sniffing and sneezed before perking his ears. *"Only one wolf down there now. There's music playing. He might not hear the door."*

"Someone's coming. Hide." We dashed away from the door at Red's warning, scrambling for cover. I crouched behind a crumbling column, hoping the shadows would help hide me.

A beam of light swept the area, settling on the door. As it grew brighter, I could make out the person carrying it. A girl, teenaged, with short, curly brown hair and a pale face. She looked short, maybe five-six or so. I sniffed the air currents roiling due to her presence. Human, and from the acrid taint, a scared one.

Another sniff offered more information, triggering something I hadn't consciously noticed at the time. Damian didn't smell exactly like the other humans who'd been at the parking lot. He had a little something extra in his scent.

So did this girl. *Maybe she's a witch?*

Whether she was or wasn't, why the hell had she decided to pay a visit here?

I watched her approach the door, noting the slight shaking of the flashlight. Yeah, definitely scared. She clicked it off and shoved it into the pocket of the blue coat she wore. The coat was long and the kid looked like a giant, puffy blueberry.

It wasn't cold enough for such a heavy coat. I regarded it more carefully. As thick as it was, it'd be some protection against teeth.

She threw her shoulders back, her lips becoming a thin, bloodless line, and reached for the door. Apparently, scared or not, she was going down there. She wasn't going unarmed either. I saw the crowbar she held close to one leg.

Whoever she was, it looked like we were on the same side, but all I could see was disaster looming. Five dogs and a short, teenage girl. Yeah, this totally wasn't going to end badly.

The door barely made any noise when she pushed it open. She took a deep breath and slipped through, careful not to let the crowbar bang against it.

"*Doesn't look like we need to go down*," Diablo said, hopping over a half-rotted box.

"*Fine, don't. I'm going. She's going to need help.*" I left my hiding spot and hurried to the door.

"*Wait*," Bone said, shooting out from the shadows to block my path. "*We need a plan.*"

I bared my teeth at him. "*This is my plan: I'm going to follow her, and if I have to, beat the wolf down while she opens cages.*"

Red chuffed. "*I like her plan.*"

"*It's a good plan*," Sal agreed. They looked at Bone. He looked at Diablo.

"*You in or not?*"

The black dog silently snarled. "*We're gonna end up dead.*"

"*We're going to end up dead one day or another.*" Sal edged toward the door. "*I'm in.*"

We filed through the door, one by one, Diablo bringing up the rear.

A ramp lay on the other side of the door, wide and sloping gently enough for a forklift to drive down. The girl had already made it to the bottom, but I couldn't hear her steps over the rumble of bass coming from below.

"*Diablo with me. You two stick with Cordi,*" Bone ordered as we loped down the ramp. He didn't pause when we reached the bottom, turning left. "*This way.*"

Diablo shouldered me aside to reach him, and the two of them cut right as we passed a tangle of rusty machinery. Red blocked my attempt to follow them. "*We go straight in. They'll check around and come in after us.*"

"*Okay.*" We ran on, catching a glimpse of blue ahead. By the time we reached that spot, the girl had gone through another door and I heard her speak.

"You took my dog, and I want her back."

The music shut off. We halted at the doorway, peeking in from either side. She stood with her feet spread, holding the crowbar like a baseball bat. Her statement explained everything.

Looking past her, I saw the wolf shifter, who looked about my age. He jittered a few steps toward her, his brown eyes wide and his hands fluttering. "I can't give you your dog back."

"I'm not asking," the girl said. "I don't ask sickos like you for anything."

He bent slightly forward, burying his hands into his sandy blonde hair and tugging at it. "You think I want to do this shit? I don't. I have to, or he'll kill me. He'll kill you too, he finds you here."

"I'm not leaving without my dog." She jerked her head right. "The Husky, she's mine. Let her out."

"*I told you my girl would come for me,*" a dog yipped. The sound had the girl lowering the crowbar and turning toward it.

The shifter moved, but so did I, rushing around her to snarl at him. He froze. "Call it off." Red and Sal joined me, one on either side. The guy swallowed hard enough for us to hear. "Call them off."

"They're not mine," she said. "You know, since I'm here, I think I'll take all the dogs."

"You can't." He fell to his knees, clasping his hands together. "Please don't. I'm not kidding, he'll kill me."

The lack of telepathy made me want to cry in frustration. I had no way to nudge the girl into asking the questions I needed answered, or to get the answers I wanted by listening to the shifter's thoughts.

Instead, we held him at bay while he begged and she ignored him, hurrying around to open cage doors. Most were large dogs, who took off as though their tails had been scalded without so much as a

"Thank you" before disappearing.

"*Hold him.*" I left Red and Sal to hurry over as the girl began opening the cages containing little dogs. There were only five of them. "*All of you need to stay with me. I'll take you somewhere safe.*"

Diablo's rumble announced his and Bone's arrival. "*Told you the bitch ain't nothing but trouble. What are we going to do with them?*"

After lifting the last little dog from its cage, the girl kneeled to hug her dog, who'd stuck to her side since being released. The Chihuahuas clustered around my hind legs in a shivering, multi-colored lump. The girl looked at them then at me, her forehead wrinkling. "I don't think you're an ordinary dog. Are you someone's familiar?"

I shook my head. "*Tell her you need to go. The other two men might come back soon.*"

The Husky yipped, grabbing hold of the girl's coat sleeve. "*Come on, Tonya.*"

Rising, Tonya let her dog pull her toward the door. She looked at the wolf shifter, who'd fallen silent, though his eyes darted around. "You'd better run if you're that afraid."

He whined, focusing on Red and Sal. "They're going to kill me."

"No, they won't. Everyone out!"

"*Go,*" Bone said. "*We'll keep the little ones together.*"

I left, rushing out the door with the smaller dogs on my heels. The four pits followed, with Tonya and her Husky behind them.

Not knowing where else to go, I headed up the ramp and back along the way we'd come, and called a halt at the window. "*Crap.*"

Sal leaped through it. Red stopped. "*We'll bring them after you go through.*"

I made shorter work of climbing onto his back and through the window the second time around. Bone and Red brought two each, while Diablo spat one tiny black pup out at my paws with a disapproving grunt.

Standing on my hind legs, I looked through the window for Tonya and her dog, but didn't see them. She must've come in another way, and left the same. I dropped to all fours. "*Okay, we're all going to my friend's place.*"

"*Not us.*" Bone slopped his tongue across my muzzle. "*We'll get you there, but we ain't staying with animal people.*"

"*I promised to find you homes if you helped me. How can I keep my promise if you don't stick around?*"

"Do you know when you won't be a dog anymore?"

I sighed. *"No."*

"Can't keep it until you're a human again. We'll be around." He flicked his good ear a few times. *"Come on."*

"Wait. There's empty houses down at the end of Bartley. You know which street that is?" When he responded affirmatively, I continued. *"Go there every night. When I'm human again, I'll go there to find you and keep my promise."*

"Okay."

"You're not going to ask how you'll know it's me?"

Bone chuffed. *"You'll be the only human who knows our real names."*

Oh. *"I really appreciate you guys helping stop the dog fights."* The four large dogs traded glances. I perked my ears. *"What?*

"We didn't stop nothing, except for keeping those dogs from going into the ring. They keep the dogs already used in the ring somewhere else." Bone's tail drooped. *"Outside of town somewhere, someone's place. Don't know where, because they always took us in van when we left it."*

Well, crap.

"Quit wiggling." The black pup obeyed, but it still felt weird carrying him in my mouth. Only a few months old, he'd proven the youngest of the little dogs, and had quickly tired. If not for Red, he might've been left behind. I'd taken over carrying him once we reached the alley that ran behind the garage. It had been nerve-wracking, crossing the busy streets with the little ones, and had taken a lot longer to get back.

"Don't forget." My reminder earned a quick tail wag from Bone.

"We won't. Go on. We'll watch until you get there."

"All right, and thanks, guys." I set off with the other four Chihuahuas, dodging pedestrians. *"Stay close. It's not much farther. Don't be scared of these animal people. They're my friends. Princess is staying with them."*

They were too tired to care, panting like crazy, with tucked tails and folded-back ears. We went into the first open bay door, marching past the half dozen tiger shifters working on cars, and stopped at the door to the stairway.

I put the pup down as gently as possible, and barked.

"Hey, the dog's...what the hell?" The one I'd bowled over during my mad dash that morning rolled out from underneath a car. "It brought puppies."

I sat down, let my tongue flop out, and grinned at him.

Sixteen

"Here." Alanna passed the third Chihuahua over to Terra, who wrapped it in a towel. "Two more to go."

"Aw, the widdle baby is cold." I watched the teen dry the little dog off from my sprawl on the couch. Princess lay on my neck, and the two who'd already been washed and dried were curled on and around me, snoring their tiny tails off.

Rescuing dogs was exhausting work. I let a burp escape. The first thing I'd done upon entering the apartment had been to eat and slurp down most of a bowl of water while ignoring Terra's alternating between scolding me and cooing over our new guests. Alanna had pitched in to feed, water, and bathe them, though she griped about it until Terra growled at her.

Princess licked the fur over my right eye. *"I didn't believe you'd save them, but you did. Even though you're a puppy!"*

"I had help. Four other big dogs." I closed my eyes, more than ready for some sleep. She subsided, dropping her head so that it hung over to rest between my eyes and I dozed off, feeling pretty pleased with my day's work.

Being a dog made things tougher, yet like Human Me, Doggy Me had found friends to help make it through.

The two women finished bathing and drying dogs. Alanna left the apartment as the last three Chihuahuas joined our pile on the couch. Vaguely aware of Terra clearing things away, I wondered what time it was.

Everything went quiet for a while, until I heard, "Discord."

Princess slid off my head when I jerked fully awake and turned to look at Terra, who sat in the recliner. She smiled as I wondered how long she'd been watching me. "It's you, isn't it?"

I wagged my tail, drawing sleepy mumbles of complaint from my nap buddies.

"Logan's going to think I'm crazy when I tell him. I'm not sure I'm not crazy, but," she hesitated. "One wag for yes, a bark for no. You were talking to Precious last night, weren't you?"

A wag of my tail caused an eruption of pissed-off puppy. He sounded like a miniature Tasmanian Devil, and went completely nuts on my tail, biting and slapping at it. Terra giggled, jumping up to grab him. "Hush, Speck."

She sat back down and settled the puppy in her lap. "Okay. I'm guessing you were talking to her about these dogs?" Wag. "Logan mentioned you had a case looking for a lost dog. Are one of these that dog?"

I nosed Princess while giving the required tail wag.

The teen smiled again. "Good. I'll have to convince him to take us to your office so we can show them Precious, and that should make it easier for them to believe you're you. He should be home soon. It's getting dark." Her smile faded, and she worried at her bottom lip for a minute. "Um, do you want to take a bath or anything?"

I thought about it for a minute or two before barking.

"Okay. I bet being a dog is really strange for you, but you figured it out fast. The first time I changed shape, I couldn't walk without tripping all over my paws." Terra grinned. "Logan helped me learn to walk. He held me up by the scruff of my neck so I wouldn't fall."

She told me a little more. Logan was twelve when she was born, and had been named her protector nearly the second she'd popped into the world. They'd barely begun establishing a territory when the Melding occurred, throwing everything into chaos. "A dragon found us, and flew me back home."

"Rroo?" We had dragons? I hadn't heard anything about dragons.

Terra misunderstood the sound I'd made. "Really. Dragons are the oldest living beings, and that one was huge. He looked white, but when the sun came up, the light turned his scales into rainbows. It was so cool."

Okay, dragons probably weren't anything to worry about, especially since I'd only now learned they existed. However, I did wonder what else there was I didn't know about, and how many of those beings might be of the less friendly variety.

Seriously, vampires and demons were enough trouble. Oh, yeah, and whatever Crazy Curseman turned out to be.

"Why haven't you used your telepathy?"

The question scattered my thoughts. I barked.

Lips slightly pursed, Terra regarded me for a long moment. "You don't have your powers?"

I preferred "abilities", but whatever. I barked again.

"Maybe that's why your hound couldn't find you." We both heard Logan's footsteps in the hallway. When he reached the door and opened it, a tornado of yapping, dancing Chihuahuas surrounded him, each begging him to pick them up.

He looked down. "I kind of hoped Warren had been drinking. Guess not."

"*Quiet now.*" I barked, and they stopped yapping. Logan pulled his jacket off while glancing at me. He tossed it onto the back of a kitchen chair and sank down to sit cross-legged in the floor.

All six scrambled into his lap, pushing and shoving at each other. Logan petted with both hands until they settled down. I memorized the sight. A hunky guy with a lap full of tiny dogs seemed to be one of the things that made my heart melty.

He looked up, focusing on Terra. "Okay, now what exactly happened?"

She told him what she knew, which came down to "Angel came back this afternoon with five more little dogs."

My turn to be stared at. Logan said, "We don't have room for any more."

"Hey, didn't you say Discord had a missing dog case?"

He blinked at her question. "Yes."

"Maybe one of them is the dog she was looking for. Will you take me to her office tomorrow, so we can ask?"

"We're meeting there in the morning anyway, so sure. I'll have Alanna and Teague follow us. They can bring you home afterwards." Logan surveyed his full lap. "We'll need a box."

"I'll take care of it," Terra promised, getting up. "Are you hungry?"

"No, I grabbed something a little while ago. Did you name these too?"

"Only the smallest one. His name is Speck." She began transferring them from his lap back onto the couch with me. "They'll need to go outside soon."

Logan rose from the floor, the last two Chihuahuas in hand, and passed them to her. "I'm going to take a shower. I'll help you take them out after that."

My third night as a dog I again spent sleeping on Logan's bed. Speck, the little black puppy, threw a fit until Terra brought him in to join us.

Early the next morning, a yawning Teague and Alanna helped get everyone downstairs for potty time, and back upstairs afterward for breakfast. By ten after eight, we'd loaded up into two vehicles and were on our way to the office.

I hoped, sitting between Logan and Terra, who held the box of little dogs, that they'd listen to her. That my witch buddies could reverse the curse, and once they had, that I'd have my abilities back. As interesting as being a dog was, I'd gotten tired of it.

Besides, I had a mystery to solve and a bad guy to catch. Make that two: I still had to figure out if my other client's grandson was her thief or not. Well, I did if the boss hadn't reassigned it to Kate by now.

Terra laid her hand on my back, and smiled when I looked at her. The best I could offer in return was a tongue-lolling doggy grin. The fact the teen had been the only one to figure out the stray dog was actually the person everyone had been looking for made me wonder how she'd done it.

I supposed she'd explain, after dropping the bombshell of who the stray dog really was on them.

When we arrived, Kate's car sat in the parking lot. A hoofed demon had once used it as a landing pad, but it hadn't taken nearly as long to be repaired as mine had after being demolished by a couple of vampires.

The witch huffed into the phone, her scarlet-painted nails tapping furiously on the receptionist's desktop. Mr. Whitehaven hadn't hired a new receptionist yet. The last one had quit because Percy, Kate's parrot familiar, kept crapping on his head.

Said familiar stood on his brass perching stand, preening his feathers and grumbling in French. I barked, startling him into a puffy mess of mostly green feathers and flared wings. He screeched. "No dogs allowed!"

"Sorry." Logan's apology earned a harried glance from Kate, who waved them by with a flick of her free hand. He twitched the leash. "Come on, Angel."

As we paraded by Percy, he settled his feathers and focused a bright, black eye on me. The flutter of wings caused Logan to duck just before we reached Mr. Whitehaven's office door, and the parrot flew past, squawking at those within to "Move, dog breaths" before he landed on the boss's desk lamp.

Hackles rising and legs stiffening, I stalked into the office beside Logan, trying to control my building growl. Nick and Patrick were there, along with another four wolf shifters.

"Why the hell did you bring that damn..." A storm of yipping and yapping interrupted Nick's complaint. I barked several times, telling the Chihuahuas to hush, and they finally subsided. There were mutters of "Stinky animal people" from the box.

Logan and Terra ignored the wolves in favor of crossing to the boss's desk. Whitehaven smiled. "Good morning. What have we here?"

"Logan told me that Discord had been looking for a missing dog. I'm wondering if one of these might be the dog?" Terra moved around the desk's side to set the box down. "Maybe this one?" She bent, plucking Princess from it, and held her up.

"That's the dog. Princess." Silence followed Nick's affirmation for a few seconds. The teen held Princess out, and Mr. Whitehaven took her, nearly engulfing her in his large hand.

"Where did you find her?"

"I didn't." I heard Terra draw a deep breath. "Discord did."

Logan dropped the leash, jumping between her and my boyfriend when Nick lunged across the room at the teen. He stopped, baring his teeth at the tiger. "Where is she?"

I bit him on the butt.

Nick spun around, swinging a fist, but Logan caught his arm. "Don't hit the dog."

"The dog bit me."

"The dog is Discord." Terra's announcement, delivered in a calm, firm tone, briefly froze everyone. Every pair of eyes in the room landed on me. Lips drawn back in a silent snarl, the hair from neck to tail standing on end, and ears back, I'm pretty sure no one believed her.

Except maybe for Logan, whose dark brows drew together even as Nick scoffed at her claim. "That dog isn't Cordi."

Terra lifted her chin and crossed her arms. "And you know that how?"

"Because Cordi likes me. That dog hates me. It just bit me," he reminded her.

She shrugged. "I don't think she can help it."

"If this is Discord, why hasn't she said anything?" Logan asked. "She has telepathy."

"Not right now, she doesn't. I asked her and she doesn't have any of her powers."

Mr. Whitehaven spoke. "Why do you believe this dog is Discordia?"

"She was in the Palisades and found Logan. He's not afraid of dogs, but he's never brought one home before. You didn't even think twice about doing it, did you?" She dropped her arms to her sides.

"No." Logan released Nick's arm, and my boyfriend backed away from me. "I didn't."

Terra pointed at me. "I left her in the yard, she dug out, and found the car. After we went home, she somehow found Princess, and ran off two wolf shifters who came sniffing around our place."

"The dog found the car?" Patrick's question earned a narrow-eyed frown from Terra.

"We saw her, and chased her all over that parking lot. She didn't stop running and dodging until she saw the car. She was looking for it." The teen spread her hands out. "That night, I watched her with Precious, I mean, Princess. Princess did this thing," Terra mimicked the gestures the Chihuahua had made, trying to show me how to open cages. "And I knew they were having a conversation."

"Yesterday morning, she ran away and came back in the afternoon, with these other little dogs." She wrinkled her nose. "They smelled as if they'd been somewhere no one had bothered to clean up for a long time, and I remembered that Princess smelled the same way at first."

While she'd explained, I managed to calm and sit down. Ears perked, I wondered if she might be interested in becoming a private investigator. The girl had some mad deductive skills.

"There were a couple of other small things. Like when you came home and told me her keys and wallet were found. You were worried a demon had her, and Angel, I mean, Discord huffed and jumped on the couch. She looked," Terra clasped her hands together. "Disgusted."

"Discordia." At Whitehaven's call, I stood and lifted my front paws to the edge of his desk. Percy shoved his head into my face, gazing with an eye into one of mine. I stared back. *It's me, bird brain. Help her out and tell them.*

The parrot clacked his beak and kept staring. I held my breath. *Come on, Percy.*

He drew his head back, shook it, and squawked. "*La petite déesse!* Cordi, Cordi, Cordi!"

Kate rushed into the office. "Where is she?"

Percy trilled, stretching to his full height and spreading his wings wide. "Cordi is dog!"

My tail wagged so hard, I nearly fell over.

Seventeen

Kate snapped at Nick over my rising growl. "You're not of any help if you can't communicate with her. Go away, Maxwell."

He and Patrick were the only two wolf shifters left in the office, since the others no longer needed to help search for me. Nick sighed and backed away, lowering his hand. "Why doesn't she like me anymore?"

"Because she's a damn dog right now. Not only a dog, but one from a herding breed. It's instinct, little brother," Patrick said, taking hold of Nick's arm and pulling him toward the door. "Don't take it personally."

I sneezed, but didn't miss the nearly identical looks they shot in Logan's direction before moving out of sight. They weren't pleasant looks. The tiger didn't seem bothered though. He shut the door and took a seat on the couch.

Mr. Whitehaven ruffled Princess's side with his fingertips as the white Chihuahua sat on his desk before him, and he had the phone to his ear. "Hello, I need to speak with Miss Vera Headley, please. Ah, excellent. Thank you. Miss Headley? Yes, it is. I'm calling to inform you that Miss Jones found Princess. I have her at my office." He smiled. "Yes, that will be fine. We'll be expecting you then."

After ending the call, he leaned back in his chair. "She'll be here on her lunch hour."

"*Your mom's coming to get you,*" I said, and Princess stood, her thin tail whipping back and forth.

"*I'm going home!*" She pranced in a circle before rearing to wave her front legs at my boss, who chuckled.

Terra took the box over to the couch and sat down on the floor close to Logan. Percy walked around me, his head bobbing up and down while he muttered. "Cordi is dog. Cordi needs changing. Cordi is dog."

Kate whipped out her cell phone. "I'll call the others and have them meet us at the shop. We'll try a cleansing spell."

I wagged my tail to let her know I approved. Her familiar

warbled. "Cleansing not work. Cordi cursed more big than other time."

"Drat." The witch shoved her phone back into the pocket of her yellow dress, which looked like something Jackie O would've worn as First Lady. All she needed was a pillbox hat. I couldn't remember Kate ever wearing yellow before. "What do we do?"

That wasn't what I wanted to hear.

"We'll need the assistance of someone skilled at transforming other people into animals." Mr. Whitehaven learned forward to reach for the phone again. "I'll make the arrangements."

Definitely more like it.

Vera Headley arrived barely ten minutes after noon. A short, plump woman with shoulder-length, light brown hair, her hazel eyes brimmed over with tears upon seeing Princess. "Oh, thank God. My precious baby."

The boss gave them a few minutes to greet each other before introducing Logan and Terra. "They've been caring for her until Discordia could inform us she'd found her."

"Thank you so much." Vera nearly squished Princess, hugging each of them in turn. "Do I owe you anything?"

"No, ma'am. It was our pleasure." Logan's assurance resulted in another hug from her.

She turned from them to Mr. Whitehaven. "Where is Miss Jones? I'd like to thank her."

"I'm afraid she's busy with another case at the moment, but I'll let her know." He walked her to his office door, where Kate took over. Princess yipped good-bye over her owner's shoulder as they walked out of sight. I sighed as the other five Chihuahuas responded, tipping their box over in the excitement.

"I think we should probably take them home and see about placing an ad," Logan said.

Terra shook her head. "I want to see Discord be changed back."

"I believe Kate sent Nick out for lunch for everyone." Mr. Whitehaven knelt to help collect squirming little bodies. "If Discordia doesn't mind aiding us, we can take them outside for a few minutes."

"*Potty*," Speck agreed, his toothpick legs wind milling as Logan scooped him up.

Needing to potty myself, I followed them out to the parking lot and one of the strips of grass lining it. The Chihuahuas took care of their business under our watchful eyes, but I moved around to the side of the building, heading for the alley once they'd been gathered up.

"She needs a little privacy. I'll go with her," Terra said, handing Speck and a long-haired, black and tan dog to Mr. Whitehaven. Logan opened his mouth, closed it, and glanced at me.

I won't let anything happen to her, dude. Sheesh.

As though he understood, he nodded. "Okay. Try and make it quick."

The teen followed me around back and turned to give me privacy. "This is a first. Logan never lets me go anywhere alone. I mean, I'm not really alone because you're here, but you know, alone without him or Alanna or Teague."

I grumbled.

"Oh, I know it's his job. I just kind of want to know what it's like being a regular girl sometimes." She sighed. "Guess I won't ever get to."

Done, I walked up and nosed her hand. Poor kid. At least I'd gotten some time as a regular girl before the Melding. None after, but we can't have everything.

We walked back around and went inside to find lunch laid out on the break room table. One of them, probably Nick, had thought to stop and pick up some small dog food for the Chihuahuas. Or Kate had told him to when she'd sent him out for the food.

I, on the other hand, had a couple of steaks waiting for me, and fell on them like a starving wolf. Medium rare, the way I liked them. They tasted so good, I whined in pure pleasure while gobbling the first down.

Nick asked, "What have you been feeding her?"

Logan actually squirmed. "Leftovers and organic dog food."

Patrick snickered, elbowing my boyfriend in the side. "At least it wasn't plain old kibble."

I growled around a mouthful of steak. Patrick and Nick ducked their heads over their plates and concentrated on eating. As far as I was concerned, Logan and Terra had done a bang-up job of taking care of a dog. It wasn't their fault they hadn't immediately known that dog was me.

After lunch, the assistance Mr. Whitehaven had called for finally arrived. The last person I'd expected it to be was Thorandryll. I hadn't seen the elf since I'd sort of blackmailed him into letting me have Leglin.

His wintry blue eyes immediately focused on me. I had a less than a minute to admire how the dark blue, leather jacket he wore fit his broad shoulders before he knelt and offered his hand.

"She doesn't do tricks," Nick said.

"I'm merely greeting Miss Jones, as is proper." Thorandryll inclined his head ever-so-slightly. Mentally rolling my eyes, I lifted a paw to shake, but the elf didn't shake. He gave it a light squeeze. "Hello, Miss Jones. My apologies for not arriving sooner. I had a matter to attend to."

The elf's scent filled my nose and proved to be one that Doggy Me found nearly irresistible. However, I did resist the sudden urges to show my belly and lick his face. The Chihuahuas didn't as his scent reached them. Four of them rushed over to dance wildly, begging for his attention.

Speck ducked under my side and looked at the elf from around one of my front legs. His soft growl made it perfectly clear he didn't like Thorandryll one bit.

Maybe I had room for another dog in my life. The pup was obviously a fantastic judge of character.

Thorandryll released my paw and spent a few minutes gently petting the others while speaking what I presumed to be Elvish to them. The sound of it made my ears perk, and when I realized my tail had begun wagging, I forced it to stop.

It really sucked that he looked so good riding to my rescue. Even though I knew he'd lie whenever it suited his purposes, there was something about his slightly triangular, movie-star face and long, golden-blonde hair that made it hard to hold a grudge.

Even harder as a dog. I swallowed a mouthful of drool before it escaped to drip on the carpet. Speck growled louder when the elf's hand moved toward him, and Thorandryll chuckled. He didn't try to pet the little guy after all, but said something that sent the other four Chihuahuas off to Terra.

"There's more than one way to curse another into animal form. Did the person who did this to you speak a spell?"

I shook my head.

"Was there any object involved, such as necklace?" When I shook my head again, he frowned. "Were you forced to drink a potion?"

I barked. The elf's frown deepened. "Hm, that will make things a bit more complicated to reverse. There are at least a dozen possibilities, and I'll have to create something able to counter them all."

"We need to discuss your fee before you begin," Mr. Whitehaven said, his voice a little deeper than normal. Thorandryll rose to face him, and Speck took the opportunity to scoot out from underneath me and join the other little dogs.

For a second, I felt tempted to bite the elf on the butt as I had Nick. Of course he wouldn't do something like this for free or out of the goodness of his heart, because he was a jerk.

A hot, drool-worthy jerk, but a jerk all the same.

"My fee for this service is small. I merely wish the company of Miss Jones for dinner on an evening of my choice."

"No way." Nick stepped away from the door, his hands clenching into fists. "Not happening."

Yes, because sharing a meal with the elf was so much worse than staying a dog. I barked at him, but my boyfriend shook his head. "He'll glamour you."

Oh, that could well be a possibility. I had a bit of a history of going hazy-minded around the elf.

Logan glanced at me and spoke. "One meal, no glamour or other form of coercion."

"Hey," Nick snarled. "How about you not setting my girlfriend up on a date with the guy who nearly got us all killed?"

"Your girlfriend's currently a dog who'd rather rip your throat out than cuddle." Logan jerked his chin in the elf's direction. "Unless you have another suggestion, it looks like he's the only one who can turn her back."

"Those terms are agreeable, as I have no intention of coercing Miss Jones in any fashion." *I don't need tricks*, Thorandryll's haughtily smug expression said. "Surely your relationship can survive one dinner?"

Nick scowled, but didn't say anything.

"If you renege on these terms, I'll be the one collecting recompense." Mr. Whitehaven's eyes began to glow. It wasn't the first time I'd seen them do it, but that time, they'd been red. Now they looked yellowish, and I wondered if they would glow different colors depending on his mood or something.

The elf bowed to my boss. "Understood."

Everyone looked at me, and Whitehaven asked, "Do you accept this agreement?"

Hm, hard decision: One dinner versus being a dog for the rest of my life. I glanced at Nick before barking. He looked away.

"Very well. We are all witnesses to this agreement. It is done."

The elf smiled and slapped his hands together. "I'll need to take her…"

"Oh, no." Kate stomped over to him, Percy on her shoulder, and stabbed him in the chest with fingernail. "You'll work under our supervision, at the Blue Orb. We likely have everything you'll need there."

The elf wisely chose to agree.

Eighteen

I loved David's book and magic shop, the Blue Orb. Walking into it as a dog proved to be a whole new experience. The smell of the herbs and oils were so sharp and distinct, I felt dizzy. Logan held the door for Kate and Terra, who'd pointed out he'd promised her a trip to the shop once I'd been found. He didn't hold the door for Thorandryll, who paused outside to answer his cell phone.

"Quite the parade," Jo said, hurrying out from behind the counter to bend down and hug me. "Hi, Cordi. I'm so glad you're found."

I hadn't licked anything but my chops—okay, the seat in Logan's truck once too—as a dog, but for her I made an exception and laid a sloppy dog kiss across her cheek. She laughed and scruffed the fur on my neck.

"Cordi." The rusty croak wasn't a familiar voice. David stood behind the counter, glasses propped on his head, a dark blue cardigan hanging crookedly from his shoulders. He pointed at his familiar, who stood on a hunk of quartz displayed on the counter. Copernicus tilted his head. "Cordi."

Jo whispered in my ear. "He's never spoken when anyone other than coven members are around. He's been worried about you."

I hadn't known the raven could talk, and trotted to the counter to look up at him. Copernicus leaned down, gazing into my eyes. It felt as though someone touched me on the cheek with something soft, maybe the tip of a feather. The raven settled back. "Dog is Cordi."

"Said that." Percy took flight from Kate's shoulder and landed next to the raven. "First."

Copernicus swatted the parrot with a wing. Percy ducked his head, feathers fluffing, and twisted, bumping the other bird with his rear. David intervened before a bird brawl broke out in earnest. "Enough, you two."

They subsided, grumbling quietly while settling wings and feathers. The warlock folded his arms and rested them on the counter top. "So you've been turned into a dog. I'll have questions later."

Behind me, the bell jingled as the door opened, and I turned, expecting to see the elf finally coming in. He did, right before Leglin shouldered him aside and trotted down the aisle. Nick followed the hound, handing my hairbrush to Kate when he reached her.

Leglin halted a couple of feet away, cocking his head and perking his ears. *"Mistress?"*

"Is that what you call me?" After being around other dogs, none quite as tall as I was, I felt suddenly short compared to the hound.

Leglin dropped his chest to the ground, butt still in the air, and somehow bounced forward. He ducked his head and licked the bottom of my muzzle. *"Mistress! I couldn't find you."*

"It's okay, neither could anyone else—even with me right under their noses."

He lay down. *"You sound different."*

"I'm a dog right now," I pointed out while sitting. His head wasn't much lower than mine in spite of his position.

Leglin inclined his head. *"Of course. But the Prince will soon set things right."*

Thorandryll was a prince? Wow. *"I hope so."* Opportunity had landed in my lap. *"Are you happy?"*

"Yes, you're no longer lost."

"No, I mean, are you happy the way things are? You know, living with me and ah...being a dog?"

His tail thumped twice. *"I am a royal hound, and you are my mistress."*

That didn't exactly answer my question. *"But are you happy? Would you rather be free?"*

"No."

I tried a slightly different approach. *"Are you happy being my hound?"*

Thunder sounded as his tail drummed the floor. Leglin stretched his head out to lick the bottom of my muzzle again. *"Yes."*

Any more questions had to wait because Kate's voice rose. "No. The brush stays in my possession. I'll take care of adding her hair to the potion."

"I gave my word..."

She cut off the elf. "You gave your word not to pull any tricks the night you take her out for dinner, old man. You haven't given your word not to pull any before then."

"I'm wounded by your distrust."

He didn't sound wounded, but snarky. I barked at them. *"Enough already. Get with the changing me back!"*

"She is wise to distrust the Prince," Leglin said. *"I've seen him*

do terrible magic with a single strand of hair or drop of blood."

Oh. I remembered that she took care of poking my finger when the elf first brought the hound to me. I should be patient and let Kate handle things. After all, it might be the only time I'd be able to have an actual conversation with my four-legged roomie.

"My workroom's this way." David left the cover of the counter for the hallway beside the staircase. Both birds fluttered after him. Kate spun away from the elf and followed. I waited until Thorandryll passed us before falling in line, and Leglin rose, bringing up the rear.

The others stayed in the store area, and I heard Jo ask, "What's in the box?"

"It's adequate." Thorandryll's assessment of the workroom made David's shoulders slump. I growled and the elf glanced at me, before adding, "Quite impressive for such a young practitioner."

The compliment brightened David's face. "What do you need first?"

As the elf began listing ingredients, I glanced at Leglin. *"He didn't tell me how old you were."*

"Three, mistress."

Speck peeked in the open doorway, and scooted across to hide under me. The hound sat down. *"What is that?"*

"A Chihuahua." I craned my neck to look between my front legs. *"What's wrong?"*

The pup blinked his overlarge, brown eyes. *"Sleepy."*

Not seeing any reason to stand in the middle of the room, I said, *"Let's use the couch."*

The coven met here, so David had designated one corner as a sitting area and put comfy, dark blue chairs and a couch there. I had to pick up the pup because he couldn't jump high enough, but in short order, Leglin and I lay facing each other, with Speck curled into a ball between my front legs.

The hound gazed at the puppy. *"Are we keeping him?"*

"I'm thinking about it, if no one claims him. He's cute, and then you'd have some company when you don't go to work with me. Unless you'd rather not have another dog around?"

"I haven't been allowed around small ones before." Leglin flicked an ear. *"I think I would like company."*

That settled that, as long as no one responded to the ad Logan intended to put out. *"Okay. What did you think about my idea? Us getting a house?"*

"I am happy wherever you are."

"Look, I know you're bound to me and stuff, but I like to think of us more as friends, and as a team. This may be the only chance we ever have to really talk. I want to know what you think about stuff."

Leglin nodded, a few wrinkles appearing on the top of his broad skull. *"I would like a room of my own for when I'm not guarding you. With a bed."*

"A people bed?"

"Yes, please."

Not a big demand, but it made me happy he'd asked for something. *"I can do that. What else?"*

The hound hesitated, glancing at Thorandryll. *"I would enjoy visiting my pack mates from time to time, yet…I'm not certain it's wise to for you to spend much time near the Prince."*

"Why not?"

"Elves are tricksy beings, mistress."

In other words, liars. A lesson I'd learned pretty damn well. *"I can deal with him when you want to visit your family."*

Leglin changed the subject. *"What happened to bring you to this state?"*

I told him, and the hound bared his teeth. *"We will hunt him, and I will tear him limb from limb."*

"Let's not get all blood-thirsty, dude. Oh, and there's another thing. I made a promise to some dogs that helped me." I explained all of that to him. *"If I get changed back today, I want to go out there tonight and find them. They may have to stay with us for a while."*

"You have a kind, honorable heart. I am proud to be your hound."

The compliment kind of choked me up for a minute or two. *"I'm just trying to do the right thing."*

"Wait." More than happy to, I looked up from the bowl. The dark liquid in it didn't smell the least bit appetizing. Kate dropped her hand to her side. "We need something to put over her, in case her clothes weren't part of the transformation."

Trust her to think of that, and thank goodness she had. Being naked in front of David would be bad enough, but in front of—I glanced at the door, counting—seven people, one of them Thorandryll? No, thank you.

"Be right back," Jo said, leaving the workroom. She'd closed the shop more than an hour before. The elf might've finished the potion faster if not for Kate's demanding an explanation for each ingredient, and David's desire to discuss the pros and cons of each compared to something else.

Terra sat to one side of the door, her back against the wall, an arm over the box of Chihuahuas next to her. Logan leaned on the wall beside her, his arms crossed. Nick squatted on the other side of the door, his gaze traveling between me and the elf.

"Is it going to hurt her?" he asked.

"There won't be any pain." Thorandryll took out the band he'd used to pull his hair back. Jo returned, carrying a quilt from one of the upstairs guest beds. She shook it out and draped it over me.

"There you go."

I looked around then down at the bowl, feeling everyone's eyes on me. Heaving a sigh, I began lapping up the potion. It tasted of licorice, which wasn't one of my favorite things, and fizzed on my tongue. Once I'd finished the dregs, the elf drew a glowing, golden symbol in the air with his finger and blew on it.

It floated over to me, hovered right above my head for a breath, and then exploded like a tiny firecracker, fountaining sparks all over me.

They didn't burn, but faded into my coat. An itching sensation spread over every inch of my doggy body, and I had to fight the urge to scratch. The itching intensified to the point I felt like ants were crawling all over me.

Next thing I knew, I was waving away a cloud of yellow smoke. With hands. "I'm me again!"

"Cordi." Nick rushed toward me, pulling me to my feet. "Are you okay?"

My clothing had been a part of the transformation, and boy, did I need a bath. "Yeah, I think so."

He hugged me and I bit him on the neck. "Ow, what'd you do that for?"

"You smell bad." The words growled out from between my clenched teeth. I pushed away, shaking my head. "What the hell? I'm sorry."

"Some of the non-physical effects of the transformation may take a bit longer to fade." Thorandryll walked around us, studying me. "Have your abilities returned?"

Kate? I glanced at her. *I thought your dress was yellow.*

She smoothed the red skirt. "I heard you. Telepathy online."

"Catch," Jo said, tossing a pink candle at me. I flung out a hand and stopped it in mid-flight. "Telekinesis, check."

Concentrating on the candle's wick, I lit it. David clapped. "Pyrokinesis, check."

I froze a coke someone hadn't finished, and then teleported a few feet. "Cryokinesis and teleportation, check. Those are the only ones I want to test. I need a shower, and I have something I have to do. I'll need a truck."

"I'll drive you."

Shaking my head, I held a hand up as Nick walked toward me. "I'm sorry, but I don't think it's a good idea for us to be in close quarters right now. I might bite you again. Plus, they don't like wolves."

"Who doesn't?" Terra asked, climbing to her feet. I hugged her and Logan both.

"Thanks for taking care of me. Sorry about running off. And I am totally going to pay you back for the vet and stuff."

Logan smiled and shook his head. "Don't worry about it. Sorry I fed you dog food. What do you need a truck for?"

"There's some dogs that helped me. I promised to find them homes, and I have to go to meet them after dark." I paused for air. "After that, I'm going to show the police where they've been keeping the dogs so that they can bust up the dog-fighting ring, and someone involved in that better volunteer some info about Crazy Curseman." I turned to Thorandryll. "Thanks for helping me."

He smiled. "You're welcome. I'll be in touch, Miss Jones."

"Oh, yeah, about that," I stopped, because he had disappeared. "Man, I hate when other people do that."

Nineteen

Kate and Jo followed me upstairs. We all kept emergency bags at the shop, with changes of clothes and whatnot in them. I explained everything that had happened since I'd left the garage in my car, and Kate went to call Damian and fill him in.

"I wonder how long the growlies are going to last."

Jo snorted. "I'm wondering if the elf slipped something in the potion to make them permanent. Be hard to keep a relationship going with Nick if you bite him every time he gets close."

Shampoo stung my eyes. "Ow." I splashed water. "Kate watched him, wouldn't she know?"

"Elves know a lot more about magical uses for herbs than we do. He could've slipped something past her."

I scowled at the ceiling while leaning back into the spray to rinse my hair. "If he did, I'll smack him into a wall until he undoes it."

She chuckled. "I want to watch."

"Deal." I conditioned my hair and let it set while scrubbing. "I'm guessing someone called my parents?"

"Mr. Whitehaven. Oh, I'd better check and see if anyone's called and told him it worked." She left the bathroom.

I'd call my parents myself, and go see them both as soon as possible. Hurrying through the rest of my shower, I rinsed and turned the water off. While drying, I wondered how to get around the leftover doggy instincts. It'd be nice to spend the night cuddled up to my boyfriend. It wasn't fair to have to keep him at arm's length after he'd spent the past couple of days trying to find me and worried to death.

Dinner with the elf wasn't a big thing. I'd go since that was the price I had agreed to, and he couldn't use any magic on me.

I dressed, skipping makeup. Logan and Terra were waiting to drive me to the Palisades to pick up Bone and his pack. After gathering my dirty clothes, I went downstairs, where David silently offered me a shopping bag to stick them in. "Thanks."

"My nose's pleasure. Did you roll in garbage?"

"No. Geeze. Leglin."

The hound turned his head. "*Mistress?*"

"Hey, I can still understand you. Cool. Do you want us to drop you off, or you going with?"

"*I prefer to stay by your side.*"

"He's going with," I said to Logan.

"So am I." Nick blocked my path toward the door and stuck his hand in my face. "Feel like biting me?"

I sniffed. "No. What did you do?"

He pointed at a small cloth bag hanging from a leather cord around his neck. "David whipped up a scent blocker."

"Yay!" I threw my arms around his neck. Nick's lips met mine, and I almost forgot I needed to get moving. Places to go, dogs to see. Breaking off the kiss, I fanned my face and stepped back to grab his hand. "Come on. We'll see you guys later."

"Don't get it wet!" David called as we trooped out the door.

"We can work around that," Nick assured me.

Since he could go, I double-checked if the other two still wanted to. Terra answered for them both. "I want to see how everything turns out. Besides, they'll need baths and stuff. It'll be faster if you have help."

Logan agreed, and they took his truck. We followed in Nick's, with Leglin in the back seat. "I'll stay in the truck or whatever, so I don't spook them."

"Okay." I laid my head on his shoulder and raised my hands to wiggle my fingers. "Feels weird to be me again. Oh, I need to call my parents. Where's my phone?"

"Evidence. Use mine." He pulled his from a jacket pocket.

I called Mom first, and she rushed to speak before I could say hello. "Nick? Have you found her?"

"It's me, Mom. I'll explain it all later. Just wanted to let you know I'm fine and everything's okay now. I wasn't hurt or anything."

"Oh, Cordi." The relief in her voice caused a wave of guilt to wash over me. She always worried about me so much. "Are you sure you're all right? Where've you been?"

"I, uh, kind of got turned into a dog. I've been with Logan and Terra, but they didn't know it was me." Dead silence. I pulled the phone away to make certain the connection hadn't dropped. "Mom?"

"You were a dog?"

I had to laugh at her disbelief. "Yeah, it's weird, I know. I'm so sorry I worried you like that."

"A dog," she repeated. "What was that like?"

"Really weird and interesting. I promise to tell you all about it soon. I need to call Dad, okay?"

"Right. Okay. Call or come see me as soon as you can."

"I will. Love you." Ending the call, I dialed my dad's number. Betty answered.

"Hello?"

"Hi, Betty. It's…"

She shrieked my dad's name. "Ben! It's Cordi!" In a less ear-piercing tone, she asked, "Are you all right? What happened?"

Hearing the real concern in her voice, I smiled. "I'm okay. I…"

"Here's your father."

"Cordi?" Dad sounded as relieved as Mom had.

"Hi, Dad. I have to go with the short version: I was turned into a dog by the dude who's been cursing people. I've been with Logan and Terra, they just didn't know I was me. But I'm me again, and not a dog any more, and I'm so sorry I worried you guys."

He started laughing. I heard Betty ask him why, and he tried to explain, sputtering words out. Her "She was a what?" set me off into a giggling fit.

"I demand a full accounting as soon as possible." Dad hiccupped, chuckled, and hiccupped again.

"Promise. Love you."

"Love you too."

Call ended, I gave Nick the phone back. "Thanks."

"No problem." He sounded a little cool, and there was a faint frown on his face.

I snuggled back against his side. "I'm sorry."

"You've got to quit taking off by yourself."

Aw, crap. "I tried to call you. It went straight to voicemail."

His frown became a full-fledged scowl. "You could've taken Leglin with you. Damn it, Cordi, every time you go off alone, you end up hurt."

I sat up. I hadn't actually gotten hurt this time. Just, you know, changed into a dog. "Can we not fight right now? Please?"

"Who's fighting? I'm stating facts." The steering wheel creaked as he tightened his grip. "Let's see, right after we met, you went off by yourself and got attacked by a fake elf who nearly strangled you. Then you went off, and got your skull cracked. After that, you went off and got attacked by vampires. That was two cases I know of. And now this time, you went off and were turned into a damn dog. Plus, before we met, you…"

I crossed my arms and stared out the windshield. "Enough,

dude. I told you this job doesn't exactly come with a guarantee of safety."

"Then you should quit and find something else to do."

"Excuse me? Now you're telling me what I can do for a career?" Unbuckling my seatbelt, I scooted down to the passenger side and buckled back in. I needed the distance, little as it was. "I can't believe…"

"I love you."

Mouth open, I turned to look at him with absolutely no clue how to respond. We hadn't been dating long enough for the L word to fly out of anyone's mouth. At least not in my book. Closing my mouth, I swallowed. "What?"

"I love you, and I want you to be safe. You're not safe doing this work." Nick glanced at me. "Guess that makes me a bad guy, wanting you to find something where you're not always getting hurt, huh? A, what do you call it…egotistical male pig or something?"

"No, it doesn't, but," I had to stop, my anger warring with disbelief and the fact I did really care for him. It took me a couple of minutes to figure out what to say. "I have to believe I have these abilities for a reason, Nick. I don't think that reason's to stand behind a cash register or whatever. I think it's so I can help people who need it, and I'm not going to quit my job. Not as long as I'm able to help people."

"What about helping yourself? Cordi, you're in danger all the time just because you're a psychic. A powerful one. You heard what the mayor said: You're on lists." He shook his head, narrowly avoiding rear-ending Logan's truck as the other braked for a light. "You don't want to be on those kinds of lists."

"Dude, I'm on them whether I quit or not. It's not like I can disappear." I hadn't even thought about what the mayor had said.

"You could." Nick licked his lips. "You could marry me and come live with my pack on our territory. You'd be safe there."

He may as well have punched me in the stomach, because all the air whooshed out of my lungs, strangling my voice. "Marry you?"

Letting go of the steering wheel, Nick stuck a hand inside his jacket and I caught a flash of something gold and shiny from his mind. Oh, God, he had a ring? I shook my head. "Oh, don't. Not right now, please. I can't handle it right now."

He stopped, his shoulders rounding, and turned his head to look out the side window. "You're saying no."

"I'm saying this is too much right this second." I sounded like a coward, but what else could I say? My emotions were trying to strangle me. I cared for him a whole lot, and enjoyed being with him, but love? Love and marriage? Those were big steps, especially for someone still freaking out over the idea of buying a house. I needed time to process everything. "I'm not saying no."

"You're not saying yes," he pointed out, letting off the brake as Logan's truck began moving again.

"But I'm not saying no." Boy, that sounded lame. When had I turned yellow? "I'm saying it's a big thing to think about and I just became me again. Don't be mad, Nick."

"I'm not mad." He didn't look mad. He didn't look anything, his expression smooth and offering absolutely no hint of what he was feeling. I winced.

"I just need some time to think about it, okay? I mean, we've only known each other a couple of months. That's not long to be making a huge decision like this."

"I know that I want to spend my life with you," he quietly said. "I can wait until you feel the same way."

"Okay. Good." I forced a smile. "Time is a good thing."

His return smile didn't look any more real than mine felt, and we didn't talk for the rest of the drive.

Nick stayed in his truck once we arrived. I let Leglin out, and bent to hug him before we joined Logan and Terra by the other truck. They traded a glance before Logan asked, "Is everything okay?"

"Yeah, sure. Let me try calling them." I turned away from them. "Bone! It's me, Cordi! I'm here!"

No response. I sighed. "Maybe they haven't gotten here yet. It's only been dark for a few minutes."

"We can wait." Terra moved to my side and slipped her arm around my waist. She leaned her head against my shoulder. "What's wrong? You're nervous."

I really wanted to talk to someone, and none of my witch buds were on hand. Taking a deep breath, I let it out slow. "Nick wants to get married."

She lifted her head, and I heard a weird sound from Logan's direction, like he'd sucked in a bug and was trying to quietly spit it out. "Oh. Um, do you want to get married?"

"Sure, some day, I guess. I mean, maybe someday. I don't know. It's a big thing." I ran my hand through my hair, which was still damp. "A really big thing."

"What did you tell him?"

I covered my eyes. "I wimped completely out. Told him I needed to time to think about it." Dropping my hand, I scowled at the broken-down porch of the house we were facing. "I mean, I care for him a lot and like being with him, but getting married? That's like the biggest thing ever except for having kids. I'm still running a few years behind and trying to catch up to where I should be. I don't even know if I want to get married at all yet."

"Then don't. If he loves you, he'll wait," she said.

"That's what he said." I put my hands up to my mouth. "Bone! Hey! Where are you?"

Leglin growled, the sound faint. We all looked at him. "What?"

"*I smell tigers.*"

"Well, Logan and Terra are right here."

The hound shook his head and sneezed. "*Not them. Others.*"

Uh oh. "He says he smells tigers."

Logan's eyes widened as he looked around, sniffing the air. "Get in the truck, Terra."

She began to obey, but I grabbed her arm as things began moving on the roofs of the houses. "Wait."

Nearly a dozen figures settled on their haunches, staring down at us. I heard Nick getting out of his truck. Another figure walked out of the house right in front of us. He was a tall guy with more muscles than I'd seen on anyone other than body builders on TV. "We've come for the White Queen."

"That's too bad, because you can't have her," Logan replied, stepping in front of us.

The other man grinned, picking his way off the porch. It creaked with each step. "I don't have a problem going through you."

"Wait a minute, let's not jump straight to the bloody stuff." I'd barely finished speaking when Nick grabbed my arm. "Hey."

"This isn't our business," he said, tugging me away from Terra. "We're leaving."

"Are you freakin' kidding me?" I yanked loose. "It may not be your business, but they're my friends."

"Go with him," Logan said, removing his jacket. He handed it to Terra, whose face had gone dead white. "He's right, this isn't your business."

I snarled, surprising them and myself. "Shut up. I'm staying."

Leglin brushed my leg as he walked to stand beside Logan. "*We fight to save her?*"

"You betcha, bub." I looked at Nick. He shook his head and

backed away, his hands up in surrender.

"I can't, Cordi. It'll start a war between my pack and their clan."

Disappointment landed like lead in my stomach. "Get out of the way then."

"I need a Queen, and she'll do nicely," the shifter said, halting at the foot of the steps.

"Dude, you're like forty." I saw Bone peek around the corner of the house. He ducked back out of sight. "You're not exactly a teenager's dream."

"And you're a loud-mouth bitch who I'll enjoy ripping apart and eating the heart of."

"Eww." I moved back to Terra's side and put my arm around her shoulders. "He's gross. I don't like him."

She swallowed, hugging Logan's jacket. "I don't either."

I could teleport them both away. Logan was close enough for me to grab his shirt. But that would leave Nick and Leglin alone, and I didn't know if the other shifters would turn on them. Plus, I now knew Bone was around, and probably the other three too. They might not come back again after seeing this, or if they saw me apparently abandoning Nick and Leglin.

"You got him?" I asked, and Logan nodded. "Okay, Leglin and I'll keep the others off both of you."

"Be careful," was all he said before walking toward his opponent. Though not a small man, he looked like a kid compared to the other shifter, who cracked his knuckles and strode forward to meet him.

Four streaks rushed out from the side of the house and Leglin leaped forward to join them. The big shifter flinched, his shoulders hunching as much as they could, as the dogs surrounded him.

Bone darted forward, nipping at the big shifter's thigh. He ducked away to avoid a strike, and Diablo closed in to nip at the shifter's other side. Logan stopped. "These your friends?"

"Yup. Hey, guys." I caught a shifter who jumped off the roof with my TK and put him back on it. Hard. "Bad kitty. No tuna for you."

Terra choked on a laugh, burying her face in Logan's jacket. The four pit bulls and Leglin drove the big shifter back onto the porch. He wasn't trying very hard to hit them. Guess he had doggy phobia too.

"Okay, you get her into the truck. Go to my place." When Logan nodded, I turned to look at Nick, who'd stayed close in spite of saying he couldn't get involved. "Open the doors and start your truck. We're blowing this pop stand."

He hurried to obey, and I called the dogs. "Come on, guys. We're leaving."

They began backing off, but a couple of shifters jumped down. I swatted them with my TK, and decided to do my part for city beautification after mentally scanning our surroundings. We were the only people around. "It's about to get hot here."

Turning, Logan rushed over and grabbed Terra, throwing her over his shoulder before running for his truck.

I set the houses on fire. Calling the dogs, I ran for Nick's truck as shifters yelled and jumped, smoke billowing to hide them from sight. One loomed in front of me, and I ducked to avoid a claw swipe before throwing him with my TK.

Bone yapped, streaking past me. *"You did that?"*

"Yes." I nearly ran into the front of Nick's truck. "Everyone in."

Tires squealing, Logan sped past. Another shifter appeared and grabbed the tailgate, throwing himself into the bed of the truck. I used my TK to throw him out while counting heads as the dogs jumped into the back seat. Nick yelled, "Get in!"

I did, and he threw the truck in reverse, throwing us all forward. The dogs squealed, thumping into the back of the front seat, and I smacked both hands on the dashboard. "Crap!"

The truck slewed around, slinging me into the door and the dogs into each other.

"Damn!" Red yelped. *"Get your paw outta my..."*

Nick threw it into drive and punched the gas. He was laughing. "My Alpha's going to kill me, but that was...God, Cordi, you're fantastic."

I shoved back and yanked the seatbelt on. "Give me your phone. I need to call in the fire."

Twenty

"Shh." I unlocked the door of my apartment and pushed it open. "Inside, quick."

My living room felt a lot smaller with ten dogs and four people in it. Terra had let the Chihuahuas out of their box before I turned around from shutting the door, and sniffing filled the air. I dropped onto the couch. "The pet rent's going to be a thousand dollars a month. I don't even have any dog food."

Nick grabbed the doorknob. He'd been the last person in. "I'll go get a couple of bags."

He left before I could agree or say thank you. Logan sank into a chair, staring at the carpet. Terra looked at him then me. "Want me to start giving baths?"

"If you feel like it, sure." I pointed at Sal. "Why don't you go first?"

The old dog huffed but followed her down the hall to my bedroom. Bone sat at to my feet, and rested his chin on my knee. *"You really are a human, and you came back."*

"I promised I would."

Logan looked up. "You can talk to them?"

"Yeah." I petted Bone, and said, "At least for now. It's probably going to wear off."

The shifter leaned back in his chair, folding his hands over his stomach. "How long can you keep them here before you have trouble with the manager?"

"I don't know, but don't worry about it. I have backup plans." We were quiet for a few minutes, long enough to hear the water start running and Terra politely asking Sal if he needed help getting in the tub. I leaned over Bone, examining his missing ear nub. "Did I cause more trouble?"

Logan's response came too quickly. "No."

"Dude, I saw you and Nick glaring at each other."

He grinned. "We do that all the time."

"Not like that, you don't. What gives?" I waved a hand. "Whew, you stink, Bone. Why don't you guys go get in line?"

He snorted, but went down the hall with Red and Diablo following. The black dog glanced back at me and offered a tiny wag of his tail. I smiled and toppled over, swinging my legs over the arm of the couch, before meeting Logan's gaze. "Tell me what I did. I can't fix it if I don't know what I broke."

"Okay." He let out a sigh. "Two things: By standing with us, you've declared yourself our ally, and now it'll spread from one end of the city to the other that the White Queen's Protector requires help to keep her safe."

I closed my eyes, buried my hands into my hair, and groaned. "Shifter politics."

"Yep."

Cracking an eye open, I said, "You totally could've whooped his butt."

"Beating him down wouldn't be enough. One of us would've died back there." Logan grimaced. "Probably me. Did you see the size of that guy?"

"Nearly as tall as the boss and wide as a wall. Couldn't miss him." I let go of my hair and rubbed my face with both hands. "Let me get this straight. I maybe saved your life, and doing it means what? That they'll try harder now?"

"Well…" He shrugged. "They were going to try anyway."

"Great." I wanted to sleep for two days, not deal with problems. "They can't try if they can't find you."

Logan shook his head. "You've done enough for us, Discord."

"I made things worse. It's my fault they tried tonight. If I hadn't dragged you with me to pick up the boys, and then distracted you moaning about my relationship issues, aw, man. I'm still going to have to deal with that too." I smacked the back of the couch with my fist. "Being an adult sucks!"

"Tell me about it." Logan slid down further in the chair and let his head fall back. "I need to call the others, have some of them come here so that I can get Terra home safely."

I waved a hand at him. "It's late. Just stay here tonight, and we'll figure things out in the morning."

"I don't think Nick will go along with that idea."

"My place, my rules." I covered a yawn. "Terra can sleep with me. You take the couch. Nick can go home. I can't deal with him bitching at me or thinking about the whole 'marry me' thing right now. I'm too tired."

There was still Crazy Curseman to find and stop too. I hit the couch again. "I need a vacation from my life."

"I've always wanted to see Tahiti. Maybe after Terra's settled." The shifter sighed. "If I live that long."

"Don't talk like that." I saw Sal coming down the hallway. He stopped in the middle of the living room, looked at each of us, and then shook. The Chihuahuas went nuts, running around and yipping their little heads off. "Dude, no. Gah! Everything's going to smell like wet dog now."

The dog grinned, his tongue lolling out, and sat. "*Sorry. Where's dinner?*"

"It's on the way." I caught Logan watching us. "What?"

"I'm trying to figure out what he's saying."

"He's hungry and wondering where dinner is." My stomach growled. "Crap. Should've asked Nick to pick up some pizza or something."

That turned out to be unnecessary, because he returned shortly with food for everyone. "Chinese."

"Bless you." I rolled off the couch, almost landing on Bone. Terra hurried down the hall with a towel in her hands on the heels of Red, the last one in the tub. He started to shake and she threw the towel over him.

We managed to find enough bowls to feed all the dogs, and settled at the table to eat our own meal. About to take a bite of my sweet and sour chicken, I had a question. "What day is it?"

Nick and Logan answered at the same time. "Thursday."

"How many more suicides have there been?"

"Two or three each day, but I don't know if they were all cursed or really suicidal. You'll have to talk to Damian." Nick dumped soy sauce on his beef and broccoli.

"I will, tomorrow." We still didn't have a motive for Crazy Curseman. My brain refused to offer up any ideas, and I concentrated on eating.

After dinner, we took turns taking dogs outside by twos and threes. Once the potty breaks were over, I left Terra and Logan corralling the little dogs while I herded the larger ones toward my bedroom.

"They're sleeping in here?" Nick stopped just inside the door.

"Yeah, and so is Terra. They're staying the night, so I guess you'll have to go home." I opened my closet door.

"No. I'll sleep on the floor or whatever, but I'm not going home." Nick's whisper burned my ears. "It's bad enough you…"

"You know what? You want to stay, fine, but no telling me how badly I've screwed things up. Not tonight." I shoved two pillows and a couple of blankets at him. "Take these for you and Logan."

Teeth bared, he growled while taking them. "I have a right to be mad."

"Sure, and I have a right not to put up with you being mad when I'm tired as hell. You can save your mad for when we have time to deal with it. We don't right now." I twirled my finger and pointed at the door. "Go, sleep. No arguing with Logan. He's a guest."

Nick gritted his teeth, lips pressed tight and then pecked me on the cheek. "Fine."

He passed Terra in the hall. She ducked under as he lifted the bedding, both of them somehow pretending the other didn't exist in spite of their dodging efforts. The teen set the box down. "I brought the little ones."

"Cool. PJs in the top drawer there, help yourself." Furry bodies littered my bedroom floor. The pits and Leglin had already fallen asleep. Diablo snored. I shut the door and toed my shoes off before releasing the mini-Krakens from the box. "Find a spot and curl up. No pottying unless you really have to, and if you do, do it in the bathroom."

Speck scratched at my leg. *Sleep with you.*

"Okay." I shut the door and picked him up before heading straight for the bed, too worn out to even care about changing. After setting the puppy on the bed, I skinned out of my jeans and climbed in. Terra turned out the light a couple of minutes later, and slid in on the other side.

I could hear the low murmur of voices from the living room. "No fighting!"

"We're not!" Nick yelled back. "Go to sleep!"

"Bossy butt," I muttered, and Terra giggled. Speck climbed onto my chest, walked around, and settled on my stomach.

Eyes closing, I hoped nothing else would happen before morning.

Twenty-one

A cold, wet nose against my cheek woke me. I cracked open an eye to find Diablo in my face. *"I need to go outside."*

"Okay." After peeling Speck off my throat, I climbed out of bed and tucked the little guy under the covers before pulling on my jeans. Leglin woke, yawned, and stretched. I petted both on the head on my way to the bathroom, emerging a few minutes later to grab my shoes and take them outside.

Nick sprawled bare-chested on the floor, his blanket bunched under him. Logan slept like a child, lying on his side with both hands tucked under his pillow, his blanket down around his hips. He'd taken off his shirt too. Nothing better than waking up to eye candy, except for coffee.

The morning chill caused shivers and goose bumps on my arms. Rubbing them, I tried to pretend alertness by checking the parking lot. My car, coated with morning dew, sparkled in the rising sun. It looked gorgeous.

A truck pulled into the lot, driving slowly past before pulling in next to Nick's truck. I recognized Patrick and intercepted him before he could reach my apartment door. "Can I help you?"

"I'm looking for Nick Max…oh, you're her." The corner of his lips quirked. Giving me a slow up and down scan, he added, "I recognize your scent. Smelled it on him often enough."

"Okay, that's just TMI. They're still asleep, and I have a houseful of dogs." Leglin bounded up with Diablo. They halted, one on either side of me, and studied the shifter. The black pit bull growled low in his throat. I realized my teeth were bared, and closed my lips.

Patrick's eyes flashed gold. "I hope you can keep it under control. Hate to…"

I stepped forward, poking a forefinger at his nose, and let my teeth show. "Here's a little tip: If you want to get along with me, you'll keep your damn threats to yourself. My dog buds are off-limits to you, Nick, and anyone else in your pack. Anyone ignores that, and I," I dropped my hand lower to poke him in the chest with each word. "Will come down on them like a ton of bricks. They are *my* pack. Got that?"

He pushed my hand away, a grin forming, and I got hit by a flash of memory. Running through the forest, chasing something. Hot blood flowing down my throat. Blood lust turning to lust and sinking a body part I definitely wasn't equipped with into slippery heat.

"Argh." I shook my head, trying to dispel the images. "Don't touch me without an invitation, dude."

Grin fully formed, he asked, "Is there going to be one?"

What a horn dog. "Oh, good night. No."

Patrick edged forward, ignoring Diablo's rising growl. "You sure? I'm not as tame as my little brother. You might like the change."

I put a hand on Diablo's head, and tilted mine. "Do you always hit on Nick's girlfriends?"

He laughed. "Yes."

"Pretty damn scum-sucking of you." I nudged Diablo with my knee. "Let's go in."

Inside, I found Nick awake and stretching. "Your douchebag of a brother's here."

"And you, little brother, are in major trouble with the Alpha." Patrick walked in behind the dogs and me. "He got a complaint from a tiger clan. Something about you interfering with a takedown."

My boyfriend groaned. Logan proved he was awake by sitting up. "He didn't aid us. He stayed because Discord wouldn't leave."

"All I did was help her get out of there." Nick scrubbed a hand over his face and hair.

Patrick shrugged, dropping into a chair. "Don't tell me. Tell Dad."

I shut the door, looking from him to Nick. "Your father's the Alpha?"

His brother chuckled. "Do you tell her anything? Yes, Dad's the Alpha of our pack."

There it was, in a nutshell. I couldn't even think of saying yes to marrying Nick when he'd never shared that kind of information with me.

"Dad said…"

Patrick interrupted him. "She's not one of your little human playmates. You've been spending all your spare time with her, and sleeping with only her." He raised an eyebrow. "I might think that means you're serious about Psychic Girl, even if she made you sleep on the floor last night. Are you in the dog house?"

Nick growled. His brother growled back. Logan knuckled sleep out of his eyes, tossed the blanket aside, and rose. "It's too early for this crap."

"Yeah. Coffee?" I headed for the kitchen, and he followed.

"Please. Mind if I borrow the bathroom?"

"Go ahead." He turned down the hall and I began setting up the coffee pot, ignoring the thump from the living room. Sounds of wrestling followed it. Diablo stalked in, his ears pinned back. Leglin stopped at the entrance, turning around and sitting, his ears perked as he watched the brothers rolling around on my living room floor. "You guys break anything, you bought it."

"*Why do you let them in your place? They ain't got no manners.*" Diablo sneezed and rubbed a paw over his nose. "*And they stink.*"

"Nick's my boyfriend." I started the coffee and began collecting bowls. "I know it's asking a lot, but try not to bite either of them, okay?"

The black dog turned his head, giving me the damaged side. "*Whatever.*"

"Keep stirring them." I'd remembered my vow to give Terra cooking lessons, and had her taking care of the scrambled eggs. The wolf brothers were gone, though Nick promised he'd be back as soon as a possible. I turned bacon with one hand, busy scribbling a list of groceries with the other.

Logan sat on the floor, sipping his coffee while rolling a tennis ball for Speck. My potential Chihuahua adoptee skittered around on the tile, bouncing off the other little dogs as they ate breakfast. The larger dogs were lounging around in the living room. A glance through the doorway showed them having a conversation with Leglin. From what I caught, they were asking him about living with me.

I'd planned to see if Mom or Betty could help find them homes, but catching that, I realized the idea of keeping them suited me just fine. That way I could be certain of what happened to them since I wouldn't lose touch.

Scooping the bacon out to drain on paper towels, I said, "I have got to find a house."

"For you and Nick?" Terra asked.

"No, my pack and me. I can't have that many big dogs in an apartment. Those are done. Hot pads are in that drawer. Just take the skillet over to the table." I turned off burners while she followed directions, and carried the bacon over. Logan swatted the tennis ball into the living room, and Speck bounded after it.

He stood, sniffing, and took a seat. "Looks good, ladies. Thank you."

Terra sat down, but I grabbed my notepad before joining them. I tore my shopping list free and stared at the blank page. After a few seconds, I sighed and tossed the pen down in favor of serving myself some eggs. "I got nothing on this guy. No motive for him cursing people into killing themselves, no clues except he's involved with the dog fighting."

"Blood?" Logan and I focused on Terra. The teen shrugged. "I don't know, I mean, blood's life, and it's used for a lot of things aside from keeping people and vampires alive. We have a sharing ritual when someone new joins our clan. It's used to seal oaths, for spells, for…"

"Sacrifices to demons." I scowled. "I swear, if demons are involved, I will personally introduce Curseman's face to a brick wall. Like, a dozen times."

"Not just to demons. To gods too." Logan speared a couple of pieces of bacon. "I know the One True God thing really took root with humans, but there's not one god. There's hundreds, maybe thousands."

I shoveled eggs into my mouth, wishing he hadn't said that. Oh, sure, I realized people thought there were a lot of gods—my witch buddies picked personal gods to appeal to from the Aztec pantheon—but to hear someone say there were loads and loads of omnipotent beings out loud seriously tilted my world outlook twenty degrees past "batshit crazy" and caused beyond-serious doubt in my ability to survive.

"Did I say something wrong?"

His question tuned me into the muffled growling. My muffled growling. Swallowing, I shook my head. "Nope, I'm just wondering how crazy things have to get before I end up drooling all over a straitjacket with my name on it at Happyville Manor."

Terra ducked her head while snagging a couple of pieces of bacon. I grabbed a few slices before they all disappeared. Shifters were hell on a girl's bacon supply. "Okay, let's go with her blood theory. All the suicides I know about did involve blood splattering everywhere, and so does the dog fighting. But if it's not being collected or spilled in like, a circle or whatever, what good does it do Curseman to be painting the town red?"

Logan straightened and pointed a piece of bacon at me. "Intent. Spells are intentions, and curses are spells. Magic practitioners always choose a personal..."

"God," I finished. "Yeah, that I did know. So he's..."

"Creating the curses with the intention of the victims being sacrifices to his god." Logan paused, lifting one shoulder slightly. "I'm sticking with a god over demons. They can be capricious and cruel, but people are agents, more of an investment for them. Demons just use and kill anyone who calls on them."

Made sense to me, and I said so. "Which means our next step is what? Find where any gods are hanging out at in Santo Trueno and ask who's been getting a lot of bloody presents?"

He chuckled. "I don't think it'll be that easy, Discord."

"Nothing ever is." I chomped down on a piece of bacon and ground it to paste before swallowing. "Oh."

"Oh, what?"

"That means it's time to call the witches in. They can ask their personal gods to lend us a hand." I popped the rest of my bacon into my mouth and smiled at them.

Twenty-two

Terra and I were in my bedroom, changing clothes before leaving for the Blue Orb, when a crash came from the living room. "What the hell?"

Dogs began barking, and the Chihuahuas came hauling into the room, screaming about bad animal people. I pointed at Terra. "Put them in the bathroom and stay here."

Not waiting for her agreement, I ran out the door and down the hallway. My front door hung from one hinge, the top of it leaning toward the wall. Leglin stood in the remains of the doorway, indecision plain in the way his ears couldn't settle on perked or flattened. Logan wasn't to be seen, and the pits were outside. "What is it?"

"*Tigers.*"

"Guard Terra and the little ones. I'll yell if we need you. Take her to Mr. Whitehaven if you have to get her out." I rushed past as he jumped out of my way, and barreled right into the shifter I'd thrown out of the back of Logan's truck the night before.

He snarled and swung as I stumbled backward and fell, landing on my butt. "Ow."

Planting my hands, I lifted my rear and kicked with one leg, catching him square in the family jewels, and then under the chin when he bent over. He went sideways and I scrambled to my feet, already scanning the courtyard.

Leglin could handle him if he went after Terra.

My short-sleeved blouse flapped open as I ran toward the circle of shifters surrounding Logan and Mr. Bodybuilder, who'd apparently already swapped a few blows from the blood decorating their faces and shirts. Bone and his pack darted in and out, their snarls filling the air as they bit at legs and arms. "Break it the hell up!"

"Not this time, chickie." Mr. Bodybuilder spat blood. "Your wolf's not here to protect you once I've ripped his," he spat more blood in Logan's direction. "Head off."

"Stay out of it, Discord."

I felt a gentle mental touch and stopped. Logan said *Please get Terra out of here. Don't let them take her. Teague knows what to do.*

A shiver made my heart skip a beat. He sounded grim and resigned. *I will if I have to, but I'm not leaving you without any backup. Leglin's guarding her right now and will get her out if needed.*

Diablo lunged, catching one of the tigers by the arm, and dragged him out of the circle. Red leaped and hit the man in the back, knocking him down. Another tiger, a woman, turned around and went for the red dog, but Bone darted between them and her, his growl warning her away.

How the hell had they found us? I scanned minds, trying to ignore the meaty-sounding thwacks as Logan and Mr. Bodybuilder began knocking each other around again. It proved damn difficult to find out anything, because the shifters' excitement over the bloody entertainment and winning the White Queen blocked most other coherent thoughts.

Then I caught a glimpse of Patrick in one mind. Son of a bitch. They'd followed him.

I whistled for the dogs, who were dancing away from every attempt to hit or grab them. They broke off their attack and ran to me, their eyes gleaming. Bone snapped at one shifter who aimed a kick at Sal's back end.

"*We can take'em,*" Diablo barked. "*Freakin' pussycats, coming on our territory.*"

"I know." I knelt and grabbed his head. "But they want the girl. Someone could go through the window in my room. Try not to kill anyone. Just disable them, okay?"

"*You heard her,*" Bone panted. "*Let's go.*"

They raced back to my apartment and disappeared inside. A roar wrenched my head back around in time to see Mr. Bodybuilder staggering backwards, with four bright red lines across his face.

It looked like a good time to bust the party up, while Logan had the upper hand. Concentrating, I threw my hands out, palms forward. Just before I released the surge of TK, I heard a click in my head.

Bright white lightning boomed into being and, crackling noisily, settled around the group. What an absolutely fantastic time for a new ability to arrive. I gulped and kept my hands up, afraid of what might happen when I lowered them. "I said, break it the hell up! I don't have time for this crap."

The repeat wasn't necessary, as they'd already frozen. Logan moved, extremely slowly, until he could watch Mr. Bodybuilder and see me. No one else moved anything but their eyes. The weight of them made me nervous, but I took a deep breath and seized on something I'd seen in a movie once. "I gave them sanctuary."

A slight shake of Logan's head said that hadn't been a good idea, but I didn't have another one handy to run with.

"Who the hell are you?" Mr. Bodybuilder had a scowl that could melt steel without the extra oomph the rips in his face gave it. My knees didn't like his scowl, and I had to lock them to keep from backing away.

"Discord Jones, douchebag, and in case you didn't notice, I'm also pissed off. You broke into my home and attacked my guests. I should fry your ass right now for coming onto my territory." That sounded appropriately angry. I hoped. "Here's how the rest of this is going down. You and your friends are going to leave. Anyone who doesn't is going to dance the Electric Slide until their brains turn to ash."

Mr. Bodybuilder jabbed a finger in Logan's direction. "You won't be around to save him next time."

"I wouldn't bet on it, but it looks to me like I saved your life just now, bub." I grinned, praying the fact my head was beginning to pound didn't show. The lightning didn't let up at all. "He was an inch away from taking your head off."

Logan's wry sounding *Right* echoed in my mind. Geeze, he should have more confidence in himself. I tried to point that out. "You're not much of a challenge to a guy who's fought and killed hundreds of demons, dude."

A tiny flash of uncertainty tightened Mr. Bodybuilder's lips. He snarled and turned around. "We'll go, but this isn't the end."

Man, I wanted them to go really, really bad, and had no clue how to stop the lightning. My arms were beginning to shake from behind held straight out for so long. If I lost control of it, Logan would fry along with the rest of them. *Okay, I can do this. Deep breath, let it out slow...*

I lowered my arms, willing the lightning to fade away, and to my immense relief, it obeyed. "I won't hold him back next time."

The shifters left, trying to saunter, but the tightness in their bodies said it was all for show. Logan stayed put, watching until they were out of sight, and then turned to me. "I haven't seen you do that before."

"Didn't know I could." My legs gave out, and I fell to the grass, banging my knees. Sparkles danced across my vision, and I groaned. "Not sure I want to again."

The grass felt soft and taking a nap on it seemed like a superb idea. I crumpled onto my side, closing my eyes, and thought about calling Mom.

Logan knelt next to me and tugged my blouse closed. "Are you okay?"

"Head hurts."

"What can I do to help?" His fingers brushed my skin as he began buttoning my blouse.

Leave me here? Naw. "I kind of want my mommy."

He chuckled and scooped me off the nice, inviting grass. "I'll call her after I get you inside."

My headache went from ax in the brain to a dull sawing when I rested my head on his shoulder. Maybe I'd screwed up things even worse, but calm flowed from Logan, making it clear he wasn't angry.

Good, because I was angry enough for both of us.

"My word." Mom's voice announced her welcome arrival. "What happened? Cordi, are you all right? Oh," she squeaked when Logan turned around from talking to the security guard. "You're bleeding! Sit down."

"I'll be okay. Discord has a major headache."

Mom scooted through the doorway and perched on the edge of the couch, her hand cool against my forehead. "You're running a fever."

"New ability." I closed my eyes, feeling my lips curve a little. Though potentially not safe for her to be here, Mom's presence made everything better.

Not only that, but she was hell on wheels at getting things done. In less than five minutes, she'd brewed me a cup of her special herbal headache tea, called my father, and shooed out the security guard. I sipped the tea, listening as she called maintenance.

Done with that, she nagged Logan until he sat down and let her take a look at his wounds. "What did this?"

"Another shifter." He winced when she gently prodded at the gashes across his chest. "I'll heal, Sunny. You don't have to…"

"Nonsense. Stay right there." She turned to Terra, who sat in the hallway with Leglin, blocking the other dogs from the living room. "There's a first aid kit under the bathroom sink. Will you bring it to me?"

"Yes, ma'am." The teen jumped to her feet and hurried down

the hall without stepping on anyone furry. Mom disappeared into the kitchen, and water began to run.

Logan grimaced before whispering. "She doesn't have to clean me up."

"Yes, she does, or you'll never hear the end of it. Mom likes taking care of people." I took another sip of the tea, ignoring the taste. Whatever she put into it always worked on my psychic-induced headaches. "Did you call the shop?"

He nodded, checking his swollen eye. The split skin over it had already begun knitting closed. "They think the same thing, someone using curses to sacrifice to a god. He said the familiars being really upset with whatever they found clued them in. They aren't scared of demons, but they are of gods. Ah, what did they find?"

I told him about the first curse that hit me, and passing it to Dad so that they could examine it. "Someone should've told you about that."

Logan shrugged off being left out of the loop. "We were all busy looking for you."

By then, Mom had gotten his shirt off and was busy cleaning the gashes. Terra shifted from foot to foot, holding the first aid kit. Her gaze went from Logan to the open doorway. "Someone's coming."

"Probably the maintenance man or Ben." Mom rose and walked to the door to look out. "Maintenance."

Once again, she took charge. I snuggled into the afghan she'd tucked around my shoulders and finished my tea.

Dad arrived just in time to deal with the apartment manager. "Well no, I can't explain the dogs..."

"Rescues. Trying to find their owners," I said, rubbing my temples. The last of my headache faded while he tried his best to keep me from being kicked out. It didn't work, but at least he negotiated a week's time to vacate.

"The dogs have to go immediately. I'm sorry, honey." He dropped down onto the couch next to me and patted my knee. "How are you feeling?"

"Loads better. Thanks for the tea, Mom."

She nodded, clucking over Logan. She'd finished cleaning the blood off him, and had begun smearing antibiotic ointment over his wounds. Terra stood behind the chair, stroking Logan's black hair with nervous fingers. The gashes had mostly closed, and his bruises were already turning yellow and green. He'd relaxed, laying his head back and closing his eyes.

I looked at the hallway and twenty-two pairs of bright eyes

stared back. "I need a house. A big one with a huge backyard."

"I'll call Rita," Dad said, naming a family friend. "She received her real estate license last year. In the meantime..."

"You can move home. I'll take the dogs with me when I leave." Mom stood up and flipped her braid over her shoulder. There was more gray in her blonde hair than I remembered being there. "You said you rescued all of them?"

"Well, not the big ones. I'm keeping them. And the tiny black one, I want to keep him if no one claims him." There, I'd made it even more official, after telling Patrick they were my pack. Soft thunder crept from the hallway as tails pounded carpet. "But I can't move home, Mom."

"Why not? Because of your job?" She put her hands on her hips, narrowing her blue eyes. "That's it. I've had enough."

"Uh..."

"You deliberately don't tell me things, Discordia Angel Jones, and I'm tired of not knowing what's going on."

Dad flinched and leaned away from me at her use of all three of my names. She stabbed a finger in his direction. "And you aid and abet her, Benjamin Thomas! We are still family, and I'm sick of the two of you trying to, to...whatever it is you think you're doing."

"Protect you." Logan's quiet comment yanked her head around. His shoulders hunched under her glare. "That's what they're trying to do."

"I'm a grown woman and a mother. I don't need to be protected. What I need is to know what's going on so that I can help. Or at least not worry constantly." Mom's bottom lip trembled. She stopped it by turning a scowl on Dad and me. "Am I, or am I not, a member of this family?"

"Yeah, Mom, but..."

Dad put his hand on my knee. "Of course you are, Sunny. You're right, and I'm sorry. Cordi's sorry too, aren't you, honey?"

"Ah...yes. Yes, I am so sorry, Mom." Crap, how did this turn from keeping her safe and worried as little as possible to her feeling like she wasn't part of the family anymore? So not my intention. "I just...I hate worrying you, and my job's not roses all the time, and I've made some enemies."

"Then you're doing things right." Mom smiled. "I knew before you woke up that you weren't going to be the exact same little girl anymore. The news was full of coma victims waking up with special powers. I'm proud that you decided to use yours to help people. But I don't need to be helped, Cordi. I don't need to be protected, but informed."

When she put it like that, I felt about two inches tall. Mom wasn't finished. "I'm your mother. It's my job to worry about you. Don't keep me from doing my job."

"Okay. I won't, Mom." I pushed the afghan off my shoulders and stood. She met me halfway and we hugged. "I really am sorry."

"You're forgiven. I know you did it because you love me." She kissed my cheek and took hold of my hands while stepping back. "Now, are you going after the person who's done all this?"

"Yes." And by damn, I was going to nail his hide, whatever flavor it was, to the wall.

Twenty-three

"Go with Discord." Terra's urging resulted in a shake of Logan's head.

"I'm your Protector."

"I'll be okay with Sunny and the dogs."

He glanced at me, tapping his fingers on his thighs, indecision marring his face with tiny lines. "I'm sorry, I have to stay with Terra."

"That's okay. I think I can get to the office on my own." I didn't want to be the cause of any more trouble for them. The teen's bottom lip jutted out. "Seriously, it's okay. I'll feel better if he's with you guys."

Terra uttered something between a growl and swear word. Maybe it was a swear word in tiger talk. Logan started to speak, but she slashed her hand through the air. "Then I'll go with you."

I bowed out of the argument, going to the kitchen to help Dad collect the dog food. We loaded it in the back of Mom's station wagon. Mom was busy making friends with the furry crowd. She cooed over the little dogs, but talked to Leglin and the pits as though they were human.

"I'll call Rita tomorrow. When you have a chance, come over for dinner, and we'll take a look at your finances to see what we have to work with." Dad held out his arms, and I stepped into them for a hug. "Be careful, honey."

"I will."

He gave Mom a hug too, whispering something in her ear that caused a smile to bloom on her face. I began putting the Chihuahuas in her station wagon, and gave instructions to Leglin and Bone. "Keep the little ones in order for her, and don't let anything bad happen to her, okay?"

"*Of course, mistress.*" Leglin inclined his head. "*You will call me if you need me?*"

"You betcha, bud." I hugged him, and on impulse, hugged the other four large dogs. "I don't know when I'll get there, but I'll see you guys later."

All but Bone jumped into the back of the wagon. I looked at him. "Get in."

He snorted and laid his good ear back. *"I'm going with you."*

"I'd argue with you, but we need to go. Okay, fine. Come on." After shutting the tailgate, I hugged Mom and told her I'd call later to let her know what was going on. Re-entering my apartment involved dancing around the two maintenance men fixing the door. "Can you lock up when you're done?"

"Yeah."

"Thanks." I grabbed my purse and jacket before looking at the two shifters. "Mom's about to leave."

"We're going with you." Terra crossed her arms, giving Logan a definite Look.

He nodded. "We're going with you."

"Then let's hit the road." They followed me out to the parking lot, where we sent Mom and the dogs off. I took my car, with Bone riding shotgun. Logan and Terra stayed on my tail the whole way to the office.

Mr. Whitehaven came out to greet us, and drew me into a hug. I felt small and a little surprised since he didn't tend to go around hugging people. But it felt nice, kind of like being hugged by a grandparent. "I'm pleased you're safe."

"Thanks, boss." I directed a grin upward as he released me. "I'm glad to have two legs and a voice again. This is Bone. He's one of the dogs that helped me while I was a dog."

Whitehaven lowered himself to one knee and held out a hand. "I'm pleased to meet you, Mr. Bone."

The dog slapped his paw into my boss's hand, offering a tongue-lolling grin. *"I like this guy."*

Once Whitehaven regained his feet, we trooped inside and straight to his office. Kate, Jo, Damian, David, and Ronnie were all there, along with their familiars. None of the latter were talking. They were huddled in a corner, fur and feathers ruffled as they glared at their respective witches.

I introduced Ronnie to the two shifters while the boss crossed to his desk and sat down. She'd colored her hair a dark brown. It looked good, and I told her so.

"Thanks." We hugged, and then I walked over to perch on the corner of the boss's desk, since the couch and chairs were full.

Taking a deep breath, I let it out slow before speaking. "So, we all think Curseman's gig is sacrifices to his god?"

"Either that, or to a god he wants to gain favor with," David responded, pushing up his glasses. His fine hair stuck up in tufts all over, indicating he'd been rubbing his head a lot. "The problem is that we don't have a way to discover which god it is. Most gods accept blood sacrifices."

I wrinkled my nose. "You guys don't…"

"We offer our own blood when necessary, Jones." Kate's crisp comment and level gaze told me I'd just lost a few brownie points for thinking otherwise. "We're white witches."

"I know, sorry, just…gah, never mind." I twisted around to look at Whitehaven. "Any suggestions?"

"Before the Melding, gods tended to keep close to their origins. Now," he spread his hands wide. "They go where they wish, at whim or in answer to calls from those who believe in them. The ah, Curseman could be offering these sacrifices to any of them."

Body slumping, I scowled at his desktop. "There has to be something we can do."

"All of the suicides have occurred at late afternoon or night, and Stannett has the entire department working overtime, patrolling the streets." Damian scratched his chin. I noticed the dark circles under his eyes. "Unless we can catch him near the scene of one, I don't know what to do. We can't set any magical traps with no idea where the next may happen."

"What about the old brewery in the Palisades?"

He sighed. "No one there when we checked it out. No one knows a damn thing. They never do in that area. It's not safe for them to."

Defeat clouded the room. It sucked to have so many people capable of doing so much, and yet here we all sat, powerless. I crossed my arms and rubbed Bone's back with the toe of my shoe. "I'm going to think out loud."

"Go ahead." Jo kicked off her shoes, curled her legs under her, and twirled a hand at me. "Beats doing nothing."

"The first we knew about Curseman was at the fair, when I stopped Rose from dying." Which hadn't actually saved her, but how was I supposed to know she'd been cursed and would finish the job? "There were six more suicides over the weekend. How many have there been now?"

Damian answered. "Ten more, for a total of seventeen."

I winced. "How many were men and women?"

"Nine women and eight men so far." He blinked. "What are you thinking?"

"Probably nothing useful. Do any gods prefer matched sacrifices? What about numbers special to them? I kind of remember something about threes and sevens, but no specifics." In fact, the only three I could think of was the Holy Trinity, but I didn't think the Father, the Son, and the Holy Ghost were on the kill-people-as-sacrifices-we'll-give-you-magic list.

Jo smacked David's leg. He jumped and rubbed the spot. "There are some who have historically required sacrifices of male-female pairs. We can work on that angle, maybe narrow things down, see if your numbers idea fits any in particular."

Terra cleared her throat with a tiny *ahem*. "Isn't one of the things we need to look at like a pattern or something? There were more of them on the weekend, and less during the weekdays. Could that mean something?"

Bone rolled over so that I could rub his chest. I slid off the desk to squat next to him, and began scratching. "It could, but I don't know what." My fingernails caught on a scar. "Unless...Bone, when do the dog fights take place?"

He wiggled, stretching his hind legs as far as they would go. *"Keep scratching. They, yeah, right there...uh, at night. Start before dark sometimes. You missed a, ooh, found it. On the..."* he rolled over, scrambling to his paws and shoved his nose in my face. *"Weekends, when more people can come watch. That's important, right?"*

"Yeah, it's important." I realized everyone was watching us and looked up. "He says the fights are on the weekends, when more people can come. Question is, how could that tie into more cursed suicides then?"

"Power." I twisted around and popped my head over the edge of the desk to look at Whitehaven. His chin resting in one hand, elbow on the opposite edge, he raised the forefinger of his other hand. "Small deaths fueling the ability to create the curses, which lead to larger deaths which will draw the attention of the chosen god."

Having always wanted to say it, I did. "Ah-hah! We can make a plan now."

Damian was already nodding. "We find where the dog fights are being held..."

"Bust'em, and catch Curseman while he's standing around, waiting to suck up power." I twisted back around and scratched Bone's neck with both hands. "Who's a good boy?"

The pit snorted, but he stretched his nose toward the ceiling, both eyes closing. *"Yeah, yeah, I can show you the places they use."*

"You're awesome. He's going to help," I said to the others. "Of course, I still have a question about all of this."

"Which is?" Jo uncurled her legs and checked her hair.

"What made Curseman focus on me? He cursed Chapman and sent him to my little brother's school, where Chapman took Sean hostage. The curse passed from Chapman to me," I paused, something not feeling totally right about that. "At least, we think it did. It didn't pass to Sean—hey, are any of the victims kids?"

Damian's "No" freed me to continue. "Okay, it didn't pass to Sean, or to Betty, but it did pass to Dad after it didn't work on me. Well, it didn't work all the way, and after that," I sighed. "He turned me into a dog. I have no clue how he knew…wait."

"Wait what? Don't keep us in suspense, Jones." Kate rose from her seat and smoothed the front of her black satin pin skirt.

"My tracking sense woke me up, but the thread was a new color: black. What all can black stand for?"

"Death." David's response made me shiver. "Mourning, sadness, but it has positive uses too. Protection, binding, banishing…"

My skin prickled all over, and I shuddered. "So the black thread could've come from someone working a spell to get me to a certain place? Can somebody do that to a psychic? I mean, my tracking ability's not really a standard one."

"True, but with a god in the mix, one receiving sacrifices that please him or her, ah," David's brow wrinkled. "I believe I may be getting a headache."

"Join the club." Coming to a god's attention had to be way worse than being on the demon hit list. "Okay, let's say that's how Curseman worked it, and it did work, because I always follow my tracking flashes. How did he know that?"

Everyone traded glances. It took a couple of minutes before someone offered up the obvious explanation, and it was Logan who took the hit for the team. "He knows you, or enough about you that he'd know you would follow through on anything like that."

"It can't be any of you. I don't think it's Nick." Yet I had no clue how much he'd told anyone, say, members of his pack, about me. Patrick had called me Psychic Girl, but that didn't mean he knew all about my abilities. I dropped my face in my hands and groaned. "It could be anyone. Someone Nick knows, or maybe even an elf, if Thorandryll gossiped. I am so stupid. I told him all about my abilities once, when we went to look at Fake Elf Guy at the morgue."

No one agreed that I was stupid, so I let my hands fall and lifted my head. Damian tapped a finger against his lips. "Or it could be someone from the government. They have lists, and we're probably all on them. I mean everyone who dropped into comas during the Melding. And people talk, even when they're not supposed to."

"I have company." Feeling better, I managed a smile. "Cool."

Kate clapped her hands together. "Alright, let's settle who is doing what."

"Knowing which god is probably important, so David and I will head back to the shop and research." Jo slipped her feet back into her shoes before standing up.

"I'll tell Stannett what we believe is going on. He'll give us some officers to help check the sites. Kate, if you'll go with me we can split into two teams and cover more ground." Damian stood, and dug into a front pocket of his dark blue slacks. He tossed something to me. "Here's your phone."

"Thank you." I dropped it in my purse.

Ronnie sighed. "I'd help check out the sites, but I'm not really good with spur-of-the-moment defense spells."

"You can help us research," Jo told her.

"What can we do?" Terra looked at me. "We want to help too."

"Ah," I met Logan's eyes. "It's probably best if you go home."

She squared her shoulders and lifted her chin. "No."

Mr. Whitehaven chuckled. "I intend to help with the research, and would be happy to have your assistance, if that's all right with Logan?"

I thought Logan would say no, after his reactions to my butting in on the steal-the-Queen episodes, but he agreed with no hesitation whatsoever. "Fine by me."

Nick had yet to turn up. "Okay, Logan and I will drive Bone around, and get addresses for the sites. I'll call you with each one, Damian, but we're not going in alone."

"Good plan."

With that, our group broke up. The silent familiars took to the air or their paws to follow their witches. Before clearing the door, Illy looked over his shoulder, an uncharacteristically serious expression on his usually smiling face. I felt a twinge of guilt and stomped it down.

It wasn't my damn fault some crazy dude had brought a bloodthirsty god into our lives. We were simply the only fools in town willing to deal with the problem.

Twenty-four

"I'm driving," I said when Logan and I stepped out into the parking lot. He agreed, watching Mr. Whitehaven leading Terra to his SUV. Once she'd climbed in and the boss had shut the door, Logan followed me to my car. He opened the passenger door for Bone and pulled the seat forward so the dog could climb into the hatchback area.

"Girls Just Want to Have Fun" blasted from the speakers when I started the engine, and I quickly twirled the dial to turn the stereo down. "Sorry."

Logan laughed. "It's okay, I'm glad you like the stereo."

"I love the stereo." I waited for everyone else to clear the lot before backing out of my spot. "Can I ask you a question?"

"Sure."

"Are you mad at me for butting in?"

It took him long enough to answer, I expected to hear a yes. "No, but I'm worried what will come of it, and about the danger you're in because of it."

"Compared to demons, shifters are easy." I aimed the nose of my car toward the lot's entrance and slipped the gear into first. "I didn't bruise your ego or anything, right?"

"I'm old enough to have learned that one person can't win every confrontation." He held up a hand when I started to speak. "My job is to protect her until she comes into her own and chooses a mate, and I can't do it if I'm dead. I may end up that way before it's over, and I've made my peace with it, but that doesn't mean I want to die. I've been living my life for Terra since I was twelve years old. It'd be nice to see my duty through and have a chance to live life for myself."

He glanced at me. "Not that I regret being chosen as her Protector, or resent her. She's my flesh and blood, and I love her. It's no more her fault she was born a white tiger than it's my fault I was the oldest, unmated male when she was born."

"That's why you were picked?" Wow, talk about random

chance. "What if you'd ended up being some scrawny dude who tripped all over his own feet and couldn't land a punch with a big red dot marking the target?"

His low laugh rolled out again. "That's why others are selected as the beginnings of each new clan. Not all Protectors have been fighters. Some were great leaders, whom others did the actual fighting for."

"Oh. Cool." We rode in silence for a few minutes. He didn't bitch or grab for anything when I made quick lane changes. Didn't even glance at the speedometer. "Why was it okay for her to go with Mr. Whitehaven?"

"Only a complete and utter idiot would cross him. He's an important figure in our community."

I chewed on that for a few seconds. "In 'our' community. You mean supes."

"Yeah." Logan adjusted until he'd turned toward me as much as possible. "You do realize you're one of us, right? You and all the other humans who gained power during the Melding."

"We are?" I'd kind of thought so, but it wasn't a thought I liked to dwell on much, since it required more adjustments to my worldview.

He nodded. "That's why the choice you made to stand with us is going to have repercussions. It's been a long time since humans with power played a part in our world, Discord. You're the first in Santo Trueno to choose to ally yourself with anyone."

"Wait, I work for Whitehaven, and you said he's important. Doesn't that mean..." I trailed off when Logan shook his head.

"You work for him, for pay. You've worked for supe clients, like Thorandryll, for pay. You didn't do what you did for us for pay, but out of friendship. It's entirely different."

"I'm dating Nick, and that's definitely not for pay," I pointed out.

"True, but that's different too because it's one on one. You haven't told anyone that if they mess with his pack, you'll fry their brains." Logan chuckled. "And make them do the Electric Side until said brains are fried."

"Well, no and hey, that wasn't bad for off the top of my aching head." I downshifted, signaling, and squeezed in between two cars in order to take the next exit.

"No, it wasn't. I would've laughed, but well," he lifted a shoulder and let it drop. "Little worried about being fried at the time."

"I was a little worried about frying you with them," I admitted.

"Kind of hoping that ability proves to be a one-time deal. It was *très* scary."

He *mm*-ed. "I bet you've never offered a supe sanctuary before."

"Nope, can't say I have, and unless I'm wrong, that was a bad move on my part. You shook your head at me right after I did it."

Logan put his hand on my shoulder, a couple of his fingers coming to rest on my neck. A faint tingle spread from the point of skin-to-skin contact. "It means more than I can say that you did, but before that, we could've downplayed your involvement. We can't now. That was an official declaration of where you stand, and it's with us. The White Queen and her clan."

"That's okay. You guys are my friends. Friends help each other out by doing stuff. You know, keeping each other alive, keeping perverts from kidnapping teenagers, things like that."

He squeezed my shoulder. "It means our enemies are now your enemies. The tigers who don't swear fealty to Terra, and any other supes who have a beef with us, now or in the future, will gun for you along with us."

Maybe it wasn't just shifter politics that were super complicated. Maybe all supe politics were. Then again, so were human politics, what with all the parties and politicians. I shrugged. "Okay."

Logan pulled his hand away. "That's it? Okay?"

"Can't change it now, right?" Not that I would. Logan had proven himself to be a friend and someone who wasn't afraid to back me up when needed. Of course now, with Terra in the city, I knew she had to be his first priority.

"Actually, it can change. You could withdraw your offer of sanctuary, and stay clear of us." He licked the corner of his mouth, settling back into the seat to look out the windshield. "That would probably be a good idea."

I braked for a stoplight. "I think that's an awful idea. All wishy-washy and stuff. I like Terra. She's a sweet girl, and I'd feel terrible if anything happened to her, or to you. I may not always be around to help, and maybe helping will cause future problems for me, but it'd be really crappy of me to turn my back on you guys. Friends don't do that to each other. They help if they can. I'll help whenever I can."

"And if you can't?"

I felt my lips draw away from my teeth. "Then I'll do my best to kick the holy hell out of whoever hurts you."

"That building, down in the cellar." Bone rested his paw on my shoulder. *"The one with the white door. Don't think they're using it tonight. Too quiet."*

"Okay." I nodded at Logan, who tapped Damian's number on my phone. "The building with the white door. He says they hold them in the cellar."

When Damian answered, he gave him the address and passed on the info. It was the second we'd called in, both in the Palisades. Ending the call, he said, "They're about to roll out."

"We need to move faster. How many more places are there?"

"There's one out on Jefferson, and one out past the edge of town in a gulley." Bone licked his chops. *"There's another in a warehouse in another part of town, down the highway from here."*

I realized that I was "hearing" him by a combination of body movements, sounds, and mentally too, with images and words. Maybe I wouldn't lose the newfound ability to talk to dogs after all. It would be cool to keep, seeing that I'd have five, or maybe six, living with me. "Let's get the one on Jefferson, the other one down the highway, and we'll come back to the one outside. Maybe by then, Damian or Kate will be free to go with us."

"Sounds like a plan."

Bone directed me to the place on Jefferson, which turned out to be an empty store. Logan called in the address though neither he nor the dog heard any activity inside. "They're rolling."

"Cool." I'd already turned around and begun heading for the highway. Even with the boost of my unnamed ability that let me know what others drivers would do, it took a good thirty minutes to reach the warehouse and call in the address. I listened to Logan explain our plan while circling the block to return to the highway.

"Damian said to call and tell him which street when we get there. He'll get there as soon as he can," he reported after hanging up.

With Bone's directions, we arrived on another street that ended in a cul-de-sac and had nothing but moldering, abandoned houses lining it. The few streetlights still standing weren't working, and the clouds had rolled in while we'd driven around, obscuring the half-moon.

I parked my car facing the way out. Logan had already called Damian, and we sat for a few minutes after he said, "They're at the first two places. It'll be a little bit before they can come out this way."

Bone looked from him to me. *"We just gonna sit here?"*

I kind of wanted to, not knowing exactly what we might see. There were enough imagined possibilities dancing around my brain, most of them involving screaming dogs and a lot of blood. "No, we'll go scope things out and come back, so we can lead them there."

Agreement came in the form of Logan opening his door and climbing out. He held the seat forward for the dog to follow suit. I opened my door and locked my car while they headed for the end of the street. "Why aren't there any other cars here?"

Bone huffed. *"There's a dirt road they use, but I don't know how to get to it. We made our break from the gulley, came back this way."*

"Oh. Okay, we find them, and one of us comes back here to meet Damian and lead his group there." Gazing at the tangle of mesquite, yucca, and cacti spreading out before us, I felt certain either Logan would have to do it, or I'd have to teleport back. It'd take me forever to trudge through the mess without someone showing me the easy way through. "Let's go."

When we started into the brush, I pulled out my phone and set it to silent. Logan noticed and repeated the action with his phone. No sense alerting the bad guys we were around, in case someone decided to give us a call.

The dog took the lead. To my surprise, the great outdoors had less interest than usual in beating me to a bloody pulp. Maybe the cool night breeze kept the insects away, but I didn't stumble or fall victim to grabby, scratchy branches or sharp cactus spines. In fact, when Bone began trotting, I fell into an easy jog, ducking and weaving, hopping over rocks and other debris.

I pinned the change on leftover doggy instincts.

By my estimate, we jogged for nearly two miles before hearing anything. We all slowed down without a word, and continued forward at a walk, only to stop a few minutes later at the edge of a gaggle of much larger trees I thought were probably elms. Over a dozen vehicles sat parked around and under them.

Both Logan and Bone sniffed the breeze, almost identical expressions of alertness on their faces. "We're clear."

The sound grew louder after we passed the vehicles and I finally realized what it was: People yelling in excitement.

Cheering.

Twenty-five

The cheering made me sick. Under it, I could make out the snarls of dogs. What kind of sick bastards found the sight of dogs tearing each other up entertaining? What the hell was wrong with people?

Logan grabbed my arm and spoke in a low voice. "Wait, I smell magic."

"You actually smell it?"

He frowned, his gaze intent on the shadows under the trees, and released my arm. "Kind of smell and feel it. It feels like a low electrical current and smells like warm metal."

I noticed the lack of sniffing from him, and drew my own conclusions, based on personal experience. He sensed it, and his mind assigned a scent to it for identification purposes. Mine preferred to assign temperatures, such as cold for vamps with psychic abilities. The colder the feeling, the more high-powered the vamp. "We can't just stand here. It could be a while before the others get here."

Logan did sniff the air then. "There's wolves here, not just humans, and something—someone—else. Almost smells like an elf." He shook his head and sniffed again. "Not an elf like Thorandryll though."

I shivered, rubbing my arms with both hands. Bone whimpered and pressed his side against my leg. "There's more than one kind of elf?"

"Not supposed to be, after the kind you're familiar with went to war a couple of centuries before the Melding." Logan scowled, turning in a circle to scan the darkness. "They supposedly wiped them out. I think they missed one, and if they did, we're in big trouble."

I hesitated, listening to the cheering rise and fall. "If this elf is Crazy Curseman and such big trouble, why am I still breathing? He could've killed me, sounded like he wanted to because I'd 'interfered', but he didn't. He turned me into a dog."

"That could've been an accident. A dog hair might've fallen

into the mix." Logan nodded to a clump of mesquite trees a few yards to the left, and I followed him with Bone right on my heels. We squatted down. "Then again, how many people wouldn't panic over being turned into a dog? He may have thought you'd get hit by a car or attacked and killed by street dogs."

"I guess." The sound of snarling had lessened, but whether because the cheering had grown louder, or the fight was almost over, I didn't know. A lump that threatened to choke me formed in my throat. Here we were, not too far away from one or two dogs probably drawing their last breaths, and we weren't doing a damn thing about it. "If he didn't outright kill me then, he might not now. Maybe he gets off on showing up another supe."

Logan's fingers caught my chin and turned my face toward his. "I know you want to help the dogs, but we're outnumbered. Not just outnumbered, but there's wolves, probably armed humans, and the dark elf."

"Help me come up with a plan." Bone nosed my knee, and I looked down at him. "What?"

"Cages aren't kept near the fighting. They're down the gulley a little. I can show you."

I repeated that to Logan. He thought it over for a minute. "If we circle around, and there's not more than one or two watching the dogs, we can free them. That'll probably end things for the night, but there might not be anyone still around by the time the cops get here."

"I don't care." I didn't, even if it meant we'd have to do this all over again whenever the bad guys rounded up enough dogs so they could restart the fights. Night had fallen over an hour before, which meant one or more dogs had already died. Maybe we couldn't do anything about the two in the ring now, but we could keep the others from dying tonight. "Let's do it."

He looked at Bone. "If things go bad, both of you need to run."

The exact same order Nick always gave me. "Right, and leave you behind holding them back?"

Logan shook his head, his lips curving slightly. "I'll be running like hell too. Elves are bad enough, but the stories I've heard about the dark ones..." He shuddered, no more hint of a smile to be seen. "Run, teleport, whatever you can do to get away as quickly as possible."

Maybe we should wait for backup after all? I tossed that thought away in favor of helping whatever dogs we could, since it would definitely be the last chance for some of them. "Okay, you heard him, Bone. Things get sticky, run."

He gave a quick wag of his tail in response. *"Follow me."*

With that, we were off. The dog led the way, darting from shadow to shadow, Logan close behind. I brought up the rear, trying to move as silently as they did. The lack of moonlight didn't help, but leftover doggy instincts again kept me from making my normal amount of not-a-woods-person noise. At some point, we passed north of the excited crowd. I gritted my teeth upon catching the faint smell of blood on the breeze and kept going.

There wasn't a damn thing we could do for the two in the ring. I needed to focus on the others.

That inability dug at me, impossible to ignore, but necessary to resist. *Can't do anything if we're caught, except run.*

Ahead, Bone stopped and looked back. Logan halted beside him and knelt, looking down. I slowed and walked to join them at the edge of the gulley. Once there, I knelt too. Roughly twenty feet below, camouflage tarps had been set up in a line of sort of open-sided tents. A figure moved restlessly from one to the other. I recognized the shifter from the old brewery. He apparently hadn't been scared enough to run.

Logan tapped my shoulder and pointed to one at the end of the line. I had to squint to make out what he wanted me to see. A pair of feet clad in white running shoes stuck out from under the hanging tarp edge. It took another few seconds of hard staring to make out the rope around the person's ankles.

Another tap and point. I looked away from the prisoner to focus on a wide crack about ten feet away from where we sat. Logan's mental voice caused a flinch because it sounded too loud. *We can climb down there.*

Okay. We both kept our heads down, moving to the crack in the earth in crouches. My legs shook, mostly from the anger I was doing my damnedest to keep control of. When we reached the crack, I peered down and shook my head. *I can't climb that. I'll teleport us to the bottom.*

He held out his hand. I took it and put my other one on Bone's back. We were down in a blink, and the pit bull slipped away from my touch. *I'll go tell them to be quiet and come back.*

Okay. We watched as he slunk around the corner of the crack's entrance. I took a deep breath, closing my eyes, and willed my anger away. Anger could be seductive, urging a person into action to right wrongs. It could also push people into believing they were doing the right thing even when they'd crossed the line and weren't. We weren't here for revenge. We were here for what justice we could manage, and we'd already decided what that justice was: Setting the dogs free.

When I opened my eyes, I found Logan watching me. *Okay?*

Yeah. We'd have to move quickly. The shifter needed taking out first so he couldn't sound the alarm. Next, release the prisoner, who might turn out to have useful information if we were lucky, and then free the dogs. *I'll smack down the guy.*

He agreed with a nod, and Bone returned. *They'll stay quiet. I told them to follow me once everyone's out of cages.*

I petted him, and on impulse, kissed the top of his broad, scarred head before murmuring, "Let's do this."

We walked out. Logan left my side to go free the prisoner, and I managed to sneak up on the fidgeting shifter as he stood staring down the gulley toward the noise. He never saw me, barely even got out "Wha…?" before he slammed face first into the rocky wall.

The urge to smash his unconscious body against the wall a few more times rose, but I fought it down by remembering how scared he'd appeared at the old brewery. He had enough trouble without my beating him into a pile of spare parts.

I turned and hurried back down to the last makeshift tent, arriving just as Logan walked out from underneath it carrying a puffy blue bundle. "She's unconscious."

"I know her. Kind of. Her name's Tonya." Her coat had provided some protection, spilling dirty white from some slashes. It hadn't protected her from a head blow, as the large goose egg protruding in shiny pink glory from her temple attested. "Her dog must be here too."

"I'll take her down a ways. Why don't you start at the other end? I'll start here when I get back."

"Sure." I said it even though something in his voice hit me wrong. "Hurry."

Logan turned and took off without another word. I hurried back to the first makeshift tent. It took me less than a second to open the four large cages with occupants there, using my telekinetic ability. The fifth cage, already open, was empty and I scowled at it before shooing the dogs out.

Under the second, there were only three large cages, and one held the Husky. I let them out, and she was the first to dash out from under the tarp. I hoped she didn't attack Logan while moving on to the third tent. Three large cages, one open and empty. Nine dogs total, so far. One of them, a German Shepherd, paused to lick my hand before joining the other dogs milling around Bone, who waited past the last tent.

Logan wasn't back yet, so I ducked under the tarp into the last one and froze as my eyes adjusted. I understood the reason he'd wanted me to stay out of this one. "Oh, my God."

Three pairs of terrified eyes stared back. The fourth and fifth pair, death glazed, stared at nothing. Both of the dead ones had been brutalized by fangs, their bodies ripped in several places. A foreleg hung from a shred of skin on one. The other was missing a hind leg. As I stared at them, numbness descended, and an eerie, calm feeling with it. Spotting a small pet carrier and a roll of trash bags, I carefully bagged the two dead, silently promising them a decent burial later, and then coaxed the three survivors into letting me move them from cages to carrier. They huddled together once inside.

Logan made it back as I stepped out from under the tarp. He winced at the expression on my face. "I didn't want you to see that. Let me have them, and let's get out of here."

"Take the carrier. The bag's a lot lighter." My voice sounded thin and toneless. "I've got it."

He came close enough to snag the back of my head with one hand while taking hold of the carrier's handle. I closed my eyes at the brief touch of his warm lips to my forehead, and he murmured, "I'm sorry."

Released, I stepped back and forced what I hoped was a smile. It didn't feel like one. "Let's go."

With a last glance around, Logan turned and set off. Bone and the released dogs were already out of sight. I did follow him a short distance. You know, before the numbness exploded in a shower of sparks I could almost see, and the anger I'd been fighting completely flooded my mind.

I'm not even sure whether I stopped or just teleported, but Logan wasn't in front of me anymore. Instead, the backs of several men were. Packed closely together, their bodies hid the dog-fighting action from me.

Some tiny part of me thought it'd be a really good idea to leave before anyone saw me. I ignored that part, lifting my arms out straight ahead of me, my fists touching, and the trash bag with its awful burden swinging from side to side.

And then I swung them apart, allowing the buildup of telekinesis to burst free. Bodies flew to either side, the cheering becoming startled yells. Marching forward, I felt crackling and heard someone screaming. I noticed the lightning crawling over my arms, and realized the scream came from me. Someone rushed me, but I hit him with a bolt of the lightning, knocking him backward and out of one of his shoes.

When I reached the square dug into the ground and looked down into it, a fresh wave of anger coated my mind. The two dogs were beyond help, the jaws of one locked onto the throat of the other even as it bled out from a gaping hole in its own neck. Neither moved.

"Hey, Electro Bitch!"

I turned into a left hook that sent me staggering sideways, one foot hitting the edge of the pit, and fell the few feet down, landing on my hip and an elbow. The crackle of electricity shut off, leaving behind an afterimage of faint, silvery lines.

The shifter who'd hit me bared his teeth and jumped down. "Forget to pay the bill?"

In response, I picked him up with my TK and threw him out of the pit before climbing to my feet. The second I stood, something slammed into my right shoulder, spinning me around and to my knees. My arm and hand quit working and I dropped the bag.

There was a freaking arrow jutting out of my shoulder, and as blood began to trickle from the entry and exit wounds, my anger dropped to basement level to give exhaustion and blazing pain a chance to rise to the top.

I choked on a sob of pain which, of course, is when the dude who shot me decided to show his face.

Twenty-six

"I thought I'd removed you from the equation, Miss Jones."

Oh, yeah, I remembered that voice. Unable to stand, I scooted around to face him while blinking tears from my eyes. Crazy Curseman flipped back the hood of his cloak, revealing his face. Definitely an elf. He had the long hair, pointy ears, and handsome face perfectly configured for the arrogant expression on it.

That's where the resemblance to the elves I'd met ended, because this guy looked like a follower of the mighty church of Goth. Pale blue streaked his ebony hair, a shocking contrast to his skin, which looked as though the sun had never, ever touched it. I'd been expecting him to look like the drows from fantasy novels. Instead, his skin was pure, fresh snow white while his lips matched the pale blue streaks in his hair.

He looked like a frozen corpse dressed in way too much black, except for his eyes, which were bright yellow.

My voice shook, ruining my attempt to sound like a badass. "What the hell is your malfunction, dude?"

A sneer curled his lips, giving me a glimpse of his teeth. I wondered if they were naturally pointed or if he'd sharpened them to look scarier. "You're nothing more than an ill-mannered child. Quite a disappointment."

The far-off wail of sirens offered some hope that help would arrive before he lifted the bow in his left hand and stuck another arrow in me. I had to survive long enough for that help to arrive first, so began gathering what I could of my TK. It didn't feel like much with the hot poker stabbing my shoulder. "You haven't seen my bad manners yet."

Beyond the confines of the pit, people were scrambling and yelling that the cops were coming. Curseman didn't seem worried about the imminent arrival of the law. "What I've seen is an infant unable to use its gifts properly. A pathetic, mewling, useless sack of flesh."

I'd been meeting entirely too many douchebags lately, which

probably meant I should reconsider my career path or something. Maybe later, when I had some downtime, if later proved a luxury I'd have. Flinging my good arm, I said, "Eat dirt."

Curseman flew to the left, and be damned if he didn't tuck, land in a roll, and come to a sliding halt on his feet, sneer still intact. "As I said, pathetic. I don't know what he sees...."

That's when Logan landed on him like a ton of furry bricks. I cheered as the black tiger's jaws closed on the elf's shoulder. Now I wasn't the only one bleeding. "Take that, you scum-sucking, low-life worm!"

Tiger and elf rolled to the side, and Curseman punched Logan in the nose with his now bow-less left fist. Logan yowled, digging his claws into the dark elf's chest, and left gaping tears in the leather vest covering it when a shouted word ripped him away from Curseman.

Logan landed on his feet and circled the elf, halting once he stood between us. His tail lashed the air and he didn't seem eager to jump back into the fight. The sirens were drawing closer, but I had the feeling rescue would be too late for us.

"Nice pet. He'll make a lovely rug."

I grabbed a handful of fur and made it to my feet, not bothering to fight the low scream of pain the move called forth. Gasping for breath, I glared at the dark elf. "Don't you hurt him."

"I will do whatever I wish." He uttered another word, and blue fire blazed into existence in his hands. Logan flinched as it streaked toward us, expanding as it came.

For a tiny second, I thought we were done for. Right up until the blue flames spattered against the shield that shimmered into existence around us, turning it dark green. A wavy flash of something white resolved into a dog at the same instant pain blared through my mind, filling my eyes with fresh tears and further blurring my vision. Fur slipped from my grasp as Logan changed shape, moving to catch me before I fell over.

Through the wavy screen of the shield, we watched the dog attack the dark elf, and I realized it wasn't Bone as I'd first thought, but Sal, and asked one of the dumbest questions of my life. "Is my mom here?"

Logan didn't get a chance to answer because Curseman screamed as Sal's teeth clamped onto one of his forearms. A thick swirl of dust rose around them, and when it settled, they were gone.

My mouth had fallen open. I closed it and swallowed. "He stole one of my dogs."

"I don't think that was," Logan paused as the shield popped and faded. "A dog."

"He stole one of my dogs," I repeated then added, "Turn the alarm off."

"Those are sirens." His face swam into sight, covered in flowery, multi-colored sparkles. "Discord?"

"Night, night." I closed my eyes, letting pain and exhaustion carry me off for a visit to unconsciousness.

My own groan woke me. "Stop it."

"She's conscious," a voice reported. I opened my eyes, only to immediately close them again due to an assault of brightness, and became aware of pressure across my legs and torso. I lay on my side, one arm trapped under me, the other held to my side by a strap.

"Where's Logan?"

"Right here."

I risked cracking one eye open and saw him sitting a few feet away. The bouncing and paramedic leaning over me informed me we were hitching a ride in an ambulance. The paramedic did something to my shoulder. "Ow!"

"Sorry, I have to secure this." He moved slightly, and I saw Tonya sitting next to Logan. She held an icepack over the lump on her noggin, and I could also see her dog's head resting in her lap. The dog carrier sat on Logan's other side, and he held the bag in his lap.

"The other dogs?"

"I sent them to the garage, and called Soames, told him to expect them," he said. "Mr. Whitehaven and Terra will meet us at the hospital."

"Are you, son of a...would you stop touching the damn arrow?" The paramedic ignored me, his cornflower-blue eyes focused on my wound. In a different situation and with no boyfriend, I might have angled for a date with him, because he was seriously cute. However, the cuteness didn't compete well against the spikes of pain caused by whatever he was busy doing to my shoulder.

"I'm fine. She's got a mild concussion," Logan said.

"Okay." I closed my eye. "I hope you're almost done, because I'm two seconds away from cussing you out."

"Cuss away if it helps," the paramedic said. "Just don't throw up on me. I hate smelling like vomit for half my shift. My name's

Mike. What's yours?"

"Discord, ahh," I gritted my teeth and swallowed. "Jones."

"Discord, huh? Pretty unique."

"Everyone says that," I muttered, wishing he'd hurry up and finish. The pain affected my stomach, and throwing up on him became a distinct possibility.

He stopped. "That'll do until we get you to the ER. Can you open your eyes and tell me how many fingers I'm holding up?"

I took a quick peek. "Three."

"Good."

My shoulder screamed as the ambulance bounced through a dip in the road. "Why don't you just pull it out?"

"Can't have you bleeding out all over my ride." Mike leaned close to check my wound, but didn't touch it again. "Dr. Allan and Dr. Jamison wouldn't be happy with me if I let that happen."

He'd named the two doctors who'd taken care of me during my three-year, Melding-induced coma and recovery from it. I frowned. "I haven't seen Dr. Allan since finishing physical therapy."

Mike chuckled. "You're going to need PT with this kind of wound."

Unless you lose the arm, I heard him think. My "What?" was a panicked shriek as I opened my eyes again.

His sandy brown eyebrows rose. "What, what?"

"I could lose my arm? Are you serious?"

"Oh, right. They told us you're psychic." He shook his head. "Sorry. Dr. Allan's a super surgeon. He'll take that nasty arrow out and fix you up good as new. Let's do some slow, easy breathing and calm down. Breathe in…"

I obeyed, but man, Curseman would pay with his hide if Dr. Allan couldn't help me. Maybe my healing ability would take up any slack? I hoped so. It'd be hard to keep doing my job with only one arm. Not to mention, I'd be spending a lot of time learning how to do things with my left hand if my right one went missing.

A lot of people learned to deal with missing limbs. I could too, but suddenly didn't want to think about it anymore. Instead, I asked Logan another question. "Did I imagine things, or was that Sal?"

"The dog that jumped in? Yeah, it was the old one you sent with your mother, but I don't think it's really a dog."

Which I'd already suspected, and the idea my Indian fairy godfather wasn't a delusion gave me enough food for thought for the rest of the ride.

A whole lot more appeared once we arrived and they were wheeling me into the ER, because I saw Dr. Allan. Only it wasn't really him. "Hey, you…"

He smiled, said something under his breath, and my voice quit working. Reduced to glaring, I tried to figure out how Thorandryll's healer, Alleryn, had taken my doctor's place. No one else seemed to notice the elf, except for Logan, who stared at him with narrowed eyes.

Alleryn leaned close to whisper, "I'm here to help you, as I have before."

Wait a minute. I plowed through my memories, snatching at one from when I'd woken from my coma. Where I'd thought, for just a second, that Dr. Allan looked different. That he'd had longer hair or something for an instant.

Allan.

Alleryn.

Argh, elves and their damn glamour. I intended to take a page from David's book and have questions later, but right then, gave him a nod. The mahogany-haired elf murmured another word, and I felt something ease in my throat. He didn't give me a chance to speak. "We'll take you right into surgery. Don't worry, I've removed arrows from far less pleasant places without any trouble. "

Five minutes later, they anesthetized me into unconsciousness, and my fairy godfather decided to pay a visit.

A point of light in the darkness grew, resolving into Sal. He sighed while looking me over. "You weren't ready to face Dalsarin."

"The dark elf?"

Sal nodded. "Now my cover's blown and I've used up one of the Avatars I'm allowed this time around."

"You're real, and you were a dog." God, how much weirder could my life possibly get? "How long were you a dog?"

"Oh, about four, no," his face wrinkled even more. "Six years."

"How could you be a dog and…"

He flapped his hand at me. "Hush, too many questions. Now, you've just received some important information. It'd be in your best interests not to forget it."

"Which part? That you were a dog or that my doctor's an elf?" When his lips thinned, I felt a surge of defensiveness. "Hey, I have a big honkin' arrow sticking out of my shoulder. Cut me some slack."

Sal made a fist and knocked it gently on my head. "Use your brain, child. That's what it's there for."

I hesitated, feeling something tugging at my shoulder. "Am I going to lose my arm?"

He snorted. "No, the elf's one of the finest healers alive and he's not one to balk at doing whatever's necessary. You'll be fine this time."

This time? I gulped. "How do we take this Dalsarin down?"

"You'll have to figure that out yourself. It's against the rules for me to hand you solutions." Sal held up his hand, shaking his head until his silvery gray hair rustled. "Don't ask about the rules. You're in enough trouble. I can tell you that you need to get the dark elf out of the city before he spills much more blood, or the city will become his."

I growled. "Sure, no problem. Maybe he'll leave if I ask him nicely."

"No, you'll have to force him out, and you don't have much time." Sal glanced from side to side before slapping his hand against my wounded shoulder.

I writhed as far away from him as possible, aware of a soothing coolness spreading into the wound. "Ahh, holy crap! What'd you do that for?"

"Shh. I just cheated a tiny bit." Sal bared his surprisingly white teeth in a grin, his wrinkles squishing together on his cheeks. "You'll be fine. Use your damn brain, girl. I'll talk to you later."

He disappeared, leaving me to sleep.

Twenty-seven

My shoulder ached. Jumbled thoughts slid across my mind, increasing as I grew more conscious. I groaned, trying to pull my mental shield into place, but the combination of drugs and the sheer volume of life around me defeated the attempt.

A warm hand touched my uninjured arm. "Remember what I taught you. Find a quiet one and focus on it."

Dr. Allan. No, Alleryn.

I'd taken his advice as a teen, and took it again because it'd worked then; searching for one mind that wasn't as loud as the others. A few more groans escaped before I found one that flowed quiet and slow, no thoughts breaking through its surface to batter at my mind.

Once focused on it, I began the laborious process of rebuilding my shield. The elf's hand rested on my arm, providing silent contact with the physical world. Nothing leaked from him, not even any emotions.

After what felt like hours, I opened my eyes to beige ceiling tiles before looking at the elf. Alleryn smiled, patted my arm once, and removed his hand. "Good. How do you feel?"

"Thirsty."

He poured water into a waiting cup, added a straw, and held it for me to drink. A few sips later, I felt ready to begin asking questions. "My shoulder?"

"It should be fully healed within a week or so. I used a rather unorthodox method to bolster your auto-healing ability. You'll need to wear a sling until then."

"Okay." Sunlight shone around the edges of the drapes covering the window. "How long have I been out?"

"Only overnight. It's nine twenty-seven AM." He didn't even look at a watch. "Do you want me to tell you what's happened, or would you rather hear it from the dozen or so people waiting to see you?"

I grimaced, certain that would be overwhelming. "You tell me."

"No suicides last night, so you apparently disrupted the curser's evening plans." Alleryn's teeth nearly glowed in the dim light when he smiled. "The deputies rounded up several of those attending the dog fight, and the dogs you freed are safe at your tiger friend's home."

Both huge pluses. Yay for the good guys. "What else?"

"The young woman you rescued will be fine. However," Alleryn hesitated, his grass-green gaze leaving my face to focus on my wounded shoulder. "I believe that a night free of human deaths hasn't helped the mayor's disposition and he's exerting pressure on the police. Your witch friend, the detective, seems to be feeling quite a lot of that pressure."

Poor Damian. Wait, what had he said a minute ago? "Did you say 'deputies'?"

Alleryn nodded. "Yes, your friend called in the Sheriff's department. I don't think that pleased his captain."

Professional rivalry. Great. I felt guilty, knowing Damian had done it because he didn't think he'd get there in time to help. Then again, the gulley was outside city limits, so technically out of the police department's jurisdiction. "Okay. What did you mean by 'unorthodox method'? What'd you do to me? And what the hell are you doing masquerading as a human doctor?"

The elf sighed. "It would take far too long to explain right now, Miss Jones, and there are some things I'm simply unable to share."

I glared. "Give me the short version."

"Very well." His brow creased slightly. "Dark, bad. Light, good. We're on the same side. Trust me."

Like I'd just take his word for it, after the things I'd learned about elves. "Right."

Alleryn straightened, his shoulders square and firm under the white lab coat. "Our behavior as a whole may leave much to be desired, but I assure you we do not wish to see this world become the horror it would if darkness held sway." He relaxed slightly, the corners of his mouth quirking. "We'd have far less time for more entertaining pursuits."

Something familiar crawled across my shield. I caught hold of it and felt my mouth drop open. It was an image of Kate. "Holy crap. You're the mysterious boyfriend."

The elf's eyes widened. "Excuse me?"

"Oh, don't try and play it off. You're Kate's boyfriend." That certainly explained her lack of checking out other guys. Who would, with a hot elf at her beck and call?

He shrugged and dropped the attempted innocent act. "I'd

appreciate you not sharing that information."

"I won't." Not for him, but for Kate, and mostly because Percy didn't seem to mind. Her familiar would've let everyone know about it, if he'd disapproved of the relationship. "You didn't answer my first question."

"Which...oh, yes. I gave you an infusion of shifter blood. The benefits don't last more than a few hours, but that was enough to speed the healing process once I'd finished repairing what I could."

I had to think about that for a minute. "Are there going to be any side effects?"

"None. Well, no physical side effects. Sharing blood's a rather serious matter for shifters." He raised an eyebrow and anticipated my next question. "Your bodyguard donated since he's a universal donor, which led to an unpleasant altercation with your extremely bad-tempered wolf after he arrived. I believe he blames the other for your injury."

My bodyguard? Who...oh, I remembered. Logan had told Alleryn he was my bodyguard, after the fight at the club the demons had attacked.

"It required Lord Whitehaven's stepping in to end it." The elf cocked his head. "Do you want to know who appeared to be winning before he did?"

"Gah." *Men.* I closed my eyes. "No. How come your glamour's not working on me anymore?"

"The combination of pain and lack of control of your abilities, I imagine. Now that you've broken it, you'll probably always be able to see through mine." He walked around the bed and began unsnapping the buttons on the sleeve of my hospital gown. "I'm going to take a quick peek. Who do you want to see first?"

Talk about a loaded question. "Who's out there?"

"Detective Schumacher, Lord Whitehaven, your bodyguard, the White Queen, two wolves, one of them yours, the young woman, a Deputy Martin, and your mother," he paused, flashing a smile. "I quite like her."

"Leave my mother alone." I gave him the fiercest glare I could manage, and winced when he touched a finger my shoulder. Pain slid down my arm to my fingers, which twitched. "Ouch."

"I'm not fool enough to harm your mother, even if I wanted to. I said I liked her. I do. She's an interesting person to converse with." Alleryn replaced the bandages and began snapping the sleeve's buttons. "The wound's sealed, and I don't think it'll leave much of a scar."

I didn't care if the injury left a big, ugly scar. That was way better than losing an arm. "Thank you."

The elf stepped back two paces and bowed. "You're quite welcome." He straightened. "Now, who shall I send in first?"

Mom bustled through the door, Schumacher on her heels. She dropped a paper bag beside the bed. "My poor baby."

"I'm okay." I'd talked Alleryn into raising the head of the bed so that I wouldn't be flat on my back. Mom kissed my cheek, smoothed my hair back, and began digging around in her purse. She pulled out a brush. I let her go to town on my hair and gave the detective my attention. "What's going on?"

Schumacher dropped into a chair and rubbed a hand over his face. There were dark circles under his eyes and his clothes looked as though he'd slept in them. "Captain's pissed. The mayor's pissed. Damian and me, we're the ones getting pissed on."

"I'm sorry. I kind of lost it last night, after seeing," I swallowed, remembering the little torn bodies. "I couldn't let them kill any more dogs."

He waved a hand at me, but I could feel the frustration and worry spilling from him. "I like dogs, Jones, and you going ballistic did some good. They picked up nearly two dozen men. Someone will talk, and there weren't any suicides last night. At least, none we've discovered yet."

"Where's Damian?"

Schumacher's expression smoothed even as his worry surged. "On break."

Mom glanced at my face, put the final touches on my hair, and we both looked at him. His gaze flicked from her to me and back. "What?"

"Why are you worried about him? What's going on?"

His lips firmed. "Are you poking around in my head?"

"No, you're worried about him and it's punching me right in the brain. I'm his friend too."

That declaration earned a loud huff of expelled air from him. "Yeah, I know. Look, he's stressed out. Has some personal stuff going on."

"Oh." Damian's girlfriend, Serena, hadn't come to the last group dinner we'd had a few weeks before. "She broke up with him?"

Schumacher propped his elbow on the chair's arm and rested his chin in his hand. "It's going that way. Or maybe has. He's been gone for about an hour."

"Damn. That sucks." Nothing I could do to help in that area, other than be there if Damian wanted to talk about it. Except figure out how to clean up the Dalsarin mess so he wouldn't have that hanging over him too.

"It didn't help that he couldn't offer any information about the symbols we found. Someone was doing something magical out there, not too far from where the dog fights were held." Schumacher raised his eyebrows. "Can you tell me anything?"

"Our bad guy's a dark elf, and he's one freaky looking, scary dude." The door of my hospital room swung open, and Alleryn stepped inside, staring at me.

"What did you say?"

"Eavesdropping is a bad habit."

The elf waved my comment aside. "I was guarding the door. A dark elf?"

"Tall, yellow eyes, looks like a corpsicle. His name is Dalsarin."

Alleryn yanked a cell phone out of his pocket. I lifted my hand, using my TK to pull it from his. It landed in my lap. "Who do you think you're calling?"

"My prince. You people are in over your heads. We'll handle the matter from here." He strode over to grab the phone. I slapped my hand down over it.

Mom and Schumacher were looking from him to me and back. She spoke first. "Dr. Allan, what do you mean, 'my prince'?"

I grinned. "Blew your cover."

I deduced he dropped his glamour from their synchronized gasps. "Prince Thorandryll, my liege and commander. I'm going to call him if your daughter will release my phone."

When I looked at Schumacher, he nodded. "Let him have it. His prince can talk to the captain and the mayor."

Picking up the phone, I offered to it Alleryn but my mom grabbed it. "This Dal-whatever turned my daughter into a dog, shot her, nearly killed her little brother, and has killed a lot of people. Can your prince really do anything about him?"

"He will. It's likely his fault Dalsarin came here." With that, the elf plucked the phone from her hand and left the room.

We stared after him until Schumacher grunted. "Life used to be a lot simpler."

"Tell me about it." I only hoped it wouldn't get more complicated, but had the feeling that hope was doomed.

Twenty-eight

It was. Right after Schumacher left, Mom gathered my good hand in both of hers. "I have something to tell you."

"One of the dogs came up missing."

She blinked. "How did you know that?"

"Because the dog is who saved Logan and me from getting roasted." I squeezed her fingers. "He wasn't really a dog. I'm not sure what he is, but it looks like he's on our side."

"Oh. All right. Um, the three new little dogs, are they dogs?"

"As far as I know. You took them?" At her nod, I smiled. "Thanks. I'm sorry you're getting saddled with taking care of them."

Mom shrugged. "It's all right. Besides, I won't be taking care of them alone. There's a girl out there, Logan said you two found her out where the trouble was."

"Tonya, yeah."

"Yes. I've talked to her a little bit. She's only seventeen and has been living in her car for the past two months. I'm going to take her home for a while."

I almost asked her if she'd gone nuts, wanting to take a stranger home, but thought better of it before anything slipped out. The girl had risked her life against shifters in order to get her dog back, and it sounded like she probably needed some help. I couldn't think of anyone better than my mom to help her. "Okay."

We exchanged a smile and she said, "Nick would like to see you, if you're not too tired."

"Okay." She kissed my cheek, gathered her purse, and left. Nick came in less than fifteen seconds later, anger preceding him in a solid wave.

He shut the door before coming over to the bed, and didn't reach for my hand. He didn't try to touch me at all. "How's your shoulder?"

"Doc says it'll be good as new in a week." I hesitated. "You're mad."

Nick's lips tightened. "You think? Tell me why I shouldn't be mad. I'm sure there's a reason."

"Maybe because I was on the job, and not alone? It's not like..."

"Yeah, having Logan as backup worked out real well, didn't it?" Nick stabbed a finger in the air, pointing at my shoulder. "He should've taken that arrow. Not you. I would've."

"It wasn't his fault I got shot." No, that had been my own fault since I'd let anger take over. "He jumped a dark elf trying to save me because I lost my temper and made a stupid decision."

Nick's lips parted, his eyebrows rising slightly. "I can't believe I just heard you say that."

"What? That I did something stupid?"

"Yeah." His brows dropped and drew together as his eyes narrowed. "You've never admitted anything you've done was stupid before. I start bitching about Logan not doing his job, and out it comes."

I took a deep breath. "It's not about Logan, okay? I did do something stupid last night. I make bad decisions sometimes, but what you're always on me about is not running away every single time things get a little hot."

Nick threw his hands in the air. "Because you end up hurt, Cordi. You think the answer is always 'Charge!' and that's what you do. Charge right into danger without thinking."

"I do too think." I amended that immediately. "Most of the time. But I can't see the future." I had to amend that too. "I mean, not usually."

"You're a psychic, not a superhero. You should use your abilities and let me take care of the physical stuff." He jabbed a thumb at his chest. "That's what Mr. Whitehaven hired me for: To handle the physical stuff and keep you safe."

"You weren't available."

Nick's head jerked as though I'd slapped him. "You could've called."

"Yeah, and what? Sat there and waited an hour for you to get there while those sick jerks were making dogs kill each other?" I shook my head. "No. It can't work that way, Nick. I have to do my job, whether you're there to back me up or not. I did it before you were hired, and somehow kept myself breathing."

He unsuccessfully fought a sneer, his hands becoming fists. "You've been lucky, but luck always runs out."

My good hand had clenched into a fist of its own. I forced it open. "Which is it you think I am, helpless or stupid?"

Sneer fading, he shook his head. "I don't think you're either.

But you're not like us, Cordi. You're fragile, easily hurt, even with your abilities. You're new to our world, and you don't know how much contempt some species have for humans."

"I don't? Funny, because I've damn sure seen enough of it from vampires, demons, and now you." His mouth fell open, but I kept going. "I watched my best friend get played by a vamp, and turned into a party favor. I've been attacked more than once by contemptuous supes who think I'm fragile, and I'm still here, still trying to do my damn job. And I'm going to keep doing it, Nick, until you and every other supe who thinks we're weak, helpless victims gets the attitude adjustment they have coming."

I threw back the covers and used my good arm to lever myself up while swinging my legs off the bed. Nick stepped back. "What do you think you're doing?"

"I'm going to see this mess through." I managed not to fall on my rear when the room spun. I'd stood up too fast. "That's what I'm doing."

"You're hurt. You need to stay in bed." He edged forward, reaching for my arm and paused, realizing he'd have to grab the injured one. "Please get back in bed."

"No." My foot touched something and I looked down to find the bag Mom had dropped. The open top offered a glimpse of clothing. Trust Mom to think about my needing some. I bent down, trying not to move my injured arm, and grabbed the bag. "I'm getting dressed. Go make sure no one comes in."

Nick crossed his arms and shook his head. "No. Get back in bed."

I snarled, tossing the bag on the bed. "Fine, don't help. Leglin."

The hound appeared between Nick and the door. His tail whacked the wall before he crossed the few feet to me. "*Mistress?*"

Goody, I could still understand him. I patted his head. "I'm going to get dressed and don't want anyone coming in here until I'm finished. Would you mind guarding the door?"

"She's hurt. She needs to get back in bed." Nick pointed to my shoulder. "Not running around after a dark elf."

Leglin growled. "*There's a dark one here, in this city?*"

"Yeah. He shot me with a freakin' arrow. Alleryn's calling Thorandryll, and I want to be in on what happens." I turned and began pulling clothes out of the bag. Mom had thought of everything, including loaning me one of her loose-fitting, button up blouses. The hound went to the door, and made sure no one would come in by sitting with his shoulder against it.

I glanced at Nick. "Sorry, he's on my side. Would you untie

me?"

"You're going to get yourself killed."

You'll be fine this time. I hoped Sal had meant more than my shoulder. "Not this time."

His shoulders slumped, and Nick moved close to untie the hospital gown. He even found the sling Alleryn had left, and helped me adjust it.

Tense didn't begin to describe the scene in the hospital meeting room the mayor had commandeered. No one was using the seats around the long conference table, except Nick and me.

"Citizens of this city have been killed by this Dalsarin." Mayor Wells held Thorandryll's gaze a lot better than I'd ever managed to. If his Snooty Highness was impressed, he didn't show it. The mayor slapped his hand down on the table. "He needs to be brought to justice. Public justice, in a court of law."

"It took the combined might of all our clans to end the threat his people posed over three hundred years ago, and many of us died in the effort." Thorandryll half smiled. He stood at the opposite end of the table from the mayor, Alleryn at his shoulder. "We took no prisoners, because they can't be held. The only way to stop him is death, and death is our sentence for those who use dark magic."

"This is my city, and I," Wells began, but I interrupted.

"Our city. It's our city, and he's telling you this guy is super bad news. Which," I rolled my eyes at Thorandryll when he looked at me. "We kind of figured out ourselves. People dying equals huge clue."

Though mad at me, Nick chuckled.

"Be that as it may, the fact remains that none of you can do much against Dalsarin, and it's best if we take over the matter from here." Thorandryll glanced at my shoulder. "I'm impressed you survived facing him, Miss Jones."

"Surviving's what I do. But," I smiled back as sweetly as I could. "I'm going with, if only to watch the corpsicle crumple."

"If she goes, I'm going." Nick crossed his arms and leaned back in his seat.

"Logan's going too," Terra said from the corner, where she stood with Logan. "I'll be Queen of this city, and should have a representative present."

Nick growled. "Why, so he can let Cordi get shot again?"

Logan stepped forward, fists clenched at his sides. "I went after her as soon..."

I lifted the heavy conference table two feet with my TK and let it drop back into place. The loud thump closed their mouths. "We really don't have time for squabbling, people. About anything. If the Cursing Corpsicle isn't taken care of soon, the city's his."

Behind Thorandryll, Alleryn gave the slightest shake of his head while his Prince focused on me. "Who told you that?"

"I figured it out all by my little self." My response caused a grin to flicker across Alleryn's lips. He just might be friend material. "I'm right, aren't I? He's doing something magical, and not just sacrificing to a god for more power."

Mayor Wells had recovered. "What the hell do you mean, the city's his?"

I didn't answer because I didn't really know what it meant, other than bad. No one else bothered to answer. Thorandryll's icy blue eyes had narrowed while he stared. I batted my eyelashes. "Nod for yes, shake for no. Keep standing there looking bugged if you don't know what's going on."

Thorandryll's expression smoothed to bland. "I believe he's trapping the souls of those he's cursed, and intends to use them..."

The door of the conference room swung open, and in came Ronnie with her ferret familiar, Saki, on her shoulder and a leather-bound book nearly as big as her torso hugged in her arms. "To cut off Santo Trueno from the rest of world."

Wow, talk about an answer I wasn't expecting. "Why would he do that? Can he do that?"

She nodded, nearly shaking Saki loose. The ferret chittered irritably, grabbing another pawful of her dark brown hair. "That's not the worst of it. Once he's cut us off, he has a captive pool of sacrifices at hand. Thousands of them, and with the power he'll gain, he could quite literally take over the entire North American continent."

Ronnie crossed to the table to put the book down, and flipped it open to a page marked with a indigo bookmark advertising the Blue Orb. David gave them out with each book purchase. "Kate borrowed this from someone, and it details the war between the elves."

I wondered if anyone else noticed Thorandryll's squinty glare aimed in Alleryn's direction. The mahogany-haired elf pretended he didn't, but I saw him flinch. Someone was going to be in big trouble later.

"It's what led to the Sundering. The dark elves did the same thing over two thousand years ago, and the power they gained from sacrificing those they trapped led to their taking over the entire southern hemisphere." She tapped a page. "It's all right here. All those allied against the dark elves decided the only way to save the non-combatants—humans—was to separate the realms. They continued to fight until they finally won a few centuries ago."

Wells snorted. "Fairytales. Historians would've uncovered..."

"The Sundering had layers. Separating the realms wasn't all it did. It also altered the memories of all those left behind." A tiny smirk appeared on Thorandryll's face. "It's amusing how humanity has filled some of the historical gaps the spell left."

I spoke before the two of them began arguing. "Why did he pick Santo Trueno? Las Vegas would've been a better choice. They have highest suicide rate in the US, and no one would've realized what was going on until it was too late. Oh, wait." I'd remembered Alleryn's remark after he'd busted in my hospital room, the eavesdropper. "It's personal, isn't it? He came here because you're here. What did you do to him?"

Thorandryll's smirk had faded, and he didn't respond immediately. After a moment, he sighed. "I slew his lover. My wife."

Oh. Well, that put an entirely new spin on the situation. Or it seemed to for Mayor Wells, who sank down into a chair, propped his elbows on the table's edge, and dropped his head in his hands. Nick, on the other hand, couldn't resist the chance to try and draw blood. Metaphorically speaking. "You murdered your own wife? Before or after you found out she fu...Ow!"

I'd hit him with my good elbow as hard as I could. For a second, I'd felt the chasm of grief the elf held inside open. "Shut up."

Nick's teeth clicked as he obeyed. No one said anything for a couple of minutes, though Ronnie slid the book a bit farther down the table from the elves, the mayor lifted his head, and Logan turned to lean his shoulder against the wall, almost completely hiding Terra from sight. She peeked over his shoulder, her gaze on Thorandryll. Under the table, Leglin laid his head on my feet.

I took a deep breath. "All right, we need a plan since we don't have time to wander around looking for Dalsarin. How can we find him fast?"

Logan cleared his throat. When we all looked at him, he pulled a folded-over rubber glove from his jacket pocket. "I have a few strands of his hair."

Twenty-nine

I sat on the couch in David's workroom, and couldn't resist reminding the few present, "This is so wrong."

"Yes, you've said it seven times now." Thorandryll continued chalking symbols inside the circle. "I apologize if my methods are making you uncomfortable, but as you pointed out, speed is necessary."

None of my witch buddies were present except David. The sight of the poor little dog corpses had briefly turned him a pale green, but he'd swallowed hard and stayed when Ronnie, Kate, and Jo had vacated the workroom.

Damian hadn't shown yet, and Schumacher wasn't pleased by being the police delegate. Deputy Martin tapped his pencil against the notepad he held. Short and compactly built, with a golden-blonde buzz cut and dark brown eyes, he'd been delegated too. I'd been answering his questions for twenty minutes about what had happened out at the gulley.

Nick sat beside me, small waves of disgust and anger gusting across my mind every time his arm touched mine. Leglin lay on my other side, his head in my lap. Logan sat in one of the chairs. Terra had gone with Mr. Whitehaven. I'd seen my boss for exactly thirty-five seconds after leaving the conference room before he escorted the young Queen to his SUV.

Alleryn assisted his prince. For all their warnings about how badass Dalsarin was, neither had called in more elfy reinforcements. Well, they hadn't yet.

Right then, they were creating a tracking spell using the hairs Logan had had the foresight to save from when he'd attacked the dark elf. The dog corpses were part of it. They were the part I didn't like and felt deep down in my bones to be so very, very wrong.

Ignoring Deputy Martin's attempt to regain my attention, I said, "They died horrible deaths. Why do you have to…"

Mr. Snooty Pants the Elf Prince sat back on his heels with a sigh. "They're beyond pain now, but their spirits will focus on the one who caused their deaths, especially since we have a physical representation of him," he gave Logan a slight nod. "And will lead us to Dalsarin."

"But you said he used the dog deaths to gather power to fuel his human-intended curses." David frowned, pushing up his glasses with a forefinger. "Their spirits won't be available."

"Yes, they will in this case, since Miss Jones disrupted his working by distracting him with her attack on the gathering." I received one of his slight nods. Thorandryll continued. "You didn't mention why he left rather than finish the task of killing you."

I wasn't about to tell the elf I had a fairy godfather who'd chosen to be a dog for a while. "Logan got him pretty good then one of the dogs attacked him, and the law got there. I guess he decided not to try his luck against bullets too."

Logan not only kept his mouth closed, he didn't look at me. Nice to have someone around who didn't make it obvious I might be skirting the truth a little. Of course, he didn't trust elves any more than I did. Since I had the chance, I brought up one of the things that had me truly puzzled. "What I want to know is why he's taken three stabs at me. He clearly made the curse for Chapman so that it'd jump to someone, and it didn't jump to just anyone, but me. And he sent Chapman to my little brother's school, had him pick Sean out of all the kids there. Then he made a potion specifically for me, and did whatever it was so that my tracking sense led me right into a trap."

"Yeah, he really has it in for you," Nick said, glaring at the elves. "I wonder why."

Alleryn proved not to be as good as Logan at not giving anything away by his quick glance at Thorandryll, who frowned. The healer raised an eyebrow, leading to the prince's lips thinning. "We have no idea how long Dalsarin's been in the city, or what he may have heard or witnessed while here. You handled the matter of the book for me, Miss Jones, linking the two of us."

"Strike two!" Percy squawked, from his perch on top of a bookshelf. "Three and you're out!"

Deputy Martin, who'd been present though silent during the meeting with the mayor, closed his little notepad. "Let me get this straight: This Dalsarin fellow, aside from being a power-hungry serial killer, wants revenge on you because you killed his girlfriend, who happened to be your wife, and he's decided you have you something going with the lady here, so he's been trying to kill her?"

He tucked the notepad into the front pocket of his uniform, shaking his head, and met Nick's gaze. "Think I get where you're coming from now."

"Glad someone finally does." Nick dropped his hand to my thigh. "Once again, he's put you right smack in the middle of danger."

"I guess."

My boyfriend huffed. "What the hell do you mean, 'I guess'?"

"I saved Rose at the fair. No one knew we'd be there until we showed up, since we didn't know whether or not we'd have to work either case that day." Which meant no one could've planned things to make certain I'd become involved then. "As far as I know, no one knew we were on the case until Wells and Stannett came to the off…oh."

"Oh? Oh, what?" David asked, pulling off his glasses to pinch the bridge of his nose.

I turned to Schumacher. "What happened to Chapman?"

"The gunman? He's under observation. Has been since," the detective paused, his lips forming an O. "But then who did it come from?"

"Chief Stannett." Everyone stared at us like we'd both sprouted second heads. "He helped me up from the stairs, and I got dizzy for a second. I think Dad felt dizzy when it passed to him."

Beefy or not, Schumacher was on his feet in a blink. "You sure?"

I nodded, absolutely certain. Something had nagged me about the whole curse-jumping theory. "None of the victims have been kids, and it didn't jump to Betty when she hugged me, but it did pass to my dad." I looked at Thorandryll. "Can a curse be, I don't know, ah, tuned to a person's blood?"

"Yes. But where would Dalsarin manage to obtain any of your or your father's blood? It would have to be from one of you, to have passed between you."

"Cordi's bled all over the damn city, since she won't step back and let someone else handle the fighting." Nick's brow furrowed. "But it has to be fresh, doesn't it?"

"Sidetracked, we're getting it." I touched my shoulder. The deep ache in it was a sign of faster-than-normal healing. I'd felt it after I'd broken both my legs. "He got it from somewhere and used it. The question is whether or not Stannett's been helping him or is just a patsy."

"A what?" came from three directions: Nick, Thorandryll, and Alleryn.

Schumacher rubbed his forehead. "Lord, save me. How about scapegoat? You know that one?"

"Ah. Can't answering that question wait?" Thorandryll held up the chalk. "We're in the middle of something."

"Yeah, it can wait. The Cursing Corpsicle," Schumacher grinned at me. "Needs to be taken down first."

I returned his grin. "I thought it sounded kind of Sherlock Holmes-y. You know. If he lived in Weird World like we do."

"Who's Sherlock Holmes?"

Logan answered Nick before one of us could. "Fictional detective. Guy named Arthur Conan Doyle wrote a bunch of stories about him." He shrugged when I looked at him. "I have a library card. I use it."

Thorandryll muttered something, but I chose to ignore what sounded like "Animals shouldn't read" and said, "Time's a wastin'. Hop to it, Elfboy."

Otherwise, giving into the temptation of knocking him on his snooty elf booty would lead to nothing but more wasted time. We were getting sidetracked again. I glanced at the circle and the two tiny corpses. Thorandryll's gaze slid from me to them, and he went back to work with the chalk.

David, for all his wandering about the workroom, appeared to be taking notes. The symbols the elf marked on the polished concrete meant nothing to me. I wondered if they did to David. He hadn't been exactly happy to learn the elf planned to raise the dead. Well, spirits of the dead.

I thought of something else. "How are we going to follow them? Won't they just go through walls and stuff?"

"It's covered," Alleryn said, exchanging gray chalk for red when his prince held up the piece. He seemed to know what Thorandryll needed without any words passing between them. After tucking the red chalk back into the box he held, he pointed at a section of symbols. "Those handle how they'll track him."

"Oh." We sat around, watching Thorandryll work. Schumacher paced until the elf shot a look at him. The detective dropped back into the chair he'd vacated, fidgeting with a loose thread on the cuff of his shirt.

After he completed the chalking, the elf rummaged through David's workbench and shelves, selecting candles, herbs, and other things. It felt as though forever passed before he'd finished mixing and placing all of that where he wanted it around and in the circle, but finally, Thorandryll began to chant.

The language even sounded wrong, full of sibilants and harsh gutturals that made the hair at the nape of my neck rise to attention. I stifled a yelp when the corpses shuddered as his voice rose to a demanding crescendo, and noticed both Schumacher's and Deputy

Martin's hands moving to hover over their guns.

Good to know they were prepared in case of tiny doggy zombies hungry for ankles. It's not as though they could reach our brains, even if the poor things could walk.

However, the Zombiepocalypse didn't begin. A thin grayness began to seep from the shuddering corpses, and swirled above them. By the time the elf fell silent after a last, stern-sounding shout, the grayness had resolved into two smoky canine figures with glowing green eyes.

"I think you called the wrong spirits," I said, surveying the two dogs. "Those aren't Chihuahuas."

"They're the right spirits, Miss Jones."

"Dude, that one's a German Shepherd, and the other's a Rottweiler."

Thorandryll spread his hands. "The forms they've taken are how they viewed themselves when alive."

Short Man Syndrome, personified in dogs. Yep, my life *could* get weirder. Not a comforting thought. "Okay. Now what?"

"Now," the elf said, touching the toe of his boot to the circle. "We hunt Dalsarin. Follow me."

He may have meant the ghost dogs, but we all rose to follow him out of the workroom and through the shop.

Thirty

Shoppers stood on the sidewalks around the cul-de-sac, staring at what could only be described as a hunting party. Two elves waited, already mounted, and another seven horses with empty saddles lined up in the middle of the street and faced the shop's front. Around them milled eight hounds.

The spectral dogs led the way to the group, their smoky figures growing more substantial in the sunlight. By the time they joined the hounds, they looked like real dogs, except for the glowing eyes. Deputy Martin paused to glance at the rest of us, before shrugging and ambling over to the waiting horses. One of them stepped forward, lowering its head, and he patted it.

The horses were tall and gorgeous, their coats shimmering in the sunlight, each one pure white and blue-eyed with long, slender legs. I listened to Thorandryll give commands in Elvish. "I hope you're telling those hounds not to attack Nick and Logan."

He half-bowed with a condescending twist of his lips. "Of course, Miss Jones. No harm will come to either by my hand this day."

Deputy Martin mounted, settling his straw cowboy hat more firmly with one hand. From the small smile he wore, he seemed thrilled by the chance to be a part of an old-fashioned posse. I glanced at Schumacher when the older man sighed. He shrugged and walked to the horses, where another one stepped out of line to greet him.

Pointing at my sling, I said, "I can't climb on a horse with this."

"I'll help you." Nick touched the small of my back. "But I really think you should stay here."

"Nope." There were nine horses total. Either one was meant for me, or I was going to ride double with someone. I left the sidewalk. "I'm going."

The horse that met me had a blue gem in the center of its bridle's headband. It matched the color of the one on Leglin's collar, before we'd been bound to one another by my blood. My teenaged fantasies of horse ownership surged to the forefront of my mind, bringing what felt like a huge, goofy grin to my lips as I petted her. "She's beautiful. What's her name?"

"Talia." Thorandryll touched her shoulder as he passed to mount his own horse, and the mare gracefully lowered herself into a kneeling position. That made it much easier for Nick to help me onto her, and I held onto the saddle with my good hand when she hopped upward.

My witch buddies stood in front of the shop, their familiars on their shoulders. I jerked my chin at them. "Where are their rides?"

"We can't go, Cordi." Jo scratched Trixie's neck. The cat's ears lay flat, and her eyes weren't more than slits. "They won't let us."

They who? Their familiars, their personal gods, or the elves? Before I could ask, Thorandryll's voice boomed. "The Hunt rides!"

Fortunately, I still had hold of the saddle horn and the reins were looped around it, because the damn elf hadn't bothered to tell us we wouldn't be traveling by ground. Talia sat back on her haunches and lunged upward, climbing an invisible staircase and quickly gaining the side of Thorandryll's horse. I glanced down to find Leglin at our other side, his huge paws flattening with each downward movement as though they were hitting ground and not air.

My hound could fly. I began giggling and looked back at a burst of noise. The shoppers were applauding as though we'd put on a show for their entertainment.

Flying horses and hounds aside, we weren't out for fun and my giggles faded. Even if things went as we hoped, people were going to get hurt and someone, the dark elf, I hoped, was going to die before we were done.

I scanned the group, making sure everyone had made the jump from ground to air. Schumacher held onto the horn of his saddle with both hands, his face pale as he stared down. Deputy Martin, Logan, and Nick didn't seem bothered by our growing altitude. Martin and Nick were whooping like cowboys, each with their reins held in one hand. They even managed to high five each other while I watched.

Logan noticed Schumacher's death grip and guided his horse to the side of the detective's. I turned to face forward again, confident he wouldn't let the other fall to his death. By then, the horses had leveled out and Talia's gait smoothed to a gentle rocking motion. I freed my hand to claw my hair out of my face.

Ahead of us, the two transformed Chihuahua spirits ran across the sky, leaving a trail of faint, green paw prints. Below us, buildings and streets passed. I looked over at Thorandryll. "How are we going to sneak up on him?"

"No one can see us now."

I didn't ask why. The answer would be "magic" because it was the reason we were riding wingless horses above the city, chasing after two ghost dogs.

"Enjoying yourself?" The elf had brought his horse closer to mine, our knees almost touching.

"I'm riding a horse through the sky. Hell, yes." That hadn't even been on my bucket list, but I mentally marked it off anyway. "I should be holding the reins, huh?"

He threw his head back and laughed. Might've been my imagination, but the blue of his eyes looked a little darker than usual. Alleryn drew even with us on his other side, a fiercely intent expression on his face. Suddenly uneasy, I checked on the others.

Nick and Deputy Martin weren't clowning around anymore. Schumacher had straightened, and held the reins of his horse in one hand, the other resting on the butt of his gun. They, and the other two elves, wore identical predatory expressions. Only Logan looked normal, and like me, he was watching the others.

One of the ghost dogs howled. I snatched up the reins after a glance at Thorandryll, checking Talia's headlong rush. The prince wasn't himself. Something else had settled on, or rather, over him. Something I couldn't see clearly, but whatever it was, it had a rack of horns that would do a buck proud.

Nearly everyone swept past as I slowed the mare more, and I caught flashes of shadows lying just above their skin. Logan had slowed his horse, and it matched Talia's canter. Leglin looked up from beside us. *"Mistress?"*

"What's happening to them?"

"The Hunt." Logan dragged a hand through his hair. "The Hunt's a thing in and of Itself, and It's in control of them now."

"I have a really bad feeling about this." They were moving faster.

"Whatever the Hunt is after, It almost always catches. We'd better keep up with them, Discord."

I nodded and touched my heels to Talia's sides. She snorted and shot forward, stretching out. Logan's horse kept pace, and I realized one of the hounds raced along its other side, as Leglin was doing. A hound ran next to every horse in the group as well.

Within moments, we'd cleared the edge of the city and taken places at the back of the hunting party. Thorandryll had said no one could see us, yet even someone as clueless about magic as me had figured out something was going on. I couldn't help but think that surely Dalsarin would be aware of something like the Hunt coming after him.

And wonder why the Hunt affected everyone but Logan and me.

Time to wonder ran short as the ghost dogs howled and began to run downward. We'd crossed over the Palisades as we left the city, and I spotted both the gulley and the now-blocked entrance to the cavern where we'd fought the demons.

I nearly fell off my horse when all of the men except Logan screamed out what sounded like battle cries as their horses began descending. We followed them to the ground and the Hunt continued. None of them looked right, with the shadows floating on them, and they didn't seem to care if we kept up or not.

Discord. Logan's mental voice broke my attempt to bring the shadows into focus. *Don't move too far away from them as long as they're mounted, and don't get off your horse. The Hunt might keep them from recognizing us.*

He didn't have to explain why that would be bad, since they were still screaming at intervals, and I could almost see the blood lust spreading from them. Made it pretty easy to figure out why the Hunt was usually successful. They were focused on accomplishing one thing: the death of Its prey.

They would remove anything or anyone that got in their way, and that included us because we hadn't fallen under the same spell.

Of course, as long as Logan stayed close enough for me to touch him, I could teleport us to safety if he proved to be wrong about staying on the horses being enough to keep them from turning on us.

I knew why Jo and the others couldn't come. No way would their familiars allow them to fall under the Hunt's spell. They'd have been at risk the same way we were, and it was more than a little scary the familiars apparently hadn't felt they'd be able to protect their witches.

Thorandryll threw back his head and bugled, the shadow attached to him definitely fitting the action. It was the head of a buck, with massive antlers.

It's Cernunnos, Lord of the Hunt, Logan said. *He's riding the elf like we're riding these horses.*

I know that name. Celtic, right? He nodded, and I remembered exactly who Cernunnos was: The Horned God. *Oh, crap. How do we make him go away?*

Logan flashed a grin. *We don't. He's a god.*

Right, because all we needed was another god hanging around. Yet if Dalsarin's god showed up, maybe having Cernunnos there would help. Unless they turned out to be buddies or something.

That would be the worst that could happen. I decided to pretend

I hadn't thought of it, because the idea scared the bejesus out of me. A more entertaining one was why a god with the head of a buck decided to become Lord of the Hunt. People, even other animals, hunted deer for food.

Leglin bayed, and was gone when I looked down. All of the hounds had disappeared from the group. They reappeared in a bunch behind the ghost dogs, and were out of sight a breath later. I realized there was a depression or something ahead.

Wrong, it proved to be a small ravine and the only reason I didn't scream when Talia went over the edge was because I was too busy holding onto the saddle. Silly of me, since she basically floated to the ground, turned and kept galloping without missing a step.

Heat had furrowed cracks across the ravine floor and rocks, but the cracks didn't faze any of the horses. Not one stumbled or fell even when rocks rolled under their hooves, or they placed one in a deep crack. At least I didn't have to worry about being thrown and breaking my neck.

I heard the baying of the hounds and howling of the ghost dogs. Little as I knew about this kind of hunting, something in their voices said they'd found Dalsarin.

They'd found a cave, and the hounds milled around the small entrance instead of diving inside. Smart dogs. The entrance, little more than a crack in the ravine wall, wasn't tall enough to walk into. We'd have to crouch and duck walk, or crawl through it.

Gathered behind the hounds, the Hunt-spelled men silently conferred. Logan and I brought our horses to a halt a few feet away from them and kept quiet. I'd never heard much about the area being riddled with caves, or for that matter, that we had many gullies or ravines beyond the one the city had been built in and around. Probably another example of the real estate changes the Melding brought.

"You."

I looked away from the cave entrance to find the buck-headed Thorandryll pointing at me. "What?"

"Go forth into yon den and issue my challenge to he who hides within."

Shaking my head, I said, "I don't think so. Dude stuck an arrow in me last time we crossed paths."

"I'll go, Lord Cernunnos." Logan slipped off his horse, leaving the reins looped over the saddle horn.

"You, a tiger who walks in the shape of a man? No. She will obey me." His deer lips drew back into a sneer, revealing long canines. I gulped and Logan dropped to his knees, bowing his head.

He tried to talk a little sense into Horned Lord. "She's injured, my lord."

I pointed at my sling. "Yeah, I'm injured. Not in shape to be crawling around a cave."

Not that I wanted Logan going in there, at least not alone. None of which apparently mattered one whit to Thorandryll/Cernunnos, because he slashed a hand in my direction, unleashing a blast of green-tinged white light.

It hit my injured shoulder, and knocked me off Talia. While I lay on the rocky ground, trying to drag air back into my lungs, the residual ache in my shoulder faded away. He'd healed it. How nice of him.

"Discord." Logan scrambled over to my side and helped me sit up. "You okay?"

"Yeah." Fumbling at the sling, I glared past him. "You hungry? I'm in the mood for roast deer."

My threat earned a deep belly laugh from Thorandryll/Cernunnos. "Go, and do as I've commanded."

Logan helped me to my feet. I dusted myself off, squinting at the cave entrance. What lay beyond could be like the Barrows: a pocket realm full of monsters. "I've never issued a challenge, and I'm not going in there alone, Bucky."

"Mortals, always afraid of dying. Very well, you may take your servant." Bucky Boy snorted, waving at the entrance. "Now go."

About to ask who he meant, I stopped when Logan touched my arm. *He means me.*

I considered arguing the matter, since the shifter wasn't my servant, but another glance at Cernunnos changed my mind. Nothing of Thorandryll showed any longer, and the god's eyes flickered with crimson light. "Okay, fine, we're going."

We chose to crawl through the crack, which meant I had a view of Logan's rear the whole way through. Probably would've appreciated it more if I hadn't been worried about our immediate future. At roughly twenty feet, the low tunnel the crack made opened to an actual cave. One with four different openings. "Great, now what?"

"Eeny, meeny, miny, moe?" Logan sniffed the air. "Or we could take the one on the very left. It's the one the dark elf used."

"You're a useful guy, Mr. Sayer."

He smiled. "Thank you for noticing, Miss Jones."

We walked over and looked. I shivered. "It's dark."

"Want me to go back and ask for a light?"

"Ha, ha. He might decide you'd make a good torch." I squared my shoulders and intoned, "I've been commanded by a god. Nowhere to go but forward."

"I'll go first." His eyes changed from dark to pale green, and he held out a hand. "I can keep you from running into walls."

"Cool." I took hold, and we walked into the dark.

Thirty-one

I could make out Logan's figure after a turn in the tunnel. "I can see. Sort of."

"There's another turn coming up, and it looks a little brighter." We continued forward, and eventually, after walking for what felt like a mile, stopped to stare at the tunnel's end. Sunlight spilled through it.

"Maybe I'm wrong, but haven't we been walking downhill the whole way?" My legs said I wasn't wrong.

"We have."

"So how can the sun be out there?"

Logan frowned. "My best guess is that maybe we're trespassing."

Cernunnos had used the word "den" and I remembered my brief trips beyond Thorandryll's home, which had been just like going outside. "Like, he has his own fairy mound?"

"They're actually called 'sithren', but yeah."

"I learn something new every day. Sometimes, it's even good. Or at least not out to get me." Neither of us moved. "We should go find him or Bucky will get mad."

Logan chuckled. "Yeah, but if it is the dark elf's sithren, there may be traps."

I snorted. "This whole situation's a trap, dude. We either find him and get him out there, or we're going to be in trouble with Bucky Boy. Who has three hostages. Well, three I'm worried about." The elves could deal with Cernunnos, since they hadn't bothered to warn us about him and the Hunt. Plus, Dalsarin wouldn't have picked Santo Trueno if it hadn't been where Thorandryll lived. "We'll be careful. Really careful."

With a nod, he moved forward. Since we were still holding hands, I went with him. Nothing moved directly outside, but we halted again. While Logan scanned the ground and checked the air, I took in the view.

Dark elf or not, Dalsarin had a talent for exterior decorating. A lush green meadow dotted with bright flowers and surrounded by mature trees lay outside the tunnel's exit. The only breaks in the ring of trees were from the path of a small stream sparkling under the sun that ran through the middle of the meadow. The sun looked brighter than the one I lived under. "I'm thirsty."

Logan kept me from walking out. "Wouldn't advise drinking from there. It smells wrong."

"Dang it." I took a closer look at the grass, which began growing a few feet away. The edges glistened. A glance at the sky said it wasn't morning, so the moisture probably wasn't dew. "Is it poisoned?"

"Probably." He pointed at a clump of bright red flowers. "Don't touch those either."

While we watched, the flowers trembled, and a few blooms snapped at a bug flying close. I blinked. "They have teeth."

"Yeah."

"That's just wrong." I fidgeted, torn between wanting to teleport us the hell out of there and the whole "return empty-handed to a god" thing. The second probably wouldn't go over too well with Cernunnos, and as I'd reminded Logan, he had hostages: Nick, Schumacher, and Deputy Martin. "We can't keep standing here."

"I know. Try not to touch anything with bare skin." With that, Logan released my hand and stepped out. Nothing happened to him, and he waved me out. We began walking across the meadow, dodging each bunch of flowers we met. The creepy things turned their blossoms to track us, and I thought I saw an eye inside one.

Shuddering, I set my gaze on the stream as we approached it. That turned out to be a bad idea. There were things swimming below the surface, long sinuous shapes I felt certain were snakes of some sort. "I'll teleport us to the other side because I am not wading through there."

"Okay." Logan offered his hand, and I suited action to words, moving us across. We dodged more of the creepy flowers while trudging through the ankle-high grass on the other side. I sent my mom a silent "thank you" for packing a pair of mid-calf, slip-on boots instead of sandals or running shoes. Logan wore his brown mechanic's boots, but the cuffs of his jeans were dark with whatever oozed from the grass.

It wasn't until we reached the trees that I realize the only noise came from us. No breeze rustled the grass or leaves, the few flying insects didn't buzz, and even the little stream ran silently. Our breathing and the shush-shush of our feet through the grass were the only sounds.

That magnified the creepy factor by about a thousand.

We'd stopped again, surveying the trees. Logan jerked his chin toward two whose uppermost branches entwined. "He went between them."

I really didn't want to walk in there, but we didn't have any other choice. Hoping to offset the gloom as we walked through the natural archway, I began humming "If I Only Had a Brain". Logan's face scrunched a bit, and he raised an eyebrow. "The Wizard of Oz?"

"You've seen it?"

He grinned. "Yeah. Come on, Scarecrow."

Barely a dozen feet into the trees, he held up a hand and then put a forefinger to his lips. I froze, wondering whether he'd heard or smelled something. Logan's head slowly turned from side to side as he scanned our surroundings. I felt my body tensing and tried to relax.

The distinct, unmistakable feeling of eyes on us didn't make it easy. When the fine hairs on my arms rose to attention, I slowly turned my head to look over my shoulder. I immediately wished I hadn't, because something that looked like a mad scientist's attempt to cross animals that shouldn't be mashed together stared back at me.

It had the body and head of a housecat, no tail, spider legs, and a mess of faceted eyes between its cute fuzzy ears and kitty nose. "Oh, gross."

Logan's turn to freeze. "What is it?"

"Spidercat." I saw another one descending from a tree behind it. "Make that plural. What do we do?"

"Keep walking. Slowly. Maybe they won't attack." He suited action to words. I forced my feet to move, unable to take my eyes off the spidercats.

"What if they do?"

"I'm going to go with 'run like hell'," he said. "If we do, we need to stay together, Discord."

"Right." Yeah, no way I wanted to be alone in Dalsarin's nightmare. Poison grass, silence, and spidercats probably weren't the only things around. "Um, there's more coming down from the trees."

"I know." I bumped into him when he stopped. "They're ahead of us too."

"Crap. Guess that takes away the run like hell option." I took a deep breath to combat the panic beginning to flood my brain. "Keep walking. If any attack, I'll swat 'em with my telekinesis."

"Okay."

The spidercats didn't attack, but they did scurry around, blocking the way between different trees. Logan growled. "We're being herded."

"That's better than being dinner."

"Unless they're taking us to the kitchen."

I smacked his shoulder. "Don't say stuff like that."

"Sorry." He turned sideways to edge between two tree trunks, careful not to touch them with his hands. "Maybe they're putting on a dance performance and need an audience."

My laughter sounded a teensy bit hysterical. I choked it off while slipping between the tree trunks. "All I know is that we need to hurry because Bucky didn't strike me as the patient type."

Logan stepped up the pace to a quick walk in response. "All good hunters are patient, and Cernunnos is the Lord of the Hunt."

"Can I ask a personal question?"

"Sure."

"Do shifters pick personal gods too? You were kind of worshippy to him." I ducked a tree branch and stepped over a fallen log, trying to step exactly where Logan did.

"He's not my god, but it never hurts to be courteous when possible. I think I see a break in the trees ahead."

I leaned to look around him. "I see it. Yay?"

"Maybe yay. I'm reserving judgment."

The spidercats kept us moving toward the break in the trees we'd spotted, but when we reached it, they didn't follow us out into the open. I put my hands on my hips, surveying the revealed landscape and castle perched on the crest of a hill. "Does he shop at Villains R Us?"

Pure bravado, because inwardly I quailed at the sight. A dirt path ran between rows of rusty cages hanging from posts. Each cage held the remains of what looked like people. Most were nothing more than skeletons with a few tatters of clothing dangling from whitened bones. Dotted among them were a few still busily decomposing. I jumped at a popping sound, and fought the urge to gag when something oozed out between bars on a cage nearby. "Ugh."

"Stay in the middle of the path." Logan pointed ahead, to a cage that looked weird. I squinted at it, and shuddered upon realizing the occupant's bony arms were wrapped around another skeleton, pinning it to the cage.

"Not a problem, dude. In fact, let's skip the whole walk of horror thing." Lacing my fingers through one of his belt loops, I teleported us to a spot just before the open castle gates. "Thank you for flying Discord Airlines."

"I didn't get my peanuts."

"Maybe next time." I wrinkled my nose, letting go of his belt loop and moving to his side. "Phew. I don't think I want to know what that smell is."

"You don't," he assured me. "You really don't."

We looked at the open gate then back to each other. "I don't want to go in there."

"I don't either. How about you shout a challenge at him from here?"

I smiled. "I like that idea. Okay, here goes." Drawing in a deep breath, I yelled, "Yoo hoo! Cernunnos is here to kick your ass!"

Logan grunted. I glanced at him, about to yell something else, and saw him start to sag. "What the...."

His knees hit the ground and he fell forward, catching himself with both hands, and I saw the arrow quivering in his back. "Logan!"

"Pull it out. Poisoned."

Oh, no. I grabbed the arrow just past the feathery part, gritted my teeth, and yanked. Logan's yowl of pain ended in a groan. Arrow in hand, I turned to look behind us.

Dalsarin already had another arrow loaded and pointing. He released it, and I ducked. It flew over my head. Logan hissed, trying to regain his feet. "Run."

"Not without you." I deflected a third arrow with a slap of my TK, sending it off to the side. It struck a cage and the decomposing corpse inside jerked upright, shoving its arms through the bars to flail at nothing.

Two more arrows whizzed toward me. I dropped the one I held, grabbed a handful of Logan's shirt and teleported twice. First behind Dalsarin, and then out of his pocket realm to the ravine. Dalsarin's fifth arrow narrowly missed Alleryn's thigh before thunking into the ravine's wall. Releasing my hold on the hem of the dark elf's shirt, I teleported once more, to the top of the ravine, which put the Hunt between him and us.

Still clutching Logan's shirt, I stretched to look down and focused, setting the arrows in the quiver on Dalsarin's back on fire with a push of pyrokinesis. He was reaching for one when they burst into flame, and yelped. I couldn't resist a giggle, watching him drop his bow and un-sling the quiver to fling it away before his hair caught fire.

Cernunnos pointed at him and Dalsarin screamed as his body contorted. I felt my eyes widening, a giggle caught in my throat, watching as the dark elf became a large, white buck. The Horned God's voice boomed. "Flee!"

Sides heaving, the buck nearly fell down as it turned to obey, but with a desperate-looking scrabble of hooves, it managed to take off down the ravine. The riders shouted, but Cernunnos decided to give the transformed dark elf a sporting chance, holding up a hand to keep them from racing after the buck.

I stopped watching because Logan collapsed. Not only collapsed, but he quit breathing.

"Oh, no." Rolling him onto his back, I pressed my ear to his chest and couldn't hear or feel his heart beating. "No."

Less than a second later, I began CPR. "One, two, three…."

After the first two breaths, a horn blew, and I heard the Hunt race after Dalsarin. Pounding hoof beats filled the air and faded as I kept going. By the third time I blew air into his lungs, my eyes were burning with unshed tears. "Come on. One, two…."

He couldn't die. Terra needed him. Hell, I needed him. I'd come to depend on his calmness in the face of any danger, and his quiet strength. "Five, six, don't die, nine, ten…."

I couldn't let him die because he trusted me. Trusted me enough to follow me into dangerous situations without batting an eye, and in spite of what Nick thought, he'd never let me down. "Fifteen, sixteen, damn it, Logan, nineteen…."

Failure wasn't an option. I couldn't fail him or anyone else, not after failing Ginger so badly. A tear escaped, and I choked on a sob. "T-twenty, twenty-one…."

Reaching thirty again, I took a breath, pinched his nose closed, sealed my mouth over his and blew, watching his chest rise from the corner of my eye. Blew again, and dragged the back of my hand across my eyes while sitting up to start chest compressions again.

Logan coughed, his eyelashes fluttering. I held my breath, clasped hands resting on his chest, and felt the heavy beat of his heart. He coughed a second time, and I scooted back as he rolled onto his side.

His eyes opened while he noisily sucked in air. I began laughing and crying at the same time, while stroking his arm.

Thirty-two

"Come on, horse." I touched the shoulder of the horse Logan had ridden, trying to get it to kneel the way Talia had. Both our horses had stayed behind, but all of the hounds had gone with the Hunt. Logan leaned against the ravine's wall, his eyes closed. "Are you going to pass out?"

"No." He opened his eyes, and began to smile, but it turned into a grimace of pain. "Last of the poison's working itself out. If you don't mind helping me get my clothes off, I can shift in a few minutes."

"And then I'll have a tiger with a hole in its back."

Logan closed his eyes again. "No, it'll heal. One of the perks of being a shifter: If we're conscious and can shift shape, most injuries we have heal during the shift."

"Oh." I left the horse's side for his, and helped him sit down. It took a bit of doing to pull his boots off without dragging him away from the support of the wall. I left his socks because the cuffs of his jeans were wet from grass residue. Next, I winced and chewed on my bottom lip while we dragged his tee over his head. The back of it was muddy with blood and dirt. "You're going to get an infection. It's full of dirt."

"Not an issue." He'd turned too pale for my liking, and his fingers plucked uselessly at his belt buckle. Head ducking, I bent and unbuckled it before undoing his jeans. He said, "I'll lift up if you'll pull them off."

"Sure." I kept my head down, feeling a totally inappropriate blush blooming. At his feet again, I grabbed handfuls of material, avoiding the damp cuffs. "Ready when you are."

"Okay." He planted his hands to either side and lifted himself. I pulled, readjusted my grip, and pulled some more, until the jeans slithered the last few inches and were clear of his feet. Keeping my head down, I tugged off his socks, rolled up his jeans, and put everything with his boots.

Meanwhile, Logan shifted shape with a bonus soundtrack of hisses and growling groans. Sounded awful, but I kept my gaze averted. Maybe one day, I'd learn not to be embarrassed around naked men whom I wasn't dating, but I wasn't going to hold my breath.

Talia snorted, pinning her ears back. I risked a peek. Logan, now fully tiger, shook to settle his thick, white-streaked black fur. I turned around. "Feel better now?"

He stretched, claws scraping across the rocky ground. Under the guise of inspecting his back, I ran my hands over his fur. In tiger shape, he was a little larger than a pony. Unable to find where the arrow wound had been, I gave him a pat on the shoulder. "You're whole instead of holey."

Logan responded with a low chirp, his head rising and ears perked. I listened, and heard the far-off sound of the horn again. "Are they coming back this way?"

Before he could answer, we saw the white buck running along the edge of the ravine. Foam flecked his muzzle, and red streaks along his sides bore silent evidence that the hunters had gotten a few shots at him.

I tried to squash a surge of pity, seeing him. Yeah, he'd done terrible things and obviously had some major issues, but being changed into a prey animal and used for target practice seemed like cruel and unusual punishment to me. If death really was the only way to put a stop to him, I preferred something quick and clean.

Logan snarled and leaped, across the ravine and a third of the way up the opposite wall. About to yell at him, I closed my mouth and hurried to Talia instead. Once mounted, I turned her head toward the ravine wall and hoped while giving her my heels.

She took off at a dead run, and I thought we'd smash into the wall, but she jumped and began climbing air. We reached the top, and I saw the Hunt coming in the distance before turning her to go after Logan and Dalsarin.

Tigers weren't really built for speed, but Logan gained quite a bit of ground on Dalsarin before I caught up with him. My heart sank when he didn't acknowledge my arrival, his attention fully focused on the white buck. It appeared the Hunt had him, now that he'd changed forms.

I glanced back and found the others were a lot closer, and had one of those moments when I had no idea what to do when I saw they were all armed with spears. Where the hell had they gotten those? They didn't bode well for a quick, clean death.

Keep riding? Call it quits, get out of the way, and let them finish things?

Try to catch the buck first?

Why would I do that? I didn't have a good answer, other than still-present pity. I could use my telekinesis, knock the buck off into the ravine, and hope the fall broke Dalsarin's neck, ending the Hunt and the problem. It'd probably be a quicker end than what the Hunt had on offer.

I kicked Talia's sides, hoping she had a higher gear. She snorted and did find a little more speed, passing Logan. The ground whizzed by beneath her hooves, more quickly than I felt comfortable with. We began gaining on Dalsarin, though maybe he wasn't running as fast anymore. He had to be exhausted and was probably suffering from blood loss. I had time to consider whether depriving the Hunt of the grand finale was a good idea or not.

Being in front of everyone, I had the best view when the white buck slewed around and slid backward, sending up a cloud of dust until he came to a halt. He lowered his head and pawed at the ground.

I nearly flew off the horse when I tugged on the reins. Talia responded like a finely tuned cutting horse, dropping her hind end almost to the ground to slide to a halt and somehow turning too, to present her side to the buck. I lost a stirrup, the saddle horn punched me in the stomach, and one side of my face made contact with her neck. "Oof! Ow, crap that hurt."

"It's about to get much more painful."

I did fall off the horse then, shocked by Dalsarin's voice. Dirty and bleeding from a half dozen places, the dark elf had become human-shaped again. He raised his arms, and I froze as a ginormous, glossy black snake's head rose from the ground to shade him. "Allow me to introduce my god, Miss Jones: Apep, the Eater of Souls."

"Sorry, don't know that one." Having landed on my rear, I scrambled back. Talia neighed, reared, and took off, leaving me alone. Only for a few seconds, because Logan stopped beside me right before the Hunt pounded up.

Dust flew and swirled, rising high in the air. I expected Cernunnos to say something, but he threw his spear. Cutting through the dust, it slammed home in the center of Dalsarin's chest and pinned him to the giant snake's body.

Eyes wide and his mouth falling open, the dark elf grabbed the spear's shaft with both hands. Crimson dripped from his lips as he tugged. Apep shuddered and rose higher, lifting the dark elf from the ground. The snake god's hiss sounded annoyed.

Two more spears flew through the dusty air. One struck Dalsarin's stomach, and the other skewered Apep's right eye. The ground shook when he began swinging his head around, his long, heavy body rolling in pain.

The dark elf disappeared into his god's coils, and I heard the spears snap. I felt it would be a great time to leave, but Nick, Schumacher, and Martin were out of reach because I couldn't tell which they were, thanks to the solidified shadows disguising the riders. Two more spears went airborne and thudded into Apep.

He struck, grabbing one of the riders off his horse, tossing him in the air, and swallowing him whole. My heart stopped; I had no idea who he'd eaten. Apep struck again, but the next rider still had a spear and stabbed it into the roof of the snake god's mouth.

Mouth snapping closed, Apep swung his head in our direction. I reached for Logan, intending to teleport, but the snake god's nose struck my shield, which appeared a split-second before he would've smashed into us. I had an up-close encounter with a snake nostril large enough to inhale my head as the shield bent inward from the force of his blow. "Oh crap, crap, crap! Go away!"

Gods do not follow the orders of mere mortals.

Apep drew back, opening his mouth. Part of the spear dangled from the roof of it. I nearly peed myself when I realized he was unhinging his jaws. He meant to swallow us whole, shield and all. Logan and I reached the other side of my shield at the same time, both huddling against it like six more feet of space would make a difference.

The snake god forced his mouth down onto the top of my shield, blotting out the sunlight. He compressed it and I shoved my hands against the top, as though I could hold him back. Pain lanced through my head.

People who've had near-death experiences always talk about seeing their lives flash through their minds. If mine did, I didn't notice because I was too busy screaming, certain my shield would fail and we'd be swallowed.

Logan snarled, straining upward, his shoulders pressing against the shield. I leaned against him, closing my eyes, and attempted to teleport us away. It didn't work. The shield didn't just keep things out, it kept me in.

Great time to learn that.

I opened my eyes and found my arms covered in tiny white lines of electricity. Saying a prayer, which went something like "Oh god, I don't want to die," I concentrated and *pushed*. Lightning surged up my arms to my hands, went through the shield and right down Apep's throat.

The world shook.

No longer screaming, I knew it wouldn't be enough even as I fed all of the lightning I could generate into him, fighting the pain thundering in my head that threatened to blow off the top of it. I needed just a little more, and reached, hoping to find it. I found something, a reserve I hadn't been aware of, and dipped into it. From the corner of my eye, I saw Logan's fur stand on end and worried I was frying him. Then my brain went supernova as more electricity poured out, and all I could do was hope like hell I didn't pass out before Apep let go.

I did.

The first clue I wasn't dead came courtesy a humongous migraine. I gagged, and hands rolled me over before I began vomiting. The sound of my own retching hurt my ears. Vaguely aware of someone holding my hair and a hand rubbing my back, I wondered what had happened.

Someone shouted in my ear. "A rousing battle."

I managed to open my eyes and glare at Cernunnos. He hadn't actually shouted, it had only sounded that way. I could hear everyone breathing, the scuff of hooves and boots on the ground, and it all stabbed into my brain. The best I could do was a whisper. "Not so loud."

Then I blinked, because Thorandryll stood next to the Horned God, who looked a little see-through. Whoever held my hair back let go of it, and the person rubbing my back pulled me into sitting position. My head screamed, but I groaned.

"Sorry, Cordi," Nick said, slowly leaning me back against him. "Do you have anything you can give her?"

"I didn't bring my bag." Alleryn's face swam into focus. He touched my forehead, only to move aside, replaced by a deer muzzle. My eyes crossed, and I closed them again.

Cernunnos's hand felt real enough and hard like wood, or maybe horn, when he laid it on my head. At least he didn't blast me. Instead, warmth spread through me, and the pain in my head slowly drained away until I felt exhausted, but didn't hurt anymore. "Thank you."

He snorted and took his hand away. "You're an intriguing child.

Look at what you've wrought."

Deciding he meant for me to open my eyes, I did. He'd already moved from in front of me, so I took a look around, taking stock of everything.

Three elves: Thorandryll, Alleryn, and one of the pair who had brought the horses. The other must've been who Apep ate. Deputy Martin was crouched by a shaking, wide-eyed Schumacher, who sat on the ground, covered in dust.

Nick had his arms around me, so I knew he was all right, and Logan squatted beside us. Nearly everyone accounted for, I scanned our surroundings, noting the horses waiting, and the hounds growling and snapping at each other while they ate something.

"Um," I said, lifting a hand to rub my eyes before taking another look. "What are they eating?"

"Roast snake," Logan said. "Well-done from head to about mid-body, medium rare from there to tail."

"But ah," I couldn't see the snake's body.

"You blew him up." Nick gently squeezed me.

"Blew him up?"

"Kerplooey," he agreed.

I looked at Cernunnos. "I blew up a god?"

"Nay, child. You merely destroyed his earthly Avatar." One of his deer ears flicked. "Quite a feat for a mortal."

"Oh." Sal had said something about Avatars. "How many more does he have?"

His horns tilted to the left as the Lord of the Hunt studied me for a long, uncomfortable moment. I'd decided he wouldn't answer right before he did. "Two more, this cycle."

"Is he going to come back here?" I hoped not, but Cernunnos shrugged.

"I know not, but vigilance wouldn't be amiss." He straightened his head. "Should he return, he'll do so hungering for your blood."

"Gee, thanks."

Cernunnos let out another deep belly laugh. It trailed off as he faded from sight.

Thorandryll gave orders to gather the horses. Nick helped me to my feet, and I yelled at Leglin. "Stop eating that! You don't know where it's been or what it'll do it to you."

My hound dropped a chunk of snake flesh and slunk over to me, his tail tucking between his hind legs. "*My apologies, mistress.*"

I bent and hugged him. "Let's go home."

Thirty-three

Late Friday afternoon, Nick held up a box I hadn't marked yet. "What's in this one?"

"Um, DVDs. I think." I taped closed the box in front of me and looked around for my marker.

"Catch." Tonya tossed the one she was using to me. I caught it and grinned.

"Thanks." After writing "BOOKS" on the top, I tossed the marker to Nick and stood up to stretch. The almost empty apartment stood testament to the work we'd put in the past two days. "I'm going to miss this place."

"Me too." Nick closed in for a kiss, the three boxes he balanced making it a quick peck. The growlies had worn off. We'd spent last night here, making up for the time we'd been separated and all the arguing once I'd been changed back to human. The supernatural grapevine hadn't spread the news about my being on the White Queen's side yet. I wasn't looking forward to Nick finding out about that. Or even sure how to handle it, now that things had settled down enough to offer time to think. "Truck's almost full, but I think we can fit the other two in the back seat."

"Okay." I watched him walk out the door, and sighed. Tonya looked up from taping closed the box she'd packed, so I asked, "When do you start at the shop?"

"Monday. Four hours of work, and four of studying."

I'd been right, she was a witch. David and Jo had offered to teach her, and Tonya had jumped at the chance. She'd left home due to an intense dislike of her new stepmother, who returned it with interest. Mom had gotten the story out of her, and taken her to see her father, who'd agreed she'd probably be better off living elsewhere upon being told she was a witch. I couldn't imagine my dad not wanting me around, and felt bad for the teen.

She seemed to be dealing with it okay though. I bent down and picked up the box. "I guess we're done here. Let's go."

Tonya grabbed her box and followed me out the door. She held my box while I shut and locked it for the last time. I'd already dropped the keys into the night deposit slot at the office. Taking it back, I let her lead the way to Nick's truck while I looked around. A circle of burnt grass in the courtyard marked where I'd first displayed my new ability, electrokinesis.

Reminding myself to call Terra and Logan later, I handed the box to Nick. He put it in the back seat of his truck and opened the driver's door for me, since Tonya had already climbed into the front passenger seat. "You look sad."

"Yeah, I am, a little. It was my first place."

He pulled me into a hug. "I'm sorry you got kicked out."

"Me too, but I'll live." I kissed his neck. The growlies may have faded completely away, but I could still understand dogs and counted that as a reward for another case closed. Only one left to finish off: The case of the suspicious grandmother. It had been put on the back burner, but I hoped to close it the following week. "Let's go."

"Wait." He moved with me when I began to step back. "I wanted to ask you something."

"Does it involve a ring?" I hoped not, but smiled anyway.

Nick shook his head. "Not yet, but it's related."

"Okay, shoot." I braced myself for the suggestion that we move in together or something. I wasn't ready for that either, but he'd been pointing out how different things would be with me living at Mom's.

"I want you to meet my parents, and our pack. Maybe next weekend?" He gazed into my eyes, tiny lines appearing at the corners of his. I could feel his anxiety before I nodded. The invitation was a step in the right direction as far as I was concerned. We needed to know a lot more about each other before the marriage question came up again.

"Sure. I'd like that. Um, is your brother going to be there?"

Nick's growing smile dimmed slightly. "Well yeah, he's family and pack."

"Right. Okay, I'll play nice if he does. And he'd better." Or I'd shock him into the middle of the following week. I needed to practice my new ability, in order to gain better control of it. Patrick seemed like a wonderful choice for target practice.

"I'll talk to him," Nick promised, lowering his head. I closed my eyes and met his lips, enjoying the simple act of kissing him until a thought popped to mind.

Pulling my head back, I asked, "Are there going to be naked people?"

"Depends on whether you stay the night or not." He grinned, kissed me again, and let go. "Come on. Your mom's cooking dinner."

"I know. Curry." He winced and I laughed while climbing in the truck, receiving a light swat on the rear from him. "Kidding. She's making stir-fry."

Nick rolled his eyes as he climbed in after me. It felt silly to feel sad, but it also felt like the end of a personal era.

One I'd really miss.

Then again, far too many people had learned where I lived and that put my neighbors in jeopardy. One of the many reasons I'd be having dinner Monday night over at Dad's place to get the ball rolling on finding a house. I couldn't stay at Mom's too long and risk the same happening there.

I shivered at a finger of cold sliding down my spine as we pulled out of the parking lot for the last time. Almost a block away, I realized it hadn't been my thoughts causing it, but my abilities sensing a vampire's presence.

Which was ridiculous, with another hour or so of sunlight left to the day.

Nick slid his arm around my shoulders. "You okay?"

"Yeah." I put the event down to leftover nerves and shoved it to the back of my mind. "Fine and dandy."

Well, as fine and dandy as life ever was for me.

About the Author

A sword-toting alien with a fetish for fur and four-legged creatures, she writes fiction and spends entirely too much time distracted by shiny things online, like Twitter.

She prefers Netflix because there aren't any commercials and she can ignore all the reality series. As a voracious reader, she enjoys both ebooks and physical books, though her ebook collection doesn't require regular dusting.

She writes scifi as G. L. Drummond, fantasy as Gayla Drummond, and other things as Louise Drummond.

If you're interested in news and future releases, you can find her on Facebook (http://www.facebook.com/G.L.Drummond), Twitter (@Scath), or visit her author web site at http://gldrummond.com.

The Discord Jones urban fantasy series has its own web site at http://discordjones.com.